THE RANFURLY MYSTERIES BOOK ONE

DANGER LIES WITHIN

K.M. KRENIK

Before you begin, have you read

Inevitable Danger [Prequel to the Ranfurly Mysteries]?

Enjoy a free copy of the eBook when you subscribe to

receive K.M. Krenik's newsletter.

Visit kmkrenikbooks.com

DANGER LIES WITHIN

Book One of The Ranfurly Mysteries

By K.M. Krenik

ISBN Hardcover: 979-8-9906296-6-0

ISBN Paperback (Amazon Edition): 979-8-9906296--5

ISBN Paperback (Ingram Spark Edition): 979-8-9906296--9

Developmental and copy edits by Jessica Powers

2ⁿᵈ edition proofreading edits by Kim Beckham

2ⁿᵈ edition cover and interior design by 100 Covers

Map design by Nathaniel R. Krenik and K.M. Krenik

Book Cover Design and Interior Formatting by 100Covers

For my readers.

You are the key that unlocks the story inside me.

Contents

A Word from the Author

Dear Reader,

The Ranfurly Mysteries series takes place in another universe. It is a world that operates on a different timeline. It is not our world's future. Unfortunately, some readers have not understood this. I hope I've cleared the matter up.

Technology is more advanced, but the world of Lord Ranfurly and Courtney Drake is a younger planet with plants and animal species that we don't have on ours (i.e. dragons!)

In many ways, though, it is a world much like ours. A bumblebee there is a bumblebee here. A land line (or blower) there looks like what we have here. Chocolate is chocolate. *Superman* is *Superman*. There isn't a list of vocabulary words for you to study. Imagine a vibrant sky and ocean, cleaner air, and a mashup of our world's fashions during the Renaissance, Victorian, 1930's, and Modern eras, and be transported.

Maps are included in the latest edition!

Trigger Warning: Mild graphic violence, references to alcohol.

Parental Guidance Advised: Scenes which mention drugs, trafficking rings, and mild graphic violence. No explicit sex scenes, symbols are used to replace swear words.

Cliffhanger Warning: Prepare yourself to meet a cliff in the sneak peek of book two. That's fair enough warning, I believe.

Affectionately Yours,
K.M.

The World - PAX Era

Exclusively for PAX Elite

PAX PERSONNEL ONLY:
Restricted Area

SNAKES IN PARADISE

LAST SUMMER

Mill Pond, Cascadia

"I didn't think paradise had venomous snakes."

I spoke the words out loud, as if the creature could understand me. Formidable, beady red eyes. Black, straight lines for pupils. I'd seen pictures of the deadly viper, but it wasn't supposed to be here. There weren't supposed to be any lethal snakes in Cascadia. Yet somehow, there it was, on my front porch, looking threatened and about to strike.

***

With a jolt, I sat up. My clothes were damp. No. They were soaked. I couldn't stop my jaw from quivering. My body was shaking.

The snake. Just a dream. Not real.

Two years. That's how long it had been since Keith went missing.

My husband had put together a rapid response team to help victims of a hurricane in The Tropics Zone. But they never came home from the trip. Two summers later, they were still missing with no answers as to where they might be.

The not knowing was the worst part.

To go on without him, not knowing whether he was dead or alive. To be honest, I'm not sure how my two teenagers and I managed it. For Laurel and me, we stayed in the denial phase of grief. We kept busy with her in sports and after-school activities.

I had a house and ten acres to deal with, which I didn't manage very well without Keith. I could barely keep my own hair combed, let alone try to maintain the overwhelming property. But at least the responsibility was a distraction for me.

For my son, Nick, the denial stage didn't last long. He fell into a deep depression and flunked all his classes in high school the year after his dad went missing. Fortunately, he eventually got back on track and ended up graduating a year later than he was supposed to–the same year as his sister, Laurel.

Time snuck past me, and it was already time for my babies to graduate high school! What a choked-up mess I was at their graduation ceremony.

When Laurel's name was announced to receive her diploma, I hooted and hollered right along with her best friends. Her bright, white smile grew wider as she walked across the stage.

To think that two months before then, Laurel had been freaking out because the orthodontist still hadn't taken off her braces. "I'm going to have to take graduation pictures with ugly teeth, Mom!" Thank God he finally set her teeth free in time for pictures. Ever since, she couldn't stop showing off her bright smile.

She'd reached her full height of five foot eight, and if Keith were with us, no doubt he would want to keep her locked up. With long legs, brunette hair to her waist, and ocean blue eyes that could charm anyone, she turned plenty of heads. I was ever-so-thankful she had no idea she was gorgeous.

Next, Nick's name was announced. He had grown to be the same height as his father – six foot three. When he was younger, he was embarrassed by it and hunched when he walked. He must have hated the way I nagged him: "Stand up straight! You should be proud of your height!" But that last year of high school, something in him changed. He began to walk with an air of confidence. He inherited his father's good looks, too. Sandy brown hair, grey-blue eyes with long lashes that his sister and I envied. A strong jaw line and broad shoulders.

We had somehow carried on with our lives without Keith.

A week after the graduation ceremony, we got a delivery.

"A package arrived, Mom!" Laurel came in from the front porch and set a medium-sized box down on the kitchen counter.

"That's strange. I'm not expecting anything." I stared at the box. "Hmm, what could it be?"

"Did Nanny and Papa send it?" Laurel asked before she left the kitchen and headed down the hall to her bedroom.

I shrugged. "Probably. Nobody else loves me enough to send gifts." I eagerly opened it.

I removed some of the packing foam balls and caught a glimpse of the red, yellow, and white colors of the object in the box. "Is this a ball cap?"

At first, I was confused. Then ... it felt like my heart stopped beating.

It was a vivid memory; what Keith wore the last time I saw him on the day he left for The Tropics Zone to be a hero. A teal, purple, and pink *Thunking Rabbits* band tee shirt, a pair of olive khaki shorts, bright orange tennis shoes, and his red, yellow, and white *Golden Eagles* ball cap.

I'd even said something about it: "Wow. Look at you. Mr. Clash Act. You always pick that same cap to wear, even though you have a closet full of other ball caps."

"It fits my head just right, Fashionista Officer," he had replied.

Staring at the box with the cap still inside, I thought, *if that belongs to Keith, his initials will be embroidered in it.*

It felt like there were two people inside me.

There was the person who wanted to pick up the cap and see if it was really Keith's, the person who wanted to finally have closure.

Then there was the person who said, "No. Walk away. Don't look at it. Keep believing he's coming home."

The need for closure eventually won.

With shaking hands, I pulled the cap out of the box, sucked in air, and flipped it over to look inside.

K.A.D. was embroidered in yellow thread, next to what appeared to be blood stains.

My knees buckled. I let go of the ball cap and watched it drop to the floor. Gripping the kitchen counter, I held on to keep from collapsing.

That's when I noticed something else was inside the box.

"What is *that*?" I reached in to pull it out. When I realized what it was, I let go of it and let out a cry. It landed with a loud bang on the granite counter. Both of my kids ran into the kitchen, alarmed.

"What's wrong, Mom?" Nick asked. He saw the ball cap I'd dropped on the floor.

Laurel caught sight of the other thing I'd dropped.

A skull. Its hollow eyes were staring at us, watching our every move.

"What's that? A skull?" She laughed. "Seriously, Mom? That can't be real."

"Who is this from, anyway? It's got to be a prank." Nick said.

I stared into the black eyes of the skull and shuddered.

Laurel laughed and rummaged through the box. She pulled out a piece of paper. A minute later, she stopped laughing. "It's on PAX letter-head." She frowned.

"What? Let me see that." Nick reached to grab it from Laurel. Laurel turned herself around and skimmed the letter first, before she handed it over to him. The color had drained from her face.

A thick silence fell. I watched his expressions change as he read. Curiosity. Then shock. Then ... anger. Red-faced, Nick stared at the letter for what felt like forever. Laurel and I said nothing.

At last, Nick looked over at the ball cap. "That's Dad's hat. I remember now," he said in a low murmur.

I didn't want to look at that letter. Seeing my kids' reactions was enough. Neither of them said anything more. They left the room, almost as if it didn't happen. Or as if they didn't care. But I knew my kids. They cared. Too much.

I pretended there was no ball cap on the floor, ignored the skull and the letter sitting on the kitchen counter, and headed outside to spend the day working on my property.

Out in the forest, it was a gamble on who would win. My excavator or the maple vine trees. Those trees put up a fight, let me tell you. I battled with the claw of my machine, more ferociously than usual. Hours later, one of the long arms of a beastly vine tree whipped back at me, gashing my cheek. I headed back into the house to clean up the wound.

The skull, the letter, the ball cap ... they were still right where I'd left them. It was a day when it felt like every enemy was winning.

Somehow, I mustered up enough courage to pick up the letter and read.

> *This letter is to inform you that Mr. Keith Anthony Drake was arrested on July 4, Year 2224, on the charges of spreading false propaganda about The Peace Alliance Ten (PAX), while in The Tropics Zone. Mr. Drake was executed as a convict on CAT 4 Island on The Day of Cleansing, October 11, Year 2224.*

That night, while the kids were out with friends, I cried. Like a volcanic eruption, a loud, ugly, messy, wailing explosion ejected out of me, and didn't stop flowing until I was at the point of exhaustion. I slept for hours, and by the next day, I felt ... vacant.

PAX. A group of billionaires. Elitists who believed they could somehow create a utopian society. Globalists who had overtaken the governments of the world by convincing us they had the solutions to bring peace. Their plans sounded too good to be true until they demonstrated their capabilities by using AI to stop an escalating war.

But Keith ... he was never fooled. And if you met him, you found out real fast what his political stance was. Unlike me, he loved to talk about religion and politics and reveled in offending people. He thought the billionaire globalists were a bunch of overgrown children who looked at the world like it was a game board. They were the kings, the rest of us were measly pawns.

I thought back to that day when Keith's team hadn't come off the plane. The embassy had no idea what had happened to any of them. Nick had said, "What if PAX arrested them?"

At the time I didn't want to believe what Nick suggested. Even though I knew deep down it might be true. Keith's team openly opposed the PAX takeover, and it was against the law to speak out in opposition of the new government.

Now we knew Nick had been right.

PAX had become so controlling that they were talking about implanting ID chips in people so they could keep tabs on everyone. "For our own safety." With test trials underway, college kids were often the ones who jumped on board as testers, because PAX offered money to test human "guineas."

Fortunately, my kids didn't buy anything PAX had to sell. Especially not Nick. He hated the thought of having a chip implant that would keep tabs on everything we did.

"We can never let them put their chips in us, Mom. Never!" Nick was so much like his dad. And now that he knew PAX was responsible for his father's death, a deep-rooted anger and desire for vengeance burned inside him.

FALL

Nick and Laurel chose private universities that hadn't enforced the chip implants. Not at that point, anyway. It was only a matter of time before PAX would find a way to force the private schools to chip their faculty and students. But for now, we embraced every inch of freedom we still could hold on to.

Nick wanted to study political science and would be six hours away by plane in The Capital Region.

Politics, of all things. Yuck. I didn't understand why he chose that career path. "How can you still want to go into politics, Nick? Now that PAX runs everything, you'll just end up working for them."

His answer: "If there's nobody good working in government, we have no hope of changing things, Mom. You know Dad would agree."

"I'm not sure he would, Nick. He despised PAX. Why not choose to be an educator, like your sister?" I asked. "You can influence the next generations to be smarter than the current ones. And Laurel is only going as far as The Goldens. She'll get to see Nanny and Papa on weekends, and she can drive home in a day from there."

"Sorry, Mom. But I don't want to teach. Maybe when I'm an old man, after I've lived a little. I need to be in The Capital Region for my career path."

What could I do? He was way too big to boss around. I had to let him be a man and choose his own way.

As I said goodbye to them, reality began to set in. All the pent-up emotion I'd been burying for two years started to inch its way up, up, up.

WINTER

Winter approached, and the darkness set in as early as four thirty in the afternoon. The dreary skies and my bleak mood were a dismal pairing. One night, lightning struck the giant cedar that Keith had once carved our initials in. As I watched from my living room window as the mighty Goliath tree split in two, something inside my mind broke.

I pulled out old photo albums of Keith and me.

Bottle of rum in one hand and a rolling suitcase of pictures in the other, I dragged the thing over rocks and holes in the ground to make my way into my forest. I left the suitcase by one of my burn piles of fallen trees and logs and went into the shop, grabbed the blow torch and propane can, and loaded them into the back of my ATV, then headed back to the wood pile and started a bonfire.

"I hate you, Keith. I hate you for destroying my life! I hate you for going to help people in The Tropics, then getting yourself killed! You and your annoying, big mouth! How could you do this to us?" I took a swig of rum from the bottle and tossed a picture of him into the fire.

"And I hate that stupid, skinny girl I used to be, who fell in love with you and got herself pregnant at seventeen!" Another swig of rum, and a few pictures of us at our wedding were thrown in. "Oh no. What have I done? My parents paid a fortune for those pictures!" I started to sob.

Too late. I couldn't save the pictures from burning. Too late.

I stayed out there half the night, drinking rum, screaming, crying, laughing, acting like an absolute lunatic. At one point, a strong wind suddenly picked up and blew through, causing the bonfire to jump to a huge, dead fir tree. The tree went up in flames. Good thing I lived in a wet climate, and it was drizzly out, or my whole forest might have burned down that night.

As I looked up at the burning tree, I thought I saw a thick mist rolling in over the hill behind it.

But then I realized … it wasn't mist.

"Holy ***!"

I later wondered if I might have been having a rum-induced psychedelic hallucination.

It looked like a snake the size of my house. Slithering over the hill. But no. Not a snake. Legs were revealed, with claws large enough for three of me to fit in its grasp. It was more like a giant lizard, about the size of the Tower of Upland.

The creature emerged, growing larger by the millisecond, until finally I saw its head. A long snout, with a huge open mouth that revealed frightening-looking, razor-sharp teeth. Horns came out of a triangular head. Seven short horns. The light of the fire reflected in its shiny orange scales.

"It's a frickin dragon!"

On many occasions, I'd climbed to the top of the mound upon where it was standing. But I'd made a point to never go down the other side of it. An old mine was at the bottom. When Keith was a little boy, his older brother went with a friend to explore inside the mine. There was a cave-in, and his brother had been trapped. After that, everyone steered clear of the area.

Could the dragon have come out of the mine? I stood, terror-stricken, watching as the overwhelming beast continued to rise. It spread its massive wings. The night air grew colder in its mighty shadow.

Did it see me? Was it my loud ruckus that disturbed it? I'd heard that some dragons didn't bother humans, while others were deadly. If I remembered correctly, the deadly kind were usually red. In the light of the fire, this one appeared to be orange. Of course, it was a dark night. I might have been mistaken.

I stood frozen. Silent. Afraid to run. It might see me as prey and give chase. I stole a glance at its yellow eyes. They were fixated on ... me.

Panic took over. Everything inside me wanted to bolt, but I didn't. I remained completely still and tried not to faint.

The dragon's wings began to flap. Its huge body was fully exposed as it lifted into the black sky, creating a gale that stoked the bonfire. The flames grew and raged. Up the dragon flew, higher and higher, until it was swallowed up by the blanket of night.

I let out a gasp as it disappeared out of sight. My intoxicated mind was more baffled than ever. "What the...! That had to be the scariest moment in my life." *Hiccup.*

Dragons were endangered, and unless you travelled to Tanai, an island out in the middle of the ocean, people didn't see them. The only reason we knew they still existed was thanks to the nature photographers, film creators, and adventure seekers who laughed in the face of danger and were crazy enough to go looking for them.

Imagining Keith was with me, I spoke out loud. "How did that dragon get here?" *Hiccup.*

The sky became even darker, and I heard the roar of thunder in the distance. "Another lightning storm. Lovely." *Hiccup.* "Come on, babe. I've had enough excitement for one night. How 'bout you?" *Hiccup.* Still holding the bottle of rum, I took another swig, and hurried back through the forest to my house, the embers of the burning tree shooting up into the midnight sky behind me.

THE SERPENT EARRINGS

❧*Lord Robert*❧

THE SAME NIGHT ~ TWO HOURS AWAY
Emer Aude, Cascadia

A girl screamed.

Drones flashed their lights down the alleyway, then continued their normal patrol route.

It was another moonless night, the sky growing darker as thunder clouds covered the huge city of Emer Aude. Not far from the city's center, in a district that had one of the highest homicide rates on the planet, a man hid himself, waiting for the drones to pass.

Thus far, he'd managed to stay undetected. He'd avoided getting the new implants people were lining up for.

PAX propaganda had convinced most people that the only way they could be kept safe from virus threats and dangerous criminals was to have an implanted chip. He knew better. The chips were nothing other than a tracking device with a person's identity. Getting one was their sure-fire way to make sure the drones would find you.

He wore a specially designed suit made of black dragon skin and encoded with a new technology that protected him from PAX scanners.

Dragon skin was the most impenetrable and flexible material on the planet, containing healing agents within. Out of the same material, he wore a face mask that conformed to his skin and concealed his identity, and gloves that covered his fingerprints.

At six feet two inches tall, his muscular frame was not easy to conceal, but with decades of martial arts training, he had mastered the art of making himself invisible at night.

It wasn't only the drones he needed to avoid. Lord Robert Ranfurly had once been a well-known figure in Upland, across the ocean in Zone A. For reasons he preferred to keep secret, he'd disappeared from his homeland five years ago by fleeing to Zone B. He kept his identity and whereabouts a secret from nearly everyone he used to know.

Another reason he couldn't afford to be recognized: it could jeopardize his work with CAPE. The Resistance.

His silhouetted frame emerging out of the penumbra, he ran towards the sound of the scream. By the time he found the girl, it was too late—her lifeless body was lying on the filthy ground in a heap of garbage. She looked like a teenager, but it was hard to tell the ages of the girls he often saw working the streets at night. They were powdered and frosted like cakes with makeup, forced to wear next to nothing by the vampire-like pimps who controlled them.

Every time he saw a young victim, he thought of his own five-year-old daughter, Elizabeth. And every time, it felt like his chest was caving in on itself. *This was somebody's little girl.*

Lord Robert bent down to get a better look at the victim's condition. Eyes wide-open, with a look in them as if the last thing she had seen was horrific. The crime had just happened. The killer must be close.

Just then, a movement in the darkness behind the girl's motionless form caught his attention. A flash of steel appeared as if floating in mid-air. The one who held it sprung out, like a wild beast, and lunged at Lord Robert. He swerved from the point of the weapon, and grabbed the wrist of the attacker, then twisted it away from his chest.

The two wrestled, but Lord Robert's strength outperformed his enemy's. Then the knife-wielding man broke loose from Lord Robert, used the wall to run up and flip over him, then darted off down the narrow passageway, out of sight.

It would catch the attention of the drones if Robert was to give chase. Instead, he searched the girl for clues. "Strange, just like the other victims, she has no signs of being cut. The killer didn't use his knife on her. She wasn't strangled. No bullets. How, then, did he kill her?"

He found words written in ink on the girl's wrist.

Behind Club Purgatory 11:45 in the evening. Wear the earrings.

"The earrings."

The other victims wore the same earrings: silver or sterling serpents, studded with emeralds and rubies for eyes. He scanned them with his wrist device known as a Digi-watch, and checked for traces of trackers, listening devices, cameras.

Poison? No. His device showed they were clean. He put the earrings inside a plastic pouch in one of the jacket pockets of his dragon suit, and quietly made his way out of the alley, careful to avoid the drones on patrol.

This was the third victim he'd found wearing serpent earrings in the past six months. *Why did the victims wear the earrings? How were they killed?* The case left him frustrated.

He pressed his Digi-watch, which signaled to Vivienne, his automobile, to pick him up.

Vivienne had the ability to either drive on wheels, hover on aluminum roads, or fly by the push of a button. It was more common to see hover cars on the highways in the past two years, as they'd become more affordable, and there were now more aluminum lanes available. Flying cars, however, were not common. Only a handful of billionaires owned them.

The difference between Vivienne and other flying cars: she had a stealth mode option, and she was undetectable by PAX drones. Also, she made a good administrative assistant.

TWO YEARS AGO

CAPE Headquarters, The Capital

Yes, PAX had some brilliant tech geniuses working on their side. But what PAX didn't know was that CAPE had their own geniuses. Dillard Doyle and Baca Gunn were the computer science whizzes in charge of CAPE Tech.

Lord Robert was by no means a technology wiz. But he was wealthy, and one way he helped CAPE was by funding CAPE's tech program. In honor of their top donor, CAPE hung a plaque on the wall of the CAPE Tech office that quoted him:

"God bless thee, anoraks,
for without wizards, we will never win."
– Lord Robert Ranfurly

Dillard and Baca often amazed Lord Robert with their inventions. He recalled the day Dillard and Baca surprised him with his new phone and car.

"Lord Robert, first off, this is your new phone. Encased in metal and outfitted with audio jammers, our CAPE phones are one hundred percent eavesdrop-proof." Dillard pushed his dark-rimmed glasses up off his nose and handed Lord Robert the phone.

"And now," Baca said, beaming, "here comes the best part. We proudly present … Lady Vivienne!" She and Dillard lifted a cover from a metallic car, shaped like a bullet. She smiled and jumped up and down.

"I feel it is important to mention that if for some reason you aren't happy with her, you can't give her back." Dillard didn't smile.

"But we already know you will love her," Baca said happily. "Shall I tell him, or?" She looked over at Dillard. "Oh, you want to tell him. I can see. Okay." When she smiled, Robert had an urge to poke his finger into her dimple, it was so prominent.

"Yes, well, first off, Vivienne comes with a chip that we, Baca and I, have designed, for you. All CAPE members have these in their vehicles now. When scanned by PAX drones, both the car and any passengers within will be warranted as clear and passable. However, should a drone lose its mind,

as one often does, each vehicle has a shield layer that protects it from bullets, fire, lasers–"

Baca cut him off. "…asteroids, lightning, arrows, swords–"

"You get the idea." It was Dillard's turn. He cut her off.

"Are-aren't you going to tell him about the gadgets?" Baca was so amped up, Robert wondered how much caffeine she'd had.

Dillard looked annoyed. "I'm getting there. Okay, Lord Robert, especially for you–"

"because you're so amazing!" Baca interrupted, smiling brightly.

"Mmhmm," Dillard continued. "We've outfitted your car with a few extras."

Lord Robert rubbed his hands together. "Extras? Really? I can't wait to see this."

"No, you can't!" Baca bounced up and down and clapped. With her blonde pigtails flapping up and down, she reminded Robert of a bunny.

"May I continue?" Dillard's inner introvert was getting agitated by Baca's burst of bubbly energy. He sighed and went on. "Of course, like most cars these days, it has an autopilot feature. Lady Vivienne will drive with or without you in the car, at your voice command."

"What if I can't talk?" asked Lord Robert.

"But you can talk." Dillard looked at Robert like he was daft.

"Yes, but what if I can't."

"You are talking now. I can hear you."

"I think he means what if, for some reason, he loses his voice," Baca said.

"That's what I meant." Lord Robert nodded.

"Oh, well in that case, there is a remote in your Digi-watch. And Vivienne also has command buttons inside her."

"Every woman has her buttons!" Baca giggled.

Dillard pretended Baca didn't say that and went on. "We also gave her a chameleon command, so she can change colors. All you need to do is say the name of the color you want her to turn."

"That's pretty nifty." Lord Robert reached out to touch the car.

"Don't! No handsies!" Dillard pointed at Robert. "I haven't given my blessing just yet!"

"Sorry."

"As you are probably aware, many of the new cars have digital license plates. We programmed yours so it can be changed as many times as you request, whenever you need it to."

"Excellent."

"And ..." continued Dillard, "with a push of a button, she has a morphing tread feature. She hovers on aluminum highways when you push silver," he pointed to the silver button, *"or push this black button and her tire tread works on normal roads. Or you can push this brown button for four-wheel drive mode."*

"Impressive." Lord Robert raised a brow.

"And–" Baca looked like she was about to burst into rainbows.

Before she could finish her sentence, Dillard cut in, "And Vivienne flies."

"What? She flies?" Lord Robert was now getting excited.

"Oh yes." A sly smile curved on one side of Dillard's lips.

"Yes! Yes!" Baca bounced. "Let me say this last part, Dillard! PLEASE let me tell him!" Her hands were folded together against her chest, as she pleaded with Dillard.

"Fine." Dillard crossed his arms.

"And ... since you are voted to be CAPE's most eligible bachelor, we programmed Vivienne's voice especially just for you, so you won't ever need to feel lonely out there in Cascadia." Baca did a strange kind of happy dance move. "Go ahead ... ask her something!"

Robert raised an eyebrow. "Vivienne, what color would you like to be today?"

"Whatever color you are in the mood for, Lord Robert." Vivienne replied in a low female voice in a sexy Uplandish accent.

With an impressed grin, Robert looked at Baca and said to the car, "Will you marry me, Vivienne?"

Baca swooned.

Vivienne replied. "That's a little premature, don't you think? Why don't we spend a little time together before rushing into something we might both later regret."

PRESENT

Lord Robert flew Vivienne out of the city of Emer Aude toward Ranfurly Manor.

As a flash of lightning lit up the sky, Robert thought he caught sight of something flying in the distance.

"I swear that looks just like a…" he started to say out loud but then decided it couldn't possibly be. *Dragons here in Cascadia? Not a chance.*

"A what?" Vivienne asked.

Robert looked out at the stormy sky and shook himself. He hadn't had a good night's sleep in over a week, and he realized he must have been imagining things. "Never mind. Probably just a strange-shaped cloud."

They reached the airspace above Ranfurly Manor, and Vivienne said, "There's your chauffeur."

The chauffeur lived on a floor above the garage and was heading out of his front door and down the stairway toward the ten-car garage.

"He rises early, doesn't he?" Lord Robert said.

"You have a note in your reminders to speak to him about getting a remote to open your front gate," Vivienne said in her sexy, programmed voice.

"Oh, right. Thanks for the reminder."

"Now would be a good time, don't you think?" Vivienne said. "Chances are, you'll forget if you wait. Your chauffeur isn't your top fan. And he doesn't drive a flying car. If he knew you did, he'd resent you even more for making him get out in the rain and punch the code in. Just saying…"

"Perhaps you're right," said Lord Robert. "I can't believe we still have to punch in a code at that gate."

"Nobody can. Perhaps you will earn a few points with your chauffeur if you talk to him right now."

Lord Robert sighed. "Vivienne, have I told you lately how brilliant you are? If only you were human."

"If I were human, I would be of no use to you, Lord Robert."

Vivienne landed out of sight, in a cleared area surrounded by thick trees, about a quarter mile from the garage.

"No peeking at me while I change, Vivienne," he said to his car.

"Don't flatter yourself. You aren't my type. But your Royal Rodney, now he might be fun to peek at when he's getting a wash."

Lord Robert changed out of his suit into jeans, a black turtleneck, boots, and a raincoat, and left the dragon suit in the car. He put the bag containing the earrings he'd found in his raincoat pocket and left Vivienne to fly back to her hidden location. Robert kept her inside a hangar at his privately owned Ranfurly Park, a once public forested campground that had been locked up and closed for years.

A blinding light accompanied by what sounded like a gunshot sent a shockwave through him. He'd nearly been struck. It thundered, followed by hail. *Typical Cascadia weather.* By the time he reached the garage, he was drenched.

The chauffeur was already at work servicing the Royal Rodney, a popular make of car that had been driven by nobles and kings in The Green Isles for over a century. This one was a classic, popular in many films. The car was one of the many items Lord Robert's cousin Theo had left him in his Will.

Lord Robert cleared his throat, not wanting to startle the chauffeur, who was looking at the engine with the hood of the car open. "When I left the house to walk over here, the sky was perfectly clear," Robert said. "But it seems this weather is fickler than a woman, isn't it? Can't seem to make up its mind."

Despite Robert's attempt to give fair warning of his presence, the chauffeur jumped and bumped his head on the hood. "Lord Robert! Why are y'here at this hour?" He raised a bushy, silver eyebrow.

"Actually, I was thinking we might have a break in the rainy weather today and was planning to take my motor bike out for a ride to catch the sunrise, but now that the weather decided to turn foul, I've changed my mind."

"Ah. Well, the weather was a-same back home in Highland. I'm used to it. Better 'an livin' where it's dry and dusty."

"True. I much prefer green hills to brown," Lord Robert said. "But I'm looking forward to getting out on my motor bike again."

"Well, if you don't need a ride somewhere, can I get back to my engine?" the chauffeur asked.

"Yes, of course. But, before I forget, I wanted to see if you can pick up a remote for the front gate. That way you can open it without having to get out of the car to punch a code in. Such a bother to do that all the time, isn't it?"

"Mm," the chauffeur grumbled.

"Go ahead and find one you like. Just put it on my account," Lord Robert continued, shivering. Thunder clapped once again, and a bolt of lightning struck less than a foot from where he stood.

"Alright. I can do that." The chauffeur glowered. "I s'pose I could give you a ride back to the manor, so you don't have to walk the mile from here in this soggy muck and thunder."

"Yes, that would be nice, thank you." Lord Robert could have given the order to the chauffeur to drive him to the house. It was his car, after all, and the chauffeur was his employee. But he had too many more important issues to worry about than a disgruntled staff member.

Ever since he'd inherited the manor from the cousin he didn't know he had, he and his children had been disliked by the employees that came with the estate. If Robert wasn't a secret member of CAPE, he might have dealt with the staff. Fired them and found better, more loyal workers. But, as they say, one must pick their battles, and scrimmages on the home front were minuscule compared to the battles he faced on the outside.

He climbed into the backseat of the Royal Rodney, and his chauffeur drove him the short drive to the front steps of the manor. Robert rushed inside the house and headed upstairs.

On the way up, he was stopped when he ran into his household manager. She was up two hours before her shift started and was not looking happy. Which was nothing new for her. "Lord Ranfurly, you're home from your business trip. Good. I need to speak vith you!"

"Really? Right now? It's awfully early."

"Yes. It is urgent. Vile you were on your business trip, the new nanny quit." Lord Robert knew the household manager was upset by her thickened Gutish accent. "I didn't sleep a vink last night, thanks to your children who vere awake half the night vith no nanny to vatch after them! They refused to go to bed. I put out a request on the internet for a new nanny."

He gave her a nod. "Very well. I'm sorry for the trouble they caused you. I'll speak with the children about it."

"Hmph!"

"You should take a nap. You look exhausted," he told her.

The household manager clicked her heels and took off down the hall in a huff.

It was no surprise to Robert to hear his children didn't like the latest nanny. Ever since Peggy (their old nanny) had died, the children hadn't liked anyone he'd hired to take care of them. They just wanted Peggy back. She was like a grandmother to them.

He continued up to the third floor, where their bedrooms were. He peeked in on them. They both were sleeping soundly. He sighed. *My perfect like angels. A reminder that there is still goodness left in the world — a reason to hope. A reason to keep fighting.* After kissing each on the forehead, he headed down the hall to his own bedroom.

Once inside, he reached to pull out the earrings. That's when he realized the pouch wasn't fully sealed. Only one earring was inside it.

Where could I have lost the other earring?

HIGH TIME

THE NEXT DAY

Mill Pond, Cascadia

The day after I tried to burn down my forest, after I *thought* I saw the dragon, *could that have been real?* I sat up in bed and caught my reflection in the dresser mirror. What a fright. The puffy and swollen bags under the eyes weren't pretty. "Mm. I look like a sack of moldy potatoes."

"Did anyone else see that dragon, or did I just swig down way too much rum last night?" I asked the dogs as I let them outside through the sliding glass doors in my dining room. I stared out at the forest. The dead tree that had caught fire the night before was burned down to a stump, still smoking. Fortunately, there'd been a heavy rain overnight and the rest of the forest hadn't burned down with it.

The ducks were outside, yapping away. "Okay, okay! I hear you! Guess I'll have to wait for coffee. None of you are going to give me any peace until you've been fed."

After all the pets were happily munching down breakfast, I plopped into my favorite teal armchair with a cup of freshly brewed coffee in hand. This was the best part of the day. Mt. Ziwa was out for a grand appearance, a rare occasion. Most mornings it was cloudy. But not today. Clear, beautiful skies met me this morning.

I was grateful I lived out in the sticks, far from city life. With outrageous crime growing in the cities, and PAX replacing the police in those cities with drones, it was the last place I wanted to be. "No drones anywhere in sight here." I sighed. "All we have are lots of trees and big mountains." I recalled the dragon I'd seen the night before. "...And apparently dragons, on occasion."

The phone rang, causing me to jump and spill my coffee.

"Oh, sharks!" I know it probably sounded silly coming from a grown woman, but I once had a habit of swearing. When our son, Nick, was two and went through the parrot stage, repeating every word he heard, Keith and I agreed to soften up the profanity with cute-sounding replacements. It felt *almost* as good as really cussing.

It was my mom. "Hi honey. How are you today?"

"Great. Just fed the animals and now I'm enjoying my brew."

"Drew? Who is Drew? A new man in your life? Is that short for Andrew?"

"No. I didn't say Drew. I said brew ... B as in–" I glanced around my house trying to think of what started with the letter b. "B as in banana R-E-W. Brew. I meant my coffee, Mom."

"Oh. You know, I've been praying you would meet another nice man, Courtney."

"Well, I didn't meet a man, Mom. Where would I meet a man? I think you need to get your ears cleaned again."

"I just had them cleaned last week." Pause. "Oh darn. I was hoping you'd finally gone out and hooked up with someone."

"Hooked up with someone? Nope, Mom. Sorry to disappoint you but my first love is still coffee ... and Thor." My big dog looked up from his food when he heard his name, then went right back to chowing down.

Another pause. I knew this meant she was getting wound up and prepared myself for the unwinding.

"Courtney, now don't take this the wrong way..." *Here it comes.* "I know how you can be. But listen, with the kids gone now, and almost three years since Keith..." She sighed, then went on with her spiel. "Well, you aren't *that* old yet. You should join a gym. Get out. It's high time,

Courtney. Get out and meet people. Maybe another good one will come your way. But you'll never find him if you stay hidden out there in the woods."

"What are you trying to say, Mom? That I'm fat? Join a gym? Seriously?"

"Now I knew you were going to take what I said the wrong way, Courtney. All I meant was that it's high time you get out and live again. Before you get too old, like me. You've only got so long before all your organs start to fail, and sex can't be enjoyed anymore."

She did not just say that. I decided it was time to change the subject. "Gee, thanks, Mom. I'll think about it. So … how's Dad?"

"He's at the casino again. It used to be just Thursdays, but now he added Tuesdays and Saturdays. I told him he's going to gamble away his grandchildren's inheritance."

"Ah well, let the man have his fun. I mean, what else does he have to do now that he's retired?"

"I guess. … Hey, do you have those drones up in your area yet? We just got our first one here. It looks like a grasshopper, even hops like one, but it's about as big as a sheep."

"Really? You have a drone there? Your town isn't even that big!" I shuddered to think about it.

"It isn't nearly as fun to go out as it used to be with that flying robot bug hopping around. It's got guns too!"

"Scary."

"Well, I worry about you living all alone, Courtney. I sure wish you'd sell that place and move here. You could stay with us in our guest room if you don't want to buy another house."

"You don't need to worry about me, Mom. I'm not lonely. And you know I prefer my quiet, drone-free life in the mountains. Besides, do you really want my two dogs, three cats, and a whole flock of chickens and ducks moving into your backyard?"

"I do not."

I laughed. "I didn't think so. Well, I love you, but I have appointments today and need to jump in the shower."

The appointments were a lie, or we'd never get off the phone. But I really did need a shower.

"Okay. Well, glad to hear you're keeping busy. Love you, dear! Mwah!"

"Love you, Mom. Mwah!"

"Okay, buh-bye, dear!" she said.

"Buh-bye!" I said.

Click.

High time I get a life, huh? Join a gym? Like I can afford it.

Thanks to Keith's life insurance, both kids could attend private universities and neither needed to worry about working while in college. But I only had enough left in my savings for about six months. Facing the mirror of truth, a.k.a. my bank statement, I realized it was *high time* I get a job.

Ew.

I fired up my ancient laptop and miserably plunged into a job search.

"No, I don't want to sell printers."

"Yes, I would love to make sixty thousand pins a year and run the community center. But no. I don't have a degree."

"No, I'm not chipped."

I scrolled and scrolled, only to find *nada*. What could I possibly do that I was any good at?

I thought for a minute. When I was younger, I sang at a few weddings. I typed "wedding singer" into the search engine. That didn't lead to much. You'd think, with all the advanced technology, I'd have a little more luck with AI searches.

"Okay, what now?"

I felt like any talent I once had was long lost. Way back a million years ago in high school, I was a cheerleader, even starred in a few community theater productions. Everyone around Mill Pond used to call me a triple threat and tell me I should try my luck on the big stage in The Capital Region. My acting coach told me he thought I'd do well in the film industry if I moved to The Goldens. But the idea of me becoming a famous star dissipated like a wispy cloud when I graduated high school pregnant with my son Nick and my last acting number was when I managed to keep the pregnancy a secret from everyone.

Well, almost everyone.

In desperation, I told my best friend from The Goldens, Meg, who took it to her grave. It still breaks my heart to think about it, but she died before my wedding day.

At first, I tried to keep the pregnancy a secret from Keith, too. I didn't want him to feel trapped into marrying me. You can imagine my surprise when he pulled out a ring and proposed on the night of our high school graduation. He had no idea I was pregnant. I freaked out and said yes, of course! Afterward, I told him about the pregnancy.

Walking down the aisle pretending to be a virgin bride – that was my last star performance. And telling people Nick was a preemie because he came seven months after the wedding was the final bow before the curtain went down on that dream.

After I had Nick, I attended a few community college classes for a semester. But then came Laurel. By that time, Keith had landed a solid job as a marketing manager. We liked that I could stay home with the two kids, both still in diapers.

Now I could kick myself for not finishing college.

After an exhausting couple of hours entering my email with job-matching programs, I was ready to get up and stretch. I put the dogs out and poured myself another cup of coffee.

Swish. A notice for a job popped into my inbox.

"North Ireland, Cascadia. Looking for a live-in nanny for five-year-old twins. Room, board, full health and dental, chauffeur, in addition to five thousand pins per month for the perfect candidate."

Seriously? You had me at five thousand pins a month! I hit the **Apply Now** button.

COUSIN THEO HAD A SECRET

FOUR YEARS AGO

Ranfurly Manor, Cascadia

Robert rummaged through bottles of wine in the cellar of Ranfurly Manor when he spotted one of his favorites. "Ah! Look at that, Vintango by Joanna Martino. Year 2212. That was a hot season." He tried to pull the wine out. That's when he discovered it was a faux bottle. He pulled it and the wall in the corner of the cellar opened.

"What? A secret passage."

He headed through to explore. Once inside, the wall behind him closed and a chandelier above him flickered on. He stood in a foyer that led to more rooms.

Peering into one of the rooms, he found it had a bed with an adjacent bathroom. Next to the bed was a heart monitor, and a large cabinet of medical supplies. "A hospital room?" Robert wondered.

The next room was large and contained several mainframes and monitors. "These computers look outdated." He turned them on. "But they all seem to work. Looks like they're on a private server. ... What was Cousin Theo up to down here, I wonder?"

Not everything he found was agreeable. As he walked into the next room, he got a whiff of something foul. "Nasty." He curled up his top lip. There was a small kitchen, and a bowl of half-eaten ramen covered in mold sat on the counter. He opened the refrigerator and a rank odor blasted out. Eggs and milk had been left inside with the dates showing over a year past expiration. "Doesn't look like anyone has been in here since my cousin died."

He touched panels and pulled out books to see if more doors opened. When he spotted an eerie crystal skull sitting on a shelf, he raised his eyebrows. "Could this be…" He gripped it and turned it. A laser beam shot out of one of the eye sockets and lit up a jewel on the hilt of a sword across the room. The wall next to the fireplace opened.

A staircase behind the fireplace led up three flights. On the way up, he could hear his children talking to Peggy, the elderly nanny on the other side of the wall. At the top, he pushed open the wall and found himself in the loft above the room they called the Kiddie Bistro. The wall closed behind him.

A few months later, he discovered the entrance to a large cavern with a lake located far beneath the manor. Taped to a desk in the cavern was an envelope with his name written on it.

Dear Lord Robert,

    We've never met. But if you managed to discover this cavern, then you know I've left you with a few surprises. If only I was alive to see your reaction.

    Look to your left, you'll see the lake. Look closely, and you'll notice a dock at the edge of it. Walk onto the dock, and you'll find a boat. It's mirrored, so you can't see it unless you're above it.

Robert took the letter with him and walked to the dock. From there, he could see the interior of a speed boat. The exterior was mirrored, making it impossible to see, unless you were looking down on it. He continued to read.

    There's a hangar waiting for you over in Ranfurly Park. Inside this desk drawer, you'll find the keys to it, and to all the goodies that await you inside. I boarded up the park years ago, so it should be quiet and empty for you.

There's a way out of the cave by boat, but you won't see it until you're out on the water. Head west down river and the first dock you'll come to will be Ranfurly Park, thirty minutes by boat.

Use the gifts wisely, Cousin. Life's too short to be wasted.

Warmly,
Theodore Ranfurly II

Lord Robert marveled at how his cousin seemed to know him. "Did he know I was a member of CAPE? But of course, he couldn't have. I didn't join CAPE until after Theo died."

❧ *Courtney* ❧

Every day was the same routine. I'd wake around nine o'clock in the morning, feed my army of animals, sit in my teal armchair with a cup of coffee, and stare out my window at the glorious view. Then I'd plunge into my job search. I applied to so many jobs I lost track.

One day I got word that a new restaurant was opening in a nearby town, about a thirty-minute drive from my home in the woods. I went for an in-person interview, and the owner hired me on the spot.

The restaurant served authentic Vinosian dishes and had live music on weekends. One of the music groups was a trio with a female lead singer. They played songs my grandparents would have listened to when they were alive. I knew all the songs from hearing the recordings while growing up.

One night, the trio's lead singer was sick. During my break, I went over near the pianist and sang along to one of the songs. I wasn't as good as I used to be, but I guess I wasn't bad either, because the band coaxed me up on stage to perform more songs with them. The restaurant owner heard me sing and said, "Why have you been keeping this a secret?" He told me he wanted to hire me for his cousin's wedding. So, I was back to singing at weddings!

At last, I had purpose in life, a reason to get up beyond feeding the animals and drinking coffee. At last, I was making some money, and the tips were decent. I even got motivated to work out in the mornings and dropped twenty pounds. I was coming back to the world of the living.

SPRING

Two happy months went by like this until, out of the blue, a message was left on my voicemail. It was a woman with a Gutish accent.

"I'm looking for a Mrs. Courtney Drake. I am interested in setting up an interview. Please return this call immediately at 8-23-45-67890."

The phone number sounded like a scam. I didn't return the call.

That same night, I texted my kids, my dogs curled up next to me on the sofa.

Nick: Hey, Mom. There's so much happening here. It's a crazy time to live in Capital City, that's for sure. But I'm managing to stay under the radar. I've made some great friends, though. How are you?

Me: I'm great. I like my job at the restaurant. Keeps me from feeling sorry for myself. I'm so glad you are making friends. But I sure wish you could just come home whenever you felt like it. I miss you!

Nick: I miss you too, Mom. But I'm learning a lot about our new government. They're going to start rolling out tests to categorize people. I'll be one of the first to take it, since I plan on working for them. I'll check in again tomorrow. Love you.

What? I felt sick to my stomach. Nick had always been interested in political science. I wouldn't have minded him working for the government before PAX, when Zone B was governed by the people and we voted in our leaders. It wasn't perfect, but it wasn't as bad as PAX.

When we found out PAX killed Keith, Nick despised them. I couldn't wrap my head around why he still wanted to work in government, for *them.* "What is that college teaching him?"

PAX. The acronym stood for Peace Alliance Ten. Our new government certainly had their way of maintaining peace. *By force.*

A conversation came to mind that we'd had at the dinner table about a week before Keith went missing.

He'd asked the kids, "What's better? Big government or small?"

"Small," sixteen-year-old Nick replied.

"Why?" Keith asked.

"Because leaders can never be trusted with too much power."

"That's right. And do you think PAX wants big government or small?"

"I don't know. They want to maintain peace," Laurel said. "And they did stop the war."

"Did they, though? Or was it an earthquake that swallowed up the armies?"

"PAX claims they were the ones who created that earthquake," Nick said.

"Maybe they did," Keith said. "Or maybe they didn't. Either way, would you say things are more peaceful since they took global power?"

"Let's see … inflation, unemployment, crime at an all-time high," Nick said. "Definitely not more peaceful."

"And the newest AI developments creep me out," Laurel said.

Keith nodded. "Leaders used to have accountability in Zone B. It was the quality that set our zone apart from all the others. Who is holding The Ten billionaires who are running the world accountable?" We couldn't answer because we didn't know. And it was against the law to even have the conversation we were having, so it was a good thing we weren't having it in public.

I loved that Keith asked provocative questions and encouraged our kids to share their thoughts at the dinner table. He was outspoken, fearless. And he taught them the importance of standing up for what they believe in. I remember thinking, *not even a totalitarian regime will keep my man down.*

Now Nick had turned out like his father. Which scared me to the core. The last thing I wanted was to see him end up killed by the regime. Or worse, I worried he might join a Resistance group. People who joined the Resistance had a death wish.

Next, I opened Laurel's text. She'd sent a photo of her and Charlotte, her roommate, wearing new outfits. Each of them was hugging a giant redwood tree.

Laurel: Hey. Our latest thrift finds!

Me: Cute! What are you up to?

Laurel: We went on a beautiful hike in the coastal mountains! Charlotte somehow managed to lean against a banana slug and the slime won't come out. Made me think of you.

Me: Bummer! But why did slug slime remind you of me, exactly?

Laurel: It's totally something I could see you doing, Mom.

Me: You're not wrong! Search it up online, maybe there's something to take slug slime out of clothing.

Laurel: Yeah, we should do that.

Me: I miss you!

Laurel: Miss you too. Been a busy semester. I'm in too many classes. Lots of homework.

Me: The semester's almost over. You can do it!

Laurel: I know. I will. Just can't wait to get a break.

Me: You're coming home for summer, right?

Laurel: Yup. Charlotte wants to come stay with us too. That's okay, right?

Me: Of course. She's family.

Laurel: Okay, thanks. Love you. Gotta get some work done now.

Me: Love you too.

I put down my cell phone and curled up to read a novel. Just as I got comfortable on the couch, my landline rang. I glanced at the clock. *Nine thirty. Awfully late.*

My dogs lifted their heads, a concerned look on their faces.

"What do you think, guys? Should I answer it?"

Thor tilted his head.

"It could be someone looking for a yummy dog to eat."

They both gave me a look as if to say, *please don't let anyone hurt us.*

The phone stopped ringing. Then started up again a few minutes later.

"Oh, quit worrying. It's just Nanny and Papa. They're the only ones who have the number to that phone." My parents knew to call twice in a row to let me know it was them. I hoped nothing was wrong since they were calling at such a late hour. "Hi. Is everything okay?"

"Is this Mrs. Drake?"

Oh no.

It was the staccato voice that had left a message on my cell phone earlier.

"Who is calling, please?"

"I'm calling regarding a job you applied for."

Thor and Loki let out low growls.

"I'm sorry, there must be a misunderstanding, I haven't applied for any jobs. How did you get this number?"

"You are Courtney Drake, ya?"

I didn't respond.

"Lord Ranfurly has done extensive background checks into each candidate, and it is down to only three people. You are one of the three."

"I'm sorry, lord who? Candidate for what?"

"Lord Ranfurly. He is searching for a nanny for his twins. He needs the position filled immediately. We have an opening for an interview tomorrow at six o'clock."

A light bulb dimly flickered in my head. I vaguely recalled applying for a position involving some twins quite a while back. It felt like months ago. Then again, I realized it had only been a couple of months since I'd started working at the restaurant. I tried to remember the job post. Something about five thousand pins a month and all dental and health covered.

That was the job that sounded too good to be true. Hmm.

Her abrupt tone broke into my thoughts. "Is it true that you have not received the PAX implant?"

I wasn't sure whether it was a good idea to admit the truth. "Nooo … I haven't … yet."

"*Das ist gut.* Lord Ranfurly will not hire anyone with the chip. Our driver will arrive to pick you up at half past four o'clock tomorrow morning."

"Wait … what? In the *morning*?"

She either didn't hear me or pretended not to, because she continued without taking a breath. "I will see you tomorrow at six o'clock, Mrs. Drake." *Click.*

They know where I live and are coming for me? Tomorrow? At half past four? IN THE MORNING? Is she for real? I looked over at my dogs. "What do you guys think? Psychopath? Or real opportunity worth looking into?"

They paid me no mind. They were back to sleeping comfortably on my couch.

"Nah! Too ridiculous. I bet it's a scam. Watch. Nobody will show up."

PURGATORY

THE SAME NIGHT
Emer Aude, Cascadia

Lord Robert took Vivienne out for a spin to Club Purgatory. Invisible and undetected by drones, she dropped him off in a vacant alley, then flew to a roof top and waited there until he signaled her.

Disguised in a silver wig, mustache, and beard, and dressed like a wealthy cowboy, he showed up out in front of the club, acting drunk and pulling off a convincing drawl. He carried a suitcase in each hand.

"Howdy," he said to the bouncers at the club entrance.

"May we help you?" one of the bouncers asked.

"I hope you can. I'm feeling a little hungry for something tasty and expensive."

"Do you have a reservation, sir?"

Lord Robert had already done his homework on the club. They required a nightly password to get in. With a little help from Baca and Dillard, he knew the latest ones.

"I reckon I must, or I wouldn't waste my *scratch* and *call* here, would I?" He held up the suitcases.

"Place your suitcases, belt, and hat on the conveyer and walk through our security scanner, sir."

Robert had hidden weapons inside his boots, but Baca had devised a clever way to keep them from being detected through scanners at clubs and airports. He wasn't sure how she and Dillard did it, but their inventions had saved his neck on countless occasions. He breezed through security without a hitch.

Big picture, Robert, he said to himself. Time to become a pervy rank cowboy. *He headed into the club, fully in character.*

He scanned the club, smiling and acting interested in every half-naked girl in the room. Talking crass and pretending to drink for a good hour, he sat at the bar.

Finally, he spotted what he was looking for. The serpent earrings. The bartender saw him staring at the two teenage girls who wore them.

"Those two are always saved for later, you know. But if you want them, I hope you brought the bank."

"Who do I pay to get them?" Robert asked. The bartender pointed to the door the girls just came through.

"The Demon. In there." Robert got up, and the bartender gave him a warning. "Serious buyers only. That isn't a crowd to mess around with."

"Oh, make no mistake, sir. I'm very serious." Robert placed one hundred pins on the counter for the bartender, tilted his cowboy hat as a salute, and headed through the door. Inside, people were playing pool and slot machines.

As he walked through the room, he observed unspeakable acts being done to women and children. *Maintain control,* he warned himself. He wished he had the ability to throw flames at every violator in the room. *But that would be too light a punishment.*

He recalled the words of his friend Peter Williams, the founder of CAPE. "The wrath of the Creator is the most terrifying punishment a person will face. Vengeance belongs to Him."

In the corner of the room, a man sat on a throne made of pitch forks. On each side of the throne was a naked woman chained to a post. He held a whip, which he used on them unexpectedly from time to time. A hideous mask with horns concealed his face.

Robert approached the throne.

"Welcome, cowboy," The Demon said.

Lord Robert tipped his hat.

"You've found the place with the best variety in Cascadia. We've something on our menu for every palate. What are you craving tonight?"

"The pair of girls with the serpent earrings, for starters." Robert licked his lips.

"For starters? Oh, those girls are not starters. They are dessert."

"How much for a six-course meal, plus two desserts?"

The Demon laughed. "How much do you guess that will cost?"

"One million."

The Demon glowered. "You didn't come here to waste my time, did you, Cowboy?"

"Well, now, don't get twisted up in a knot, no offense intended, Demon. Why don't you tell me what amount is worth your time?"

"Ten million," the Demon said.

"Very well, sir. I brought Zelby with me," Robert placed a suitcase that contained ten million pins on a table and opened it.

"You named your suitcase. Adorable." The Demon eyed the pins and curled his upper lip, revealing sharpened teeth. "Ten million Zone A pins, not Zone B pins."

Knowing the exchange rate had put Zone A pins at a value of twice as much, Robert had come prepared. "Oh, you don't like Zelby? Okay." He closed the suitcase and took it off the table. "I brought Zelda along for the ride, too." He set down the other suitcase and opened it. "Ten million Zone A pins, at your service." He tipped his hat and smiled like a proud schoolboy.

The Demon flashed his fangs and motioned to one of his men to go get the girls. A moment later, four children and two teenagers were brought out.

"These ones," he pointed to three of them, "are reserved for the weekends by VIPs. Bring them all back before twenty-four hours. Return them in perfect condition. No broken bones," The Demon said.

Robert raised an eyebrow at The Demon. It took all his strength to stay in character. "I only see six courses. Where are my two desserts?"

"Ha! Well, now that'll cost you that ten million Zone B pins in your other suitcase." The Demon sneered.

"Let me make sure you are giving me the two I want before I hand over my millions. I only want the ones with the earrings." Robert stood in his cowboy boots, legs planted, ready for action.

The Demon laughed. "Bring the princesses of the evening to Black Angus here."

The two girls were brought to him, and Robert handed over Zelby.

"Twenty-four hours. No bruises on the desserts," The Demon instructed. "The earrings come back with them."

Lord Robert left Purgatory with the eight girls he'd purchased. He met Vivienne out of view of the club. When the invisible bullet shaped car suddenly became visible to the girls, they gasped.

"Don't be alarmed. This is going to be your ride." In the vehicle's trunk, he routinely kept blankets for the trafficking victims he rescued. The look of surprise came over the faces of every girl when he pulled out the blankets and wrapped them over each of their shoulders.

Next, he checked for trackers and listening devices. "Can I see those please?" Robert asked the two teenage girls wearing the earrings.

The girls paled. One shook her head and said, "We can't take them off. The Demon will punish us."

"It's alright. I promise. No harm will come to either of you," he said.

The girls hesitated.

He checked around him for signs of being followed. "But we must hurry."

The teenagers cautiously placed their earrings into his gloved hand. Robert pulled back his sleeve and aimed his Digi-watch's scanner to check for bugs and trackers. *No listening devices. Good.* But one earring in each pair had a tracker. They were also different than the other earrings he'd found. *Hmm. These have sapphire stones for eyes. That's different. The other serpent earrings had ruby eyes.* Throwing the earrings with trackers into the fountain, he pocketed the two earrings that scanned clean.

He turned to the girls, who were eyeing him with baffled expressions on their faces. "Does anyone else have any jewelry? Rings, piercings, necklaces, bracelets, other loose items? If so, hand them to me. Quickly."

The girls did what he asked. He scanned, and every article checked out clean. He handed the girls back their loose items and said, "Now I need each of you to take off your shoes."

One of them whispered, "Is he robbing us?" The others shrugged their shoulders.

"He's checking for trackers," said one of the teenagers who had been wearing the serpent earrings. She appeared to be the oldest of the girls.

Robert scanned each shoe and found a tracking device planted in every one of them.

"Here." He started handing shoes back to the girls.

One of the girls started to put the shoes back on. He stopped her.

"No, don't put them on. Do this." He pitched a shoe into the fountain.

The girls all broke into smiles, a couple even giggled. They each threw the shoes into the nearby fountain. One shoe didn't make it in. Robert ran to pick it up, and chucked it in.

"One last thing I must do before you can get in the car," Robert did a scan of each girl for implants. Sure enough, they'd all been chipped. He wasn't surprised. The Demon was just doing the dirty work of running the trafficking operation. But PAX was behind the curtain, receiving the big pins. Ultimately, these girls were PAX property.

Out of their earshot, he asked Vivienne, "Does your system have the ability to disable the PAX implants once these girls are inside the car?"

"CAPE Tech tested me in this exact scenario, and yes, my system is sufficient."

"I have the same system at Ranfurly Park, so we should be good, then. McGregor and Kila will need to extract the implants from the girls before they leave the hangar."

"Warning. Armed drones are heading our way."

Robert turned to the girls. "Hop in, quickly! Two in the front passenger seat, the other six in the back. Good thing you're all little and light, you'll have to double up on seats; she isn't made to fit more than five adults."

The girls climbed into the back of Vivienne, and Robert jumped behind the wheel. They were amazed when the car lifted off the ground.

"We're flying!" One of the girls said.

"I can't believe it," another girl whispered.

Lord Robert pushed a button and put Vivienne in fully armored stealth mode, seconds before drones with weapons rounded the corner and blasted lasers into the fountain.

The girls panicked.

Floodlights probed the alley below, searching.

Robert held a finger to his lips, warning the girls not to make a sound. Vivienne rose high above the city skyscrapers, undetected by the drones and their searchlights.

Sighs of relief could be heard as they shot into the night, away from the city.

They sat in silence during the ride to his hangar, until a little girl asked, "Where do you think we're going?"

The others shushed her, warning the girl not to speak.

"It's alright." Robert spoke in his normal accent. "You girls are safe with me. And with Vivienne, my car."

"Hello girls," Vivienne said.

The girls exchanged "wow" expressions.

"Your car can talk?" one of them asked.

"Yes, I can. I can fly, talk, protect you from trackers, and I'm invisible right now, so nobody can see us flying through the sky."

"Wow," the girls said.

"So, that's why the drones didn't see us?" one of the teenagers asked.

"Yes."

The girls became more comfortable and chattery.

"I thought you were a cowboy," one girl asked Lord Robert. "But now you talk different. Why?"

"I had to be in disguise in order to rescue you."

"Rescue?" she repeated.

The other girls began whispering to each other.

"He's rescuing us!"

"Will he bring me to my mommy?"

Robert felt a warm sensation go through him. It was for moments like this that made the risk worth it.

They arrived at Lord Robert's hangar, where CAPE team members McGregor and Kila were waiting to fly the girls to a CAPE safe house. They removed the PAX implants from each of the girls and Kila laid out sweatpants and sweaters for them to put on.

"You're free now," Kila told them. "We aren't going to let those bad people hurt you anymore."

One of the younger ones asked, "Are we going to see my mommy?"

"I hope so. We will look for all your parents," Kila told them.

"Are you a police officer?" a young teen asked.

"I was, before the bad government took over." Kila pointed a thumb at Lord Robert and McGregor. "Now I work with these guys. We do what we can to get kids like you away from bad people." She talked to the kids until they were ready to load everyone into the larger jet.

"Any trouble on your way here?" Lord Robert asked McGregor.

McGregor shook his head. "No issues or confrontations with haywire drones or traffic control towers. The chips seem to be doing their job at fooling PAX tech."

Lord Robert nodded. "Good. And thank you for making the trip. I know it's a long flight each way."

McGregor grinned. "Are you kidding? The plane flies itself! We pretty much watched movies the entire flight. You're the one who did all the hard work. And rescues like this are what I live for!"

Kila helped the girls onto the plane and McGregor boarded behind them. Lord Robert waved as the plane took off.

Once they were gone, Lord Robert checked the time. Half-past midnight.

The night was still young. Time to track down a killer. "Back to Club Purgatory we go," he said to Vivienne. He changed into his dragon-skin suit on the way.

When they arrived, he waited inside Vivienne on a rooftop behind the club. It gave them a clear view of the alleyway below. Armed drones passed, but Vivienne's high-tech armor did its work to keep them from being detected.

"The drones don't bother with the club, where crimes are committed," he said.

"No. They are operated by PAX, and the traffickers at the club are profiting PAX. The annual global market value of human trafficking is six hundred billion Zone A pins. This is a three hundred percent increase from the year 2223, when the global market value was at one hundred fifty billion. PAX's share is ninety percent of that."

"Absurd. I knew they were benefiting, but ninety percent? That is…" Lord Robert shook his head.

"Sick and twisted," Vivienne finished.

The back door of the club opened, a lone man came out the back door. He stood still a moment, then Robert saw him pull a ski mask over his head. His body movements were familiar. Agile, like an acrobat. "The Ninja," Robert said.

"Yes. You encountered him the night you found the serpent earrings on the dead victim."

"Drop me down there, then wait for my signal."

"As you wish, my lord," Vivienne replied.

Robert quietly got out of the invisible car and shadowed the Ninja.

Patrol drones were heading toward him. Robert's suit was undetectable, but not invisible. He silently darted behind a wall and crouched down, avoiding their probing lights.

Once the drones were past, Robert searched for the Ninja. He was nowhere in sight.

Blasted drones. I lost him.

The wind was knocked out of him as he was kicked from behind. The Ninja whipped past.

Robert kicked the Ninja in the face and sent him down.

The Ninja did a flip in the air and power-kicked Robert in the chest.

Blinding light flashed in Robert's eyes. A drone. He dove into a dumpster, barely avoiding being shot by its laser blast.

Vivienne blasted a shot at the drone and knocked it out of the sky. It crashed next to the dumpster. More drones were heading their way.

Apparently, Robert's dragon suit wasn't so impenetrable. He could feel the cold air on his bare skin. He recalled the knife in the Ninja's hand. When the Ninja had whipped past him, he must have sliced the suit and ripped it.

It wasn't until he was safe inside the car that he took off the suit and saw the stab wound.

On the way back to his hangar, Robert called his friend, Peter Williams, founder of CAPE.

"The Ninja got away. Yet again. Managed to stab me first." Robert pressed into the stab wound to put pressure on it.

"Are you alright?" Peter asked.

"No worse off than I ever am," Robert said. "But I'm beginning to think maybe you are right. Perhaps I could use a partner."

Peter chuckled. "I was just waiting for you to say that. I already have her for you."

"Her?" Robert groaned. "You trying to set me up now?"

Peter laughed. "Hardly. I'm assigning my niece as your new partner."

"Winnifred? Isn't she a little young? And inexperienced?"

"Don't underestimate her. She's young, yes, but she's got a lot of experience in forensics, and she can hold her own in a fight. I wouldn't send her if I didn't think she was capable. She certainly knows how to patch up a wounded soldier, and you seem to need a lot of patch-ups lately."

"Hmph. Speaking of patch-ups, why don't you talk to Dillard and Baca about making this suit *completely* impenetrable. It was ripped tonight, when the Ninja stabbed me with his knife."

"Hey, show a little gratitude. Think of how many times you would have been captured or killed if it weren't for them."

"Peter, you don't have to defend them every time I point out their mistakes. They aren't children. They told me the suit would be able to deflect bullets and lasers. Yet it failed when a knife pierced it. You must admit, it needs improvement."

Peter sighed. "Alright, I'll talk to them about it. But you could be more appreciative. They both look up to you and want to make you happy."

"I'll send Baca flowers and Dillard … I don't know–"

"He likes comic books."

"Fine. I'll send him a comic book along with a thank you card. Will that redeem me in your eyes, Peter?"

"A little. But if you can give Winnie a job at your manor so she can work undercover with you, that would certainly earn you many redemption points."

Robert sighed. "I suppose I can do that. I'll clear Winnie to work as a maid."

Peter laughed. "A maid? Isn't there something else you can have her do there? Winnie isn't exactly the type to tidy up after anyone. Not sure she even knows how."

"Oh. How about a gardener, then?"

"Uh, I don't think you want her near any of your flowers."

"I'm afraid there isn't anything else I can have her–" Robert suddenly felt ill. "Vivienne, are you spinning in circles?"

"No. I'm flying in a straight line."

"Do a scan on him, Vivienne," Peter said.

A minute later she reported, "My system detected poison has entered Lord Robert's bloodstream. It is moving slowly. If it isn't reversed, he will die within thirty minutes."

"The tip of that blade must have been…" Robert felt like he was about to pass out.

"Laced with some kind of poison," Peter finished. "Robert, put the suit back on, and push the first aid button on it. … Don't let him pass out, Vivienne," Peter said.

Vivienne blasted cold air into the car. Robert put his suit back on and pushed the first aid button, just before he lost consciousness.

TWO HOURS LATER

When Robert awoke, the stab wound was still tender. But the dragon suit had saved him from whatever poison was on that blade.

The first aid button. Dillard and Baca forgot to mention this latest feature in my new suit.

It was true what Peter said. He owed his life to those two.

Peter was also right about Lord Robert getting wounded all too often. He'd acted as his own doctor on numerous occasions. Fortunately, he'd survived this long on his own. Deep down he knew that having another CAPE team member might be helpful. But he wasn't used to working with people, and part of him felt like another person would just get in his way.

And Winnie? Why does Peter think Winnie will be a good partner for me?

The last time he'd seen her, she was only sixteen. Back then, she was a sweet kid with an afro and a wide, bracket-toothed grin, and she was starting the young officer training program at her high school.

It's been a while. Come to think of it, that was eight or nine years ago. I suppose she's a little more grown up now. Robert shook his head. Time flew.

Vivienne's bullet shape maneuvered easily through the narrow, hidden entrance into the underground cavern below the manor. She hovered over the lake and set down an automatic ramp that released by the driver's seat door. "I'm afraid this is as far as I can take you. You'll have to climb the stairs up to your manor on your own," she said.

"I'll manage it," Robert grumbled as he exited down the ramp. Every joint in his body ached, and it felt like he was dragging heavy weights as he made his way up the steep flight of stairs to reach the hidden rooms in the cellar.

As he ascended, he wondered how it would feel to share this hidden world with another human. Nobody in CAPE, not even Peter, knew about his secret hide-away beneath the manor. And he liked it that way. If Winnie was going to be his partner, could he keep his underworld a secret? But if he didn't tell her about it, how could she help him during times like this, when he was injured?

Peter said Winnie's strength was in forensics. CAPE forensics had tested the serpent earrings for poison and found no trace. "The earrings with ruby eyes are worth a fortune," Robert said out loud. "Yet they were left behind on the victims. Why didn't the murderer take the earrings? Well, perhaps with her background in forensics, Winnie will be some help in discovering more answers."

It was four thirty in the morning when he reached the bedroom in the hidden underground. *Oh, blast.* Pain seared through his forehead as he remembered he had a meeting scheduled. *This is the morning I'm supposed to interview the nanny at six o'clock.*

He had to get an hour of sleep before the interview. Throbbing pain behind his eyes clouded his ability to focus. He slipped into a dreamless sleep … and didn't wake out of it for forty-eight hours.

6

WHITE KNIGHT

∾Courtney∾

THE SAME MORNING
Mill Pond, Cascadia

Keith was throwing a rope, playing fetch with Little Bear, our chocolate lab. But then I remembered Little Bear died many years ago. I felt a chill as a shadow passed over. It was a drone that turned into a giant snake, stopping to scan the area. A doorbell rang, and Little Bear started barking.

***

I sat up abruptly. *Another dream.* I often had vivid and disturbing dreams. But in this one, Keith and Little Bear were alive, and I didn't want to wake from that part. As for the drone-snake-thingy… I wanted to forget that. I closed my eyes, trying to recall the happy moment in the dream, trying to picture Keith again. The sound of my dogs barking wildly broke into my serenity.

Then I realized my doorbell in real life was dinging.

I grabbed my cell phone off the floor. *Four thirty in the morning. Who is friggin' ringing my doorbell at half past four in the morning? And where is my sweatshirt?* I moaned, mad that it was still cold in the mornings.

Cascadia was still dark, cold, and gloomy and it was supposed to be spring. After a brief search, I found my sweatshirt at the foot of the bed. "I can't wait until the sun finally decides to shine again," I grumbled, pulling the sweatshirt over my head.

Eyes barely able to see clear through the crusts, I stumbled through the house. My dogs were waiting in the foyer. It was dark when I peered out the front door peephole.

I turned on the porch light, which revealed a man wearing a white shirt with black suspenders, white gloves, and a tweed Herringbone cap. He was whistling and gazing toward the orchard in my front yard. When the light came on, he turned around and waved at the peephole.

I held down my intercom button. "May I help you?" I managed, barely producing a vocal tone at that ungodly hour.

"I'm here to pick up a … *ahem*, Mrs. Drake?"

"And you are who, exactly?" *Need. Coffee. Now.*

"I work for Lord Ranfurly. You are set for an interview at the Ranfurly Manor. My orders were to pick you up at half past four. And here I am." He flashed a very charming smile at the peep hole.

"This has to be a prank." I said this out loud to myself, without pushing the intercom button.

Apparently, he could still hear me. "Definitely not a prank, ma'am. In fact, my job will be on the line if I don't get you to that interview by six o'clock."

I peeked out to take a second look at the guy. It was like seeing a man who stepped out of a page of the *Gentleman's Quest* magazine. He took off his cap, revealing light brown hair that was tapered on the sides, and longer waves on top. He jumped up and down as if trying to stay warm.

I pushed the intercom button again, "You do realize it's still dark out?"

He glanced at his wristwatch. An old-fashioned one with a brown leather band. Very last century, like something we used to wear before the digital world took over. He pushed the intercom button and pleaded. "Ma'am, please. The interview is a good hour's drive from here. I got up at three o'clock in the morning to come collect you. How long will it take for you to get ready?"

"Collect me?" I mouthed to my faithful guard dogs. They were sitting behind me the whole time, ears perked up, eyes alert. Only, they were more like two playful overgrown puppies than the fierce guard dogs they were supposed to be. "Why are you two looking so excited? You should be growling at him, warding him off! This guy isn't here to take you for a walk and bring you treats!" I said, apparently a little too loudly.

"Dogs love me," he spoke in the door margin.

I pushed the intercom button. "Why do you assume I'm talking to dogs? How can you be certain they're not alligators?"

"Well, if you have alligators, then you will be quite at home with Elsie," he piped back.

"Who is Elsie?"

"You'll see."

"I'll see Elsie, huh?" I took a step back and stared at Thor, who was eyeing the door, tail wagging. … "Why is this happening?" I asked him, forgetting the man at my door could hear me. "I haven't even had my coffee yet."

"Listen, I will stop for a coffee if you'll move at light speed."

The guy wasn't going away.

"Fine," I surrendered. I left him out there on the porch and hurried off to my bedroom to change. Man, was I glad I never opened the door for the guy, because when I took off the sweatshirt, I saw it was inside out, and the tag was in the front. I slipped into a black skirt and a beige silk blouse that ruffled in the front. Then I put on a houndstooth school-boy blazer and zipped on a pair of high heeled faux leather boots.

The whole morning was starting off surreal. I slapped my face to make sure I wasn't dreaming. *Yow! Okay, okay. I'm not dreaming.*

I had to admit I did apply for the job at one point, and the pay and perks had sounded too good to be true. But all this? *Was. Not. Normal.*

I hurried to the front door. Mr. *GQ* had been leaning against it, and as I swung the door open, he lost his balance. He turned to me and said,

"G'day, ma'am." Then his eyes seemed to fixate on my hair. "Ahem." He pointed at my head. "I'd check the mirror," he advised.

"Oh crunch!" I said after I ran back inside and caught a glimpse of my reflection in the mirror that hung in my foyer. Mascara was smeared under my eyes. My hair was sticking straight up on one side, fly-aways going every direction. Jetting to my bathroom, I grabbed the makeup bag, stuffed the emergency kit in it: makeup remover wipes, face powder, mascara, spray bottle of water, hairbrush and spray, lip liner, blush, lipstick.

I was about to leave when I remembered the dogs. "About how long will this interview take? I need to feed my army of animals."

"Ah, right. The alligators."

"Yes, them too."

"I'll have you back by mid-morning," he promised.

I ordered the dogs outside, where the cats were waiting at the door to come in. One of the cats shot past me and made a beeline for Nick's bedroom. I chased after her, but she escaped me by hiding under the bed. Mr. *GQ* called the cat. "Here, kitty..."

At the sound of his call, she immediately came out from under the bed and ran right to him. He picked her up, stroked her fur, and carried her outside, then set her down gently on the front porch rocking chair. "There's a good kitty." He patted her on her head.

"Wow. I'm impressed. You're a Cat Whisperer."

I stopped in my tracks when I saw the car I was about to climb into. He had opened the back door of a Royal Rodney White Gallant. I knew a little about this model. Keith's dad restored old cars, and the White Gallant was his pet project. Before his dad passed, he salvaged and restored it, then eventually sold it. Keith's mom had a picture of their family standing next to the car hanging up in their hallway.

"Beauty, isn't she?" The driver had a look of pride as if this were his begotten child.

"Hmm, impressive," I replied. "A White Gallant Edition."

"Well! Now I'm the one who's impressed!"

I climbed into the car and for the next several minutes, the leather interior of the Royal Rodney was used as my powder room. I cleaned off my face, reapplied makeup, and did my hair. Then I saw that I had gotten a little makeup on the seat. Panicking, I grabbed one of my makeup remover sheets and tried to clean the makeup off. A hint of peach color from my blush on the otherwise perfectly white leather wouldn't wipe clean. I could only imagine what this mistake might cost. I prayed the driver wasn't catching any of the action in his rearview mirror.

I shivered. It was cold in the back of the car. My hands were freezing. Luckily, I'd brought along my brown leather gloves. I put them on.

"So why is this interview so early in the morning?" I asked.

"The Household Manager can't have anything interfere with her regular schedule, so she made the interview before it begins."

Oh. Lovely. ... "You mentioned we might be able to stop for coffee?" I asked, as sweetly as I could muster without having any caffeine in me.

"You took far too long arguing with me," he scolded.

"Hmph," I pouted. I caught his glance in the rearview mirror, and I showed him my best sad face.

"You know, coffee is actually very bad for you," he said, shifting his eyes back and forth between the road ahead of him and me in his rearview mirror.

"I don't think you and I can ever be friends," I said. I eyed the pinkish-peach stain on the car's interior, guilt-ridden.

That's when I noticed an earring on the floor of the backseat. I wondered if it could belong to the driver's girlfriend. *Or wife?* I picked it up and held it in my gloved hand to inspect it. A serpent, with emeralds, and two rubies for its eyes. Beautiful. I wondered if it was real or costume. "Do you know anyone who lost an earring? I found one here on the backseat floor."

His forehead crinkled in the mirror. Finally, he said, "Probably one of the other candidates who were interviewed for the job. Here, why don't you leave it with me. I can ask around to see if anyone knows who it belongs to."

He opened his white-gloved hand, and I handed him the earring. We had just turned off the highway.

"Where exactly is this place? I've never been this way before."

He stopped in the middle of the road for a farmer who was crossing with a herd of sheep. "You see, here is another reason why we can't stop for coffee." He pointed at the sheep crossing. Then he continued, "It's on a river island, about thirty minutes from the small community known as North Ireland."

I'd never heard of it.

The last pudgy sheep made its way across the road, and then we were moving again. We turned onto a street that was lined with cedars, and the landscape went from wild and overgrown to manicured and lovely. Then I caught sight of what appeared to be a castle through an opening in the cedars.

"That isn't the manor, is it?" I asked. "It looks like a castle."

He chuckled. "Locals call it Ranfurly Castle. We used to give once a month tours, before Lord Ranfurly moved in. But no, it isn't a castle. Castles are fortified to fend off enemies. This is just a manor."

"Interesting," I replied. "Why does a lord live out here? Where is he from?"

"Lord Ranfurly is from Knoxfordshire. The Green Isles. That is where the original Theodore Ranfurly the First who built this place came from. He was nobility, too. Of course, now he's long dead. He had a daughter who had a son. The son was Theodore Ranfurly the Second. He was born here and had no title, just went by Mr. Ranfurly. He was my boss. He died a few years back and had no heirs, so that's when his cousin, Lord Ranfurly, inherited it."

"Aha. So your old boss was the grandson of the guy who built the place?"

"Very good."

"Thank you. And what made Grandpa Ranfurly want to leave his castle in Knoxfordshire and come to wild Cascadia. Some crazy scandal?"

"Ha, who knows? There could have been. But more than likely it was because he was the third son of a viscount. In the Green Isles, the law is that the eldest brother inherits everything, and if they are a decent brother, they give a reasonable allowance to the younger siblings. As a third son, he came here on a quest for gold. Like so many others. But he was one of the lucky ones. Grandpa Ranfurly struck it rich." He stopped again for an elk that was crossing the road. "Eventually, he married and built the Ranfurly Manor with his fortune."

"You say you used to give tours of the place. People came all the way out here?"

"Yes, my boss did."

"Your boss was the grandson Ranfurly. And he never married?"

"That's right. No, he did not. He held tours for people he personally invited, not to the public," he explained.

"Interesting. So, how did you like working for the previous owner?" I asked.

"I liked him. I grew up here. Learned all about taking care of horses and just about everything else. Mr. Ranfurly was like the father I wish I had. Haven't lived here most of my adult life, though. Just came back here a year ago and was sad to learn Mr. Ranfurly had died. I was also surprised to find the whole household disrupted by the new Ranfurly—the fancy lord—and his twins. Mr. Ranfurly never had children, so the elderly staff are pulling out their hair because none of them know what to do with those little tykes."

We stopped at a very fancy, expensive-looking cast iron black gate. He got out of the car to punch a code into a little box that was mounted to a post. The gate opened for us, and he proceeded to drive through. "Nice we don't have to fuss with all that AI biz out here in the middle of nowhere but punching in this code is a bit of a pain, especially when those monsoons pass over," he said.

"I bet. I'm surprised there isn't a remote for it. So, where's the mother of the twins?"

"What I was told, died after childbirth. Bled to death."

I cringed, and a flashback of my own labor experience passed through my mind. I'd almost died from bleeding too much after Nick's birth.

The driver regarded me in the rearview mirror. "Ah, look at that! You've been transformed into a lovely picture."

"Yes, what a difference lipstick and a hairbrush can make," I replied. "So, do you enjoy working for Lord Ranfurly?"

I didn't get to hear his answer because we'd reached our destination. "Look at that! Fifty-eight minutes past five. I got you here with two minutes to spare. Am I good or am I good?"

I stepped out of the vehicle and into the shadow of the manor's overpowering entrance. One of the huge double doors opened, and a large-boned woman stepped out onto the landing. She had a long, hooked nose, and her features reminded me of a Crissal thrasher. She wore a grey smock with a matching grey apron, and her dull grey hair was pulled back into a tight bun. Her stockings were brown and non-slip rubber brown shoes appeared almost comical on her humongous feet. The woman's skin tone matched the shade of her outfit – she wore a stone-cold, sour expression on her face.

MEET THE CHILDREN

THE SIX O'CLOCK IN THE MORNING INTERVIEW
Ranfurly Manor

"This way," said the woman in grey.

I followed her through the manor's overwhelming double door entrance and stepped into a room that looked like a lobby of a grand hotel: black and white checkered marble floors, curved parallel staircases rounding up to a second floor which overlooked the entrance, suits of armor standing guard on each side of the staircase. I felt pixie-size in the massive space.

The woman clicked her heels and pivoted left through another set of huge double doors into a dark, haunted looking parlor. Golden candlesticks flickered on the walls, creating spooky-looking shadows. Humongous paintings of unsmiling people looked down on us. A draft came through the vacant walk-in fireplace.

"Sit down." It was an order.

I plopped into the nearest wing-backed armchair.

"Would you like tea?" She scowled.

"Do you happen to have coffee?" I asked, trying to sound sweet and pleasant. My voice sounded more like a desperate rasp.

At that moment, an attractive young blonde who looked to be in her early twenties walked in with a tray outfitted for a tea party. She set it down on a round table between the armchairs.

"Gretchen, brew a pot of coffee. Apparently, she is not a tea drinker." Madame Stern-Face the Grey ordered.

"Oh, certainly." Gretchen smiled.

"Thank you, Gretchen," I said. "Sorry to trouble you."

Her eyes widened. "No trouble at all, ma'am. Whatever you need. I'm happy to be of service." She curtsied.

Madame Stern-Face the Grey shot her a glare. Gretchen hurried out of the room. "I am Ms. Stern, the Household Manager for Ranfurly Manor. I have worked at the Ranfurly Manor for twenty years."

I almost blurted, "Wait … your last name is actually Stern?"

"I only have a few questions for you, Mrs. Drake."

"Of course. What would you like to know?" I asked.

"How do you feel about children?"

"I love children. I raised two of my own and they are both already in college!" I beamed. "The years sure do fly, don't they? I miss the days when they were little and—"

"Ya, I'm sure you miss your children very much. The question I have for you is, how do you feel about raising twins who are five, now that you are older? Do you think you have the energy to keep up with five-year-olds at your age, Mrs. Drake?"

At my age? How old does she think I am? Fortunately, Gretchen walked in with my coffee at that exact moment and stopped me before I blurted out something I might regret.

"Bless you, child!" I said to Gretchen as she handed me my coffee. "A cup and saucer. How adorable." I giggled. "I usually drink out of mugs."

Ms. Stern's eyes widened, as if I'd said something crude.

"Cream and sugar are there on the tea tray, ma'am," Gretchen said sweetly.

"Perfect," I smiled. She returned the smile, then glanced at Ms. Stern who shot her a look that clearly meant, *get out*. Gretchen quickly turned and escaped, closing the double doors behind her.

"Uh … back to your question…" I sipped and savored the dark roast brewed to perfection. "Mm. *Very* good coffee. Yes, I'd have no problem keeping up with a couple of five-year-olds."

"You should know, these are highly active five-year-olds, Mrs. Drake. The last person we hired quit after three weeks."

I raised my eyebrows. "What exactly do you mean by 'highly active?' I mean, most five-year-olds just need to get their wiggles out every so often. Is that what we're talking about here, or is there something extra energetic about these five-year-olds?"

Ms. Stern raised her chin and frowned down at me. "Let me ask you the questions, Mrs. Drake."

Alrighty, then. I sipped my coffee and waited for her to continue the interrogation. I realized, after a glare from Ms. Stern, that I was slurping. *Oops.*

She asked, "You have one son who is studying to be a government major, ya?"

I nodded.

"Does he desire to work with the new government, PAX, then?"

I tried to think of how to answer that question. "He's been interested in political science since he was a little boy."

"Hmm. And your daughter? She is a Language Arts major now. What made her decide to go to The Goldens to study at university?"

"You definitely did your research on me and my family, didn't you?"

She didn't bat an eye. "Of course." She waited for my response.

"My daughter has grandparents who live in The Goldens. That and the fact that she loves the beach and warm weather. I used to love it too when I was a kid and I lived there, before my family moved to Cascadia when I was sixteen. In fact, I remember—"

She cut me off. "How did you discipline your son and daughter when they were young and misbehaved?"

"Oh … wow. That was a while back. Let's see, um … I would give them a time-out and take away privileges." It seemed like a lifetime ago that I had to correct my kids. These days, they were usually the ones correcting me.

"Give an example of a situation where you did this." It was an order.

"Um, let's see … I would try to make the punishment fit the crime. Like if they played video games when they should be doing homework, I would take away the video games for a time."

"Ah, that answers my next question. Lord Ranfurly forbids his children any video games, television, or electronics. But it sounds like you did allow your children those things."

A guilty pang shot through me. It felt like *Judgment Day* had arrived. "Yes, I did."

"Would you be able to keep children entertained without those things to help you babysit them?" The woman seemed to appear taller, while I felt like I was shrinking.

"I'm sure that would not be a problem for me." I shot back, mimicking her tone. *What? Why did I just say that? Ms. Stern is bringing out the worst in me.* I had no idea if I could survive raising kids without the assistance of electronics. I had never managed to ban electronics for more than a couple days when raising my own. Except for those times when Keith and I would take them camping for a week and go unplugged.

"Also, Mrs. Drake, would you be willing to set an example for these children by refraining from the use of electronics, as well?"

I spit out my coffee, laughing, and nearly dropped my cup.

Ms. Stern's look of disdain caused me to sit up straight.

"You're serious?" I asked.

Ms. Stern blinked, unsmiling.

My weak eye began to twitch. "Well, I would need to look at my phone messages. I have kids that text me every day."

"You would be allowed an hour each evening to check messages after the children are in bed." Ms. Stern lifted her chin and pursed her thin lips. "Mr. Knight can drive you to a location where there are cellular service and Wi-Fi."

I sipped my coffee slowly, fixated on a vase filled with fragrant lavender on a nearby end table. *Is she serious? This giant mansion doesn't offer Wi-Fi or cell service?* It was as if I had been transported into the past.

I decided to be completely frank with the bride of Frankenstein. "I'm not sure how I feel about that, to be honest. Plus, I have many responsibilities that would need to be dealt with. A house of my own … animals … ten acres of land. I would need to have a plan for all of that if I were to live here. In fact, I'd probably need to go home every day, until I could find someone to care for my animals."

She waved her hand as if she was swatting a fly. "That could all be easily solved, it's not a problem. *If* you are chosen as the right candidate for employment, you would have one week to set things in order."

"One week? I wouldn't be able to start work here in one week. I would need at least a month. I have another job to give notice to."

She gave me a curious look. "Hmm. We shall see." She shrugged and glanced at her old-looking watch. It was like the driver's, who I now knew was called Mr. Knight. I took a sip and contemplated the idea of working there, while she wrote notes down on a pad of paper.

Her staccato broke the momentary silence. "Now for the next segment of the interview. It is time for you to meet the children."

Ms. Stern led me up a flight of stairs to the second floor, then down a hallway. Paintings of portraits lined the walls. One especially stood out: a man with bright green eyes, white hair, and a curled mustache. He held a pipe and was dressed like a wealthy cowboy.

Ms. Stern noticed I was staring at the painting. "Striking, isn't he?" Her harsh tone suddenly softened. "That was Mr. Ranfurly the Second. A *real* cowboy. He raised cattle and kept a stable of horses, which he caught in the *wild*." She reached out to touch the cheek of the painted man. "He broke the horses and trained them himself."

It was the first time the woman showed any emotion. I could almost imagine what she might have looked like as a younger Ms. Stern. She stood there, gazing at the portrait, lost in some distant memory.

Ms. Stern, you devil, you! Crushin' on your boss!

Ms. Stern shook out of her mesmerized state. She turned and opened the door we were standing by. Inside was a large room that looked like a Kindergarten classroom. There was a mat with colored squares on the floor in front of a chalkboard. Stenciled letters of the alphabet were on the wall above.

Facing the board, two children, a boy and a girl, sat in little school desks. Neither of the children looked up when we entered but were engaged in a writing exercise.

A pudgy, older woman with short grey hair sat at a desk next to the chalkboard, keeping watch. Like Ms. Stern, she had a permanent frown on her face.

At first glance, the children were identical. They wore matching blue and white uniforms, except the girl wore a skirt, the boy trousers. Both had a mop of curly, strawberry-colored hair on top of their heads, but the girl had two long braids tied with little blue bows, while the boy had a buzz-cut above his ears.

"Mrs. Pemberley, Elizabeth, and Luke, this is Mrs. Drake. She is interviewing to be your new nanny," said Ms. Stern. Then she turned to me. "Mrs. Pemberley is one of five interim nannies, until we're able to fill the position."

The children both looked up in unison. They didn't look *at* me, but past me, with blank, emotionless faces. Almost like a pair of robots.

Poor things. They seem apathetic to life at such a young age.

Then I caught the boy sneak a peek at me. He quickly did his best to return to his indifferent expression, but it was too late. I'd seen him break character.

The little stinkers. They are putting on an act.

"Do you have your letters ready?" Ms. Stern asked them.

"Almost. We could use a few more minutes, please," replied Elizabeth, as if she were a robot.

Ms. Stern raised a brow, then said in her staccato accent, "Very well. Mrs. Drake, allow me to show you more of what is on this floor of the manor." She led me out of the classroom down the long hallway. "Whenever Lord Ranfurly is away, which as of late has been quite often, the nanny is responsible for the children twenty-four, seven. But since we have not filled the position yet, I oversee their schedule.

"Today was an exception, the children are up early for the interview. Six-thirty is the regular time that the nanny must wake the children. They must get ready and be at the breakfast table promptly at seven-thirty. It is the nanny's duty to make sure they always have clean teeth and hands, and brushed hair. They must wear their uniforms each day."

I kept my question to myself. *Uniforms for homeschooling?* I wasn't sure what the point was.

"Lessons begin in the classroom at eight-fifteen on the floor mat where the children recite the alphabet and learn the calendar. At nine o'clock, the children move to their desks and begin written exercises. These lessons would be your responsibility to teach, as well. Ten o'clock, they have a healthy snack and playtime with toys in here," Ms. Stern explained. "Speaking of snacks, I do not approve of the children eating sugar when Lord Ranfurly is away. Unfortunately, when he is home, he allows them to eat whatever they like. And of course, they like sugar. Very much. But when they have it, they act like chimpanzees." Her eyebrows rose so high they nearly collided with her hairline.

Next, we went into a room with tumbling mats, a small balance beam, a bar and rings, and mirrored walls. "At ten-thirty they come into this room, where Monsieur DuPont, the gymnastics instructor, works with them for an hour. You would be expected to stay in this room and observe the lessons."

We walked into the next room, which was decorated like a street in La Belle Terre. "At eleven-thirty, they begin their Bellais language lessons in here."

"Umm … I took a couple years of Bellais in High School. But I don't remember much. I'm afraid I won't be the best tutor in this subject," I confessed.

"Of course, you wouldn't. Lord Ranfurly hired a tutor from La Belle Terre," she said, curtly.

"Oh, right. That makes sense." *Only the best for the children of a lord,* I thought.

She shot a condescending glare in my direction. "But you would have a chance to improve while sitting in on the lessons daily, no doubt, Mrs.

Drake. Consider this another perk to employment here." She showed yellowed teeth, which I think was supposed to be her way of smiling even though the rest of her face remained a scowl. Then she turned on her heels and headed out the door.

I wanted to stay and look around at the Bellais décor, which was charming, but Ms. Stern moved at a brisk pace, so I hurried to keep up.

The house seemed to go on forever.

"After Bellais lessons, Gretchen sets out lunch for the children in here," she opened the doors to another large room, with small-sized tables for the little ones, and a larger table set for adults. Painted on the walls were stenciled letters that spelled out *Kiddie Bistro*. "The Kiddie Bistro is where the nanny eats lunch also."

"Now, as you are finding, we have many tutors," Ms. Stern explained. "The nanny is responsible to *always* be with the children. Even when the other tutors are working with them."

"I see."

I did see, and I didn't like it, any of it. First off, I'd miss texting my kids on a regular basis. Second, I'd miss my cozy house and all my animals, and third, I would hate to follow a strict regimen every day. *How awful for those children!* "So, is there any flex in this schedule? I mean, if the sun decides to shine, would Lord Ranfurly agree that Vitamin D would be healthy for his children? Would I be able to teach them outside?"

"Lord Ranfurly is not always home. That is why I oversee their schedule. Children need routine and structure or they act like monkeys, Mrs. Drake. Changing their routine brings out the worst in them. I would think a woman with two grown children should know this."

I ignored her comment. "He's not always home? So how often do the children get to see their father?"

"It is unpredictable. When he is here, he gives the tutors paid time off because he likes to spend every minute of his time with his children. But he has strange ideas about how to raise them. He often takes them into the forest, and they act like a pack of wild dogs together."

"Wild dogs?"

"Oh ya. Mr. Reed once took his gun into the woods because we all thought a pack of wolves or something was nearby. But no. It wasn't wolves. It was Lord Ranfurly and his children. They were out there howling and barking like three crazies! Mr. Reed came close to shooting one of them." She tutted in disapproval.

She went back to reciting her schedule of drudgery. "After lunch, the children have reading time in the loft. There." She pointed to a corner of the room where a ladder led to a loft. A spiral slide was one way a person could come down from it. The other ways included back down the ladder, or there was a fireman's pole. "Then it is their nap time."

I laughed.

Ms. Stern glared at me. "What do you find to laugh at?"

"I just, well, I must admit I've never had success getting a five-year-old to take a nap."

Ms. Stern shook her head slowly. "You are serious?"

Suddenly I remembered this was still a job interview. "I mean, just my *own* five-year-olds. They weren't really the napping type. But I'm sure it will be no problem for me at all to squeeze in a little naptime."

"Just to be clear, I am talking about the children napping. The nanny doesn't get to nap, Mrs. Drake."

"Of course not. I would never." The woman had no sense of humor.

We were off to another room.

"At fourteen hundred hours, it is time for violin lessons by Mr. Lee. In here." An upright black piano sat against a mirrored wall. Violins hung on the wall opposite.

"Really? Violin, Language, and Tumbling. Every day?" *Maybe those kids do fall asleep during naptime. They must be exhausted.*

"After that, the children begin their chores. They are learning how to care for plants in the Conservatory, downstairs. We will not have time to see it today, but the Ranfurly Manor has quite an impressive collection of species." Again, she flashed yellow teeth.

"After inside chores, they go to the stables to care for their horses. They stay an hour with the horses. Then it is on the schedule for them to play outdoors. If weather permits. Unlike Lord Ranfurly, I do *not* permit them to run wild through the grounds. They must play only in the playground. If it is raining, they have several play areas to choose from on the second floor, or they may stay in their nursery on the third floor."

"I see."

"When Lord Ranfurly is home, supper will be served in the Dining Room downstairs at eighteen hundred hours. Otherwise, it will be brought up to the nursery for you and the children. After supper, it will be your responsibility to ensure their bedrooms are tidy, give them baths, have them brush their teeth, read them their bedtime story, and say their prayers. Lights out at twenty hundred hours. Sharp."

She sounded so much like a drill sergeant, I did a salute. "Yes, ma'am."

Ms. Stern's face was as unmoving as a stone statue.

I wasn't used to thinking in military time and had to take a second to convert twenty hundred hours to standard. *Eight o'clock bedtime. I wonder how those kids fall asleep in this gigantic, haunted-looking mansion? I don't think I'd be able to fall asleep here. Then again, after trotting through Ms. Stern's routine, I might just fall asleep before I hit the pillow.*

Ms. Stern looked at her ancient watch, and exclaimed, "Ah, it is well over fifteen minutes now. The children should be finished with their letters."

We were back in the schoolroom. The children were quiet, sitting at their desks, hands folded on their laps. I looked from one angelic freckled face to the other and noticed that other than their hair color, they weren't identical. The girl had exquisite green eyes, and the boy had bright blue eyes, with unusual flecks of yellow. The boy had a rounded nose and round face, and the girl had a pointy nose and a heart-shaped face.

Overly energetic? They don't seem hyperactive to me.

First, the boy gave me his letter. I was impressed with the neat handwriting, for only five years old.

> Dear Mrs. Drake,
>
> I want a nanny who is always nice, who never yells.
> You are pretty. But I wish I cood have a man nanny who
> likes to go on treasr hunts and who knows stuff. Do you

know how many eyes a spidr has? Do you know stuff about dragins?

Sincerely,
Luke Ranfurly

I managed to keep a straight face. Next, Elizabeth gave me her letter. She had even neater handwriting.

Dear Mrs. Drake,

I don't acshully need a nanny. My brother is dum, so they get nannees for HIM, not for me. I could be his nanny and teach him everything he needs to know.

Something you should know about this place is that we have bad fairees. They threatened to eat the last nanny. I hope you have magic powers because you will need them here. If you ever see something in your bed that looks like a spider with wings, that is what the fairees look like.

We also have many ghosts here. They don't like nannees either.

Best of luck,
Elizabeth Ranfurly

After I read the letter, I smiled at Elizabeth. "Do you know, I am highly skilled in catching and killing bad fairies?" Then I addressed her twin. "Oh, and Luke, it is so funny that you are interested in dragons. *I* have a dragon living in my forest."

The children looked at each other, wide eyed. Ms. Stern's eyes also widened.

"Really, Mrs. Drake." She turned her chin up and looked down at me through slitted eyes.

Once again, I had forgotten I was being interviewed.

UNEXPECTED SURPRISE

IMMEDIATELY FOLLOWING INTERVIEW
Ranfurly Manor

After the interview, I was standing outside on the porch beside the monstrous front doors of the manor, trying to picture myself living in that place, with those people.

I don't think it would be easy to warm up to Ms. Stern.

Gretchen was nice enough, though.

Mr. Knight, well, he was certainly a charmer. Not bad on the eyes, either.

But those poor children! Only five, just babies, and clearly lacked a consistent parental figure in their lives. If I was at all tempted to take the job, it would be for them.

But whoa, Nelly! That schedule! Talk about structure on steroids! My natural inclination was to rebel against an overabundance of structure.

Then again, those little freckled faces plagued me. They needed somebody to love them. Somebody who would stick around. *And those fun imaginations! I miss when Laurel and Nick were that age.* I sighed.

A window must have been open upstairs because I heard voices talking from somewhere above me. "Why was he so insistent she come today? She is nothing like any of the others." It was a woman's voice. She spoke with a Bellais accent.

"Hmm." A man, also with a Bellais accent spoke. "Not at all like the others. They are always too old and impatient with *les enfants*. Or too young and addicted to their phones. *Mais celle-ci est tres sexy.*" [*But this one is very sexy.*]

"*Vraiment? Tu pense qu'elle est sexy?*" [*Really? You think she is sexy?*]

"*Oui. Mais elle ne se compare pas a toi, ma cherie.*" [*Yes, but not compared to you, my dear.*]

My Bellais was weak, but I caught the gist of what they were saying.

The beautiful Royal Rodney rolled up to a stop in front of the manor, and Mr. Knight stepped out. He came around to open the door for me.

"Your carriage awaits," he said.

Once we were on our way back to my house, he asked, "So, what did you think of the little Ranfurlys?"

"They were adorable! And angelic. Very bright for their age."

It dawned on me that I hadn't even met the children's father. *He was the one who wanted to hire me, so why hadn't he been the one to interview me? If it were my own children, I would certainly want to meet any potential caretakers.*

"So, am I finished with all the interviews here? I thought their father would want to interview me, as well."

Mr. Knight shrugged. "Lord Ranfurly is a very busy man. He doesn't often grace us with his presence."

"Right. The whole 'lord' bit. So how often do his children see him, anyway?"

"Not as much as they would like, that's certain."

"Hmm." *Absent father.* As I weighed the *pros* and *cons* of the nanny job, I added another check to the *con's* column.

Then there was the fact that I had no idea how to act around a lord. Another check.

Mr. Knight asked, "So, what do you think? If they offer you the job, will you accept?" He cupped a hand next to his mouth and added in a hushed voice, "I hear the other two candidates weren't very impressive."

I smiled. "Really? You heard that, did you? Hmm."

"They were also a lot older and far less attractive." I caught him looking at me through the mirror. He lifted his eyebrows as if to ask, "Well?"

"Well … to be honest, I don't know if this is the right fit for me," I said. I looked at him sideways, with a half grin. "Especially after reading the letters the children wrote."

"Did the children write you letters?" Mr. Knight asked, surprised. "What on earth did they say?"

"Oh, I have them right here." I held them up and read Elizabeth's aloud.

Mr. Knight's laugh was throaty and appealing. "Ah, yes, but it isn't the fairies you should be worried about. There are certainly more dangerous creatures in that castle who would find you to be a scrumptious morsel to devour." He looked wolfish through the rearview mirror.

I was sure I had turned the color of the children's hair. It had been way too long since I'd been flirted with. By an extremely attractive man, no less. I found myself tongue-tied.

After a few awkward minutes, Mr. Knight pulled through an Espresso Drive-Through. "What would you like? I owe you one."

"Ah, well, now perhaps we can be friends," I said. A funny, swirly feeling came over me – a feeling I hadn't felt in years. Attraction to a man who wasn't Keith. That was new.

As I contemplated the job, perhaps Mr. Knight was a perk to consider. A check for the *pros* column.

After Mr. Knight dropped me off back home, I contemplated.

Maybe I should take the job. I could really use the money.

Or is it that you just want to see more of that dashing Mr. Knight? As soon as the thought popped into my head, I tried to shake it out.

Of course, I don't! I hardly know the man! Besides, it isn't like he was interested in me, anyway. And he seems like the type that flirts with every woman he meets.

"Courtney, stay away. It isn't safe," Keith whispered in my ear. He kissed me on the cheek and started to leave the room, carrying his travel bag.

"Where are you going?"

He looked back at me. "I'm serious. Stay away from that place, Courtney." He left.

I wondered where he was going. And what place he was talking about that he wanted me to stay away from.

Drones flew past my bedroom window and aimed their guns directly at me.

I ducked and crawled under my bed.

Explosions blasted.

Was I dead?

***

Sweat covered my body. My heart was racing.

"Oh…" I moaned. "What an awful dream!"

I ran to the toilet and chucked up vomit.

The following evening, my cell phone rang. The number looked familiar. *Ms. Stern?*

"Hello?"

"Am I going to get to see you again, Mrs. Drake?" The Highlandish brogue was unmistakable.

"How did you get my number, Mr. Knight?"

"It was written down here … next to the blower. I figured that made it fair game," he replied.

I was baffled. "Did you just say blower? You found my phone number next to a leaf blower?"

"What? Where would you get that idea? No, next to the *blower* … you know, the landline."

"Oh. Hmph. Well, I don't know how we'll see each other. I have no plans to visit Ranfurly Manor again in the future."

"You mean you're not going to take the job?" he asked.

"As far as I know, I haven't been offered the position. Unless you know something."

"Oh, I'm sure you'll soon be offered the job. Like I said, there wasn't another candidate who holds a candle to ya. No doubt, you would be a ray of sunshine in this place."

"I—That is very sweet of you to say. Thanks." Again, tongue-tied. "Well, I'm sorry but I got to run. I work at a local restaurant and am late for my shift."

"Right. Of course. I'll let you go, then." There was an awkward pause.

"G-glad to have called you," I stammered. "I mean … I'm glad you called."

"May I call again?"

"Uh-um … sure."

"Great!"

"Okay … Buh-bye." Oops, I did it again, said buh-bye. My kids always made fun of me for that. They told me I sounded like a thirties-something mom from The Goldens, to which I always replied, "That's because I am a thirties-something mom from The Goldens."

"*Ciao!*" he said.

Ciao? Okay. Apparently, we both have quirky ways of ending phone calls.

The next morning, I was in my favorite place, sipping coffee on the front porch. My fierce dogs were on each side of me, and my two fat ducks were at the foot of the porch steps, sitting like little guard post figures.

The dogs started to bark.

To my horror, the Royal Rodney White Gallant was making its way up my long driveway.

I choked on my coffee, and it shot out of my mouth and all over my oversized flannel pajamas. I was off work that day and had no plans of seeing another human. The hair had not been touched by a comb. The teeth had not been brushed. Deodorant had not been applied. I knew it was likely that I'd already been spotted, but I ran inside the house anyway, where I transformed myself faster than *Clark Kent* turning into *Superman* in a phone booth.

He was greeting my "guard" dogs and patting a duck when I casually opened the front door. I tried to hide the fact that I was out of breath from the exertion I'd put myself through getting ready at *Kryptonian* speed.

"I didn't catch you off guard, did I?" There was amusement in his eyes.

Great. He saw me sitting on my porch when he drove up the driveway.

This time he wasn't dressed in the cute chauffeur outfit. He had dressed up in a classy business suit and was holding a bouquet of blue flag irises.

"I certainly wasn't expecting any company," I said, unable to stop smiling as swirly butterflies swarmed in my gut.

"You know, I'm surprised you don't have a gate for the front driveway. I mean, that's a half mile down there, and you can't see from here who might be coming."

"Yes, I know. I keep putting it off. But after this second intrusion of yours, I have a mind to go down to the store today and buy the best security gate I can find." I smiled at the flowers. "These are beautiful. Irises are one of my favorites."

"Oh these? These aren't for you," Mr. Knight teased. His eyes were the shade of light brown sugar.

"Really? Who are they for, exactly?" I played along.

"The fairies. Certainly, you know you have fairies here. I aim to earn their favor."

"Well, I am sure they will think these are charming. Shall I put them in a vase for the fairies to admire?" I took the bouquet and invited him in.

"Nice little place you have here," he said, looking around. He pointed to a photo on my wall. "Who is this?"

"Keith, my late husband. The kids must have been seven and eight in that photo."

"Huh." He stared at the photo for a minute. "Where are your kids now?" he asked.

"They're both away at college. My daughter comes home for summer break soon."

"Ah," he said, moving on to more photos on the wall. "This must be her?" He pointed to her high school portrait. "Stunningly beautiful, just like her mother. If I didn't know better, I'd have mistaken her to be your sister."

"Hmm. Flatterer. She's off limits to you, Mr. Knight," I warned. "Coffee?" I offered.

"Sure, if you have real cream."

"I do. I like mine with real cream, too." I pulled it out of the fridge and served him a cup. "What brings you out to my humble abode for a second visit, Mr. Knight?"

"To be honest, I was hoping to help you make up your mind about the job."

"Really? You aren't here because of my irresistible charm and magnetic powers?"

"Oh, you catch on fast. I most certainly am." He flashed his charming grin.

"Would you like to sit outside with our coffees? It's turning out to be such a gorgeous spring day. Finally warm enough to enjoy the outdoors again."

We sat in the wicker rockers on my porch and Loki, the smaller of my two big dogs, went over to Mr. Knight to greet him. Thor was too lazy to get up.

"What are their names?" he asked.

"The one you are petting now is Loki, and the one by me is Thor. Oh, and that cat that's coming your way … that's Fiona."

"Ah yes, Fiona. I remember you. You're a good little lass." She was the same cat he had charmed to come out from under Nick's bed.

"You have an accent. Highlandish?" I asked him.

"Yeah. I was born in the Highlands. Accent comes out sometimes. I lived most of my life here but moved back to live there for a few years when

I was in my twenties. My dad's from there; he still has a strong brogue." He lifted Fiona onto his lap to pet her.

"Quite the animal lover, aren't you?"

"Yes, my magnetic powers attract them." He winked.

I laughed. "You and I have so much in common."

"We should meet like this more often," he chimed. "I noticed you have a piano inside. Do you play?"

"No, my husband used to play. I sing."

"Ah, nice. I play a little piano," he said.

"Really? Do you want to show off for me?"

"Sure, why not?" He set Fiona down on the wicker rocking chair and we went back into the house. He sat at the piano and started playing an old song that was popular when I was in high school. I remembered it and sang what I knew.

He joined with me on the chorus. I almost fell backward when I heard his voice. "Let me guess? You're in a band?"

He laughed. "Used to be. Now that Lord Ranfurly has me doing his bidding, no time for fun."

"You do realize you aren't doing much to convince me I should take the job?" I lifted an eyebrow.

He laughed. "Right. That's what I came here for, wasn't it? Let's see then, you truly won't be able to find a better job. Plus, you would have weekends off. I do not. My off days are midweek. Not exactly the best nights for band gigs."

"True. Well, too bad. You should be out there showing off all that talent and good looks."

"Well, shucks … now you have me blushing." His dashing smile made my toes curl. He struck the middle C on my piano and sustained it, "On a serious note, do you think you will take the job?"

I played along. "Let me 'C' now … that is a very serious note."

He chuckled. "Well, do you?"

"I'm sorry. Especially knowing you made a trip all the way out here. … But I'm leaning toward turning it down. The thing is, I already have a job. And as you can see, I have all these animals and a lot of property to take care of. I can't just abandon everything and start a whole new life at Ranfurly Manor."

He turned on the piano bench to look up at me, his sugary caramel-colored eyes searched mine. "Mrs. Drake, may I be honest with you?"

"Y-yes?" I looked at him sideways.

He smiled. Then he looked down at the piano keys, as if he needed a minute before he began.

"… I just wanted to … I just think …" He spoke slowly. Deliberately. "I think there is a woman hiding in you that desperately wants to be discovered."

An awkward feeling came over me. It dawned on me that I'd already drained my coffee mug dry and I was still holding on to it. I set it on top of a coaster on the piano. "I don't know what you mean by that, Mr. Knight. You only just met me."

"Oh. No ... You took that the wrong way. What I'm saying is: women like you are a rare find."

"Er—women like *me*? What do you mean by that, exactly?" I laughed uncomfortably.

"What do I mean?" He took a deep breath. "Well … I mean, you're nothing like any of the others."

"The others?"

"They've tried all types of nannies for those children. Lord Ranfurly is a hard man to please."

"Oh. I see."

He seemed to be choosing his words carefully. "And I must admit, I *am* hoping selfishly to see you again."

What is happening? Is this sincerely all about a job position? I was getting mixed messages.

A chill came over me. I picked up my mug and his, which was sitting on a table by the piano. "You didn't touch your coffee."

"No, I guess I didn't."

Keith's voice came into my head, "Careful, Courtney." His ever-present ghost reminding me he was watching. He didn't want me entertaining this stranger.

I headed into the kitchen to rinse out the coffee mugs. Then I noticed the quote of the day on my flip calendar. "A prudent man sees evil and hides from it, but the naïve proceed and pay the penalty."

Okay, Keith. I get the message.

"I'm sorry for the trouble you went through to come here, Mr. Knight. I appreciate the job offer, but I'm going to have to decline."

At first, he said nothing. Then he struck a dissonant chord on the piano keys. "Right. Okay, then. Well, it sounds like there is nothing more I can say to convince you." Standing up, he said, "Well, I … ahem … shouldn't take up any more of your time, Mrs. Drake." His lips smiled, but his eyes were sad.

I followed him out the front door.

Out on the porch, he said, "You've made a lasting impression on me. One that I won't easily be able to forget, I assure you." He tilted his head in farewell. "Thank you. We sang a smashing duet." He climbed into the Royal Rodney and drove off.

I watched from the porch until he was no longer in sight.

A text came through. It was Nick.

Nick: Mom, I am having that same recurring dream I've told you about. The one about Dad. Do you still have nightmares about it?

Me: Yeah. I'm sorry, Nick. I wish I was there, kiddo.

Nick: Me too. It was a hard day. I shot down a drone today in the Capital Region.

Me: What? That is crazy! They'll send you to the island if they catch you, Nick. Why did you do that?

Nick: I had to. The drone was about to kill one of my friends. It's fine, nobody saw us.

Me: I hate that you live there.

Nick: Mom, you are living in a bubble. When are you going to wake up and realize the world isn't safe anymore?

Me: I know it isn't safe, but I'm certainly not about to go looking for danger. That's why I like it here, Nick. But I know … you're young and crazy and want to be where the action is.

Nick: I have to be, Mom. I got into studying government because I want to convince people that we need to win back freedom. I can't stand around and watch the world go to hell. I have to try to make a difference. But I'm not alone. There are many others here in The Capital who think like me. More than I ever imagined.

Me: You're so much like your dad. I admire that about you, Nick. But please try to stay alive! I don't want anything to happen to you. You see what happens to people who join The Resistance. It doesn't end well for them. Please promise me you will play by the rules and do things peaceably.

Nick: Sometimes I wish you would just get a little more fight in you, Mom.

Me: What do you mean by that? I have plenty of fight in me! Let's go … right now. Bring it on!

Nick: LOL. I know, but if you were here, you could make a difference, Mom.

Me: Nick, I am not good at speaking, or lobbying. I don't have a law degree. I don't even have a college degree! Nobody in your world would respect a thing I have to say. I'm just a mom. I don't know how to be anything else.

Nick: You are not *just* a mom. You're *my* mom. And I think you're selling yourself short.

A tear snuck out of an eye. I wiped it away.

Me: I sure did good with you, didn't I? Love you, kid.

Nick: Love you too.

After our conversation ended, I reread it a few times and sighed. *Worrying about that kid is going to give me an ulcer.*

I sent a bunch of heart memes to Laurel and headed outside to work in my garden.

9

WINNIE DROPS IN

Lord Robert

TWO DAYS LATER
Ranfurly Manor

Robert woke up in the quiet hidden room behind the cellar, sore and groggy. *Bloody hell. Feels like I've been trampled on by a stampede of elephants. Now I've got to get to that interview.*

He checked his Digi-watch to see what time it was. *Bollocks! I've been asleep for forty-eight hours!* He'd missed the interview with the nanny. God only knew what else he'd missed.

My children … I need to check on them.

Years back, when he'd first discovered the room with the old computers behind the cellar, he learned what his cousin was using the computers for. Surveillance. It was why there were thirty screens hanging on one large wall. Hidden cameras all over the house and grounds connected to the computer system.

Unfortunately, the outdoor cameras were no longer operational. It was on Robert's list of action items to replace them and update the entire system. At least many of the indoor cameras still worked.

He scanned all the surveillance screens until he spotted Elizabeth and Luke. They were in the Conservatory taking care of the plants. A smile crossed his lips and his eyes stung as he watched them talk to the plants

75

and butterflies. He quickly turned to head upstairs. He couldn't wait to swoop them up in his arms.

As soon as he began to climb the stairs, blood seeped through his shirt. "Damn!" He grunted and went to replace the bandage.

I can't risk the staff noticing I've been stabbed. It'll lead to too many questions.

He'd overheard the gossip that passed through the staff:

"I hear he has several houses! He probably keeps a mistress at every one of them."

"His poor children."

"Typical billionaire aristocrat!"

They had no idea he was right there, either under their feet, or over their heads, or behind walls between rooms, hearing everything they were saying. And he intended to keep it that way. His best option was to remain hidden until his stab wound scabbed over.

Once he had a fresh bandage on his wound, he went back into the surveillance room and checked the screens to see how his household was managing without him. "I wonder how the interview for the nanny went," he said to himself. He found the moment of the interview and replayed it.

Standing with his arms crossed, he was expecting to be slightly bored by another nanny interview. But when the mother of Nick Drake came on screen, he perked up, and his breath caught in his throat. *Dear lord! Nick didn't mention that his mother was absolutely cracking.*

He paused the replay to pour himself a drink. Then sat to take in the full interview.

Courtney Drake was a mixture of fire and water.

The fire: Long, dark and sultry waves of hair flowed down her back, with traces of auburn that looked like flames in the flickering light of the room. Dark arched brows revealing intelligence and inquisitiveness.

When she shot out the question, "Would Lord Ranfurly agree that Vitamin D would be healthy for his children?" it gave him a chuckle. He'd already managed to irritate her, and she hadn't even met him yet. *Fiery indeed.* But it didn't put him off. It only piqued his interest.

When she inquired whether the children could do their lessons outside, he thought, *I like the way this woman thinks.*

The water: Striking eyes, as blue as the ocean, reflecting a contemplative, caring soul. His favorite moment of the interview was seeing the way her eyes glistened when she met his children. There was a childlikeness, a purity about her that he had never seen in another adult.

His senses became reawakened. He hadn't been aroused since he'd been with his late wife, and it caught him off guard — to *feel* that way again — after five years.

He heartily laughed when she said she had a dragon. Her response to the children's letters was the frosting on the cake, if Courtney were cake.

"Mrs. Courtney Drake. Hmm."

His children were the number one reason he chose to fight as a member of the Resistance. With PAX in power and technology advancing rapidly in the hands of a wicked regime, the world was getting worse by the day. He feared the next generation would have no future if things didn't change.

Fortunately, Robert wasn't alone in wanting to change things. Ex-police, ex-intelligence agents, ex-military, doctors, lawyers, tech experts, and journalists alike had secretly joined CAPE in the fight against PAX.

Robert had been trained in martial arts since he was five years old. An expert archer, gunman, and fencer, he came from a long succession of warriors. When the fight with the Resistance called, he knew it was what he was made for.

It took two more days before his wound finally stopped bleeding. When he was finally able to emerge, he eagerly headed upstairs to spend time with his children. He bumped into Ms. Stern on the stairwell.

"Lord Ranfurly! You're finally home. There has been a serious situation you should know about in your absence." She was agitated. As usual.

"Yes?"

"It is Sean Knight. He took the Royal Rodney and hasn't returned."

As she was speaking, Gretchen called from downstairs. "The Royal Rodney is coming up the driveway!"

Robert and Ms. Stern hurried out front. Robert's Royal Rodney came around the circle driveway and stopped in front of the manor. It wasn't Sean who got out of the car, though. It was Sean's father. Mr. Knight, Sr.

"Where's Sean?" Gretchen asked him, peering into the car, looking as if she expected Sean to pop up any minute.

Sean's father shook his head. "Got a strange phone call from a woman. She told me she saw the Royal Rodney stranded in the Wildwoods Forest. She gave the coordinates, then hung up."

"It is Lord Ranfurly's car." Ms. Stern snapped, like a crocodile. "You're just a chauffeur. Why did she call *you*? And how did she get *your* number, unless you gave it to her? None of our phone numbers are listed."

Sean's father's face turned a deep reddish purple. "I *never* give out my blower's number!" He had a thick Highlandish brogue and bared his teeth like an angry bear. "Davey drove me oot there in the wee sma oors! Didna sleep a wink the haill nicht!"

"Nobody's heard from Sean or has any idea where he is?" Lord Robert directed his question at Gretchen, since he knew Sean recently had a little fling with her.

Gretchen burst into tears and ran back into the house, her face buried in her hands.

"It has been quite terrible," replied Ms. Stern. "She's been that way since he disappeared."

"Strange," Robert shook his head. "Sean should be more than capable of taking care of himself. Perhaps he just went backpacking – The Wildwoods are a backpacker's paradise."

"If he did, he certainly did not tell anyone here his plans. He did *not* get permission to take your Royal Rodney, Lord Robert." She glared at Mr. Knight, Sr. "Your son is a thief!"

"Is this true?" Robert asked Mr. Knight, Sr. "Your son took my car without permission?"

The chauffeur shot a look that could kill at Ms. Stern. He growled, "Ah'm stickin the bloody caur back in the garage!" He slammed the door of the car and sped off.

Lord Robert sighed. "Well, the place didn't completely burn down in my absence."

"Hmph." Ms. Stern slipped into a stronger Gutish accent. "And … vile you ver absent, a voman came. She convinced Davey Reed to let her in the gate." She was getting more worked up with every word. "She came to the front door! I had no idea vee had a stranger on the premises, so I answered it. Then she told me you hired her as a maid! I tried to turn her avay, of course! If it vere true that you hired her, you vould have consulted vith me first!"

Until that moment, Robert had completely forgotten about promising Peter that his niece could come work as a maid. "What do you mean by 'tried' to turn her away, Ms. Stern?"

"She vas quite obstinate. She sat on the front step and refused to leave!"

"When was this?"

"Yesterday afternoon. She is probably still sitting there! Like a balky boulder!"

"I'm afraid she will have to stay, Ms. Stern."

"Vat? Are you saying you ordered a new maid, Lord Ranfurly? I vould have never agreed to allow this voman on my staff." Ms. Stern exhaled out of her long, hooked nose, and it gave off a sound like a whale coming up for air.

"The last time I checked, I was the one paying the staff salaries. Not *you*, Ms. Stern. That makes it *my* staff, not yours." Lord Robert left Ms. Stern to gape after him.

He went to see if Winnie was still sitting on the front porch. There was no sign of her. *I'll have to call Peter to see if he knows where she went.*

He was about to close the front door when he heard a voice say, "Hey." He looked out but still didn't see anyone.

"Winnie?" he called out.

"Up here, Uncle Robert!" Winnie's voice said.

"Where the dickens are you?" he asked. Then he saw her.

A young woman, who looked much older than the teen he remembered, was climbing down from a two-hundred-foot Fir tree. Like Peter, she had nearly black skin. Unlike Peter, she was lean and moved like a cheetah. Her sporty shorts showed off long, muscular legs.

"I'm here." She jumped to the ground and swiped dirt off her hands. "Nice pad you got here. Big enough to house an army."

"You certainly have grown up since the last time I saw you."

"Yea, it's been a minute." She grinned. "I've always wanted to climb one of those trees. Cascadia has the best trees."

"Yes, I suppose it does. But I certainly don't make it a pastime to climb them. Most people use ropes and harnesses for that sort of thing."

"I'm not most people, Uncle Robert."

"Well, no. I guess you're not. Sorry about the way my housekeeper treated you. Don't take it personal, she's that way to everyone. Where did you end up sleeping last night? Please tell me it wasn't in that tree."

"No. I met these two cute little redheads who snuck me into the house. I slept in their playroom."

They both laughed. "You met my children!" Robert said, wondering how he managed to miss Winnie on the surveillance screens. "Very good! I must reward them for showing such warm hospitality to a guest. After I reprimand them for inviting in a stranger."

"I'm not a stranger. They knew who I was. You have lots of pictures of me in their photo albums. They recognized me right away as their cousin."

"I have told them about you. But I'm surprised they recognized you … you were a teenager in those photos … with braces."

"They still knew it was me."

"I see the braces paid off. No more crooked teeth."

"Yep." She smiled a wide, bright smile. "Well, no need for reprimands. Your kids did nothing more than come to their cousin's rescue."

"Alright, I'll go easy on them." He opened the front door and made a motion for her to enter. "Ladies first."

Winnie grinned and went into the house. "Wow! I didn't come through the front last night. Fancy, fancy, Uncle Robert!"

"Yes," Robert said.

"So, Uncle Peter told me you were stabbed. How's it healing?"

Lord Robert held up a finger to his lips, warning her to keep her voice down. She winked at him and smiled. She whispered, "So, what's this about me having to play a maid? You really don't have a better job for me? I could be a nanny for your kids instead," she suggested.

He chuckled. "I'm sure you would teach my kids all sorts of ways to make mischief. But then you wouldn't be able to help me much. Besides, I have someone in mind for the nanny position. You probably know Nick Drake from CAPE, don't you?"

"I do. Great guy! But as a nanny? You're gonna hire *him*?"

Lord Robert laughed. "No, no! Not Nick. His mother." *His very beautiful mother,* Robert thought to himself. "Strange coincidence that she applied for the job. Doesn't know anything about Nick's connection with CAPE, either. None of the staff here know about CAPE. Not sure who we can trust."

"Got it. I'll play my part. But I can't promise I'll be the best house-keeper. I like things messy." She glunched. "I don't have to wear one of those little black maid dresses, do I? I saw someone wearing one." She gave Robert a scolding look. "Were those *your* idea?"

"My idea? Good heavens, what kind of a man do you take me for? No, this place was well established by my cousin Theo before I ever came around. Take it up with his ghost. And I'm afraid you'll have to follow Ms. Stern's orders and wear the uniform, or people will become suspicious about you. Ms. Stern doesn't like changes being made. She's a Theo loyalist, through and through."

"Please don't tell me Ms. Stern is that woman who answered the front door yesterday." Winnie stared unblinkingly at him.

"Afraid so."

"Well, aren't you the boss around here? Just tell the old bag you'll fire her if she doesn't order new outfits. Those miniskirts are so degrading to women."

Lord Robert shook his head. The maid's outfits were the last thing on his mind. "Ms. Stern would have my head if I tried to make a change like that, and I don't want to start a war right here on the home front. I've got bigger fish to fry. Don't worry, you're only part time, so you won't have to wear it much. The rest of the time you'll be helping me."

"Fine. I guess I'll put up with it." She rolled her eyes.

"Let's find one of the staff who will show you the way to your new living quarters." Robert said. They ran into Gretchen as she was about to head up the stairs with a tray. The miniskirt of the maid's uniform was so short you could see the white ruffled panties she wore underneath when she bent over.

Winnie looked at Gretchen's long, bare legs and grimaced. She gave Robert a wide-eyed expression of horror, as if to say, *You aren't seriously going to make me wear that?*

Robert paid no attention. "Gretchen, this is our newest staff member, Winnie. She'll be helping you with your duties."

Gretchen smiled. "Oh! Lovely! Welcome Winnie!"

Winnie tried to curve her lips into a smile.

"Is there an empty apartment in the staff quarters where she can stay?" Robert asked.

"Yes! The one next to mine is empty! Oh good … It'll be nice to have someone closer to my age to talk to around here. All I have is Marie, but she's way older. Jasmine's not that much older than me, but she doesn't seem to like women."

Winnie raised an eyebrow.

Robert cleared his throat. "Once you're finished delivering that tray, Gretchen, come back down and show Winnie to the room next to yours."

THE NEXT DAY

Robert resumed his workouts with Simon. Fencing was on the day's agenda, and he was too proud to cancel, even though he was still healing from his injury.

His trainer was one of the fittest men he knew, which brought out Robert's competitive nature even more.

"You're a bit slow today, Lord Robert. Not feeling well?" Simon lunged at him and struck a point.

"Probably just the flu. Under the weather. Nothing major." A red-faced Robert tried to block Simon's foil to no avail. Another point went to the trainer.

"Really, Monsieur. This is going bad for you today." Simon scored again. "*Mon dieu*! Send in Luke. He would be more of a challenge than you are." The foil jabbed into Robert's side where he'd been wounded.

"Ach!" Robert cried out, unable to mask his pain. He felt blood gush out.

"What is wrong with you, old man? That was just a love tap." Simon laughed.

"I think it must be the stomach flu. I'm done for the day. But know this. You won't see me coming next time." Robert quickly excused himself and rushed out, leaving Simon shaking his head. Blood had already stained through his fencing shirt and Robert hoped Simon hadn't noticed.

"Send in Monsieur Luke! I need a real man to fight with!" Simon yelled after him.

Now that he was "home," there was a lot of frantic drama to settle with Sean Knight's disappearance. Funny, he did feel a little better knowing Winnie was there. She'd already covered for him a couple of times.

Of course, the best form of healing for Lord Robert was getting to spend time with his children. He was surprised at how often they talked about Mrs. Drake.

"I really want you to make her our new nanny. She has a dragon. She's the only person I know who has a dragon," Luke said.

Elizabeth raised her eyebrows and spoke to them as if she was instructing a class of young children. "But I'm perfectly capable of being in charge, you know. We don't really need a nanny, Daddy."

"But, Elizabeth, I like Mrs. Drake. She isn't afraid of your fairies!"

"You didn't like Mrs. Drake, Elizabeth?" Robert asked his daughter.

"Well, if we *have* to have a nanny, I guess she'd be better than anyone else."

It was Elizabeth's way of saying she approved.

"And she's the most beautiful girl in the whole wide world." Luke's smile lit up his little freckled face.

Courtney Drake. She wasn't chipped with one of the PAX implants, which was essential. She also seemed to genuinely care about children, unlike all the others, who treated Elizabeth and Luke like they were nothing more than a job.

Had he finally found someone who would be reliable for them? *If only nannies were as easy to come by as secret hideouts, boats, and airplanes.* He chuckled at the irony. *Ow.* It still hurt his ribs to laugh.

He arranged for Ms. Stern to call Courtney and offer her the position.

SILENT KNIGHT

LATER THE SAME DAY

Mill Pond, Cascadia

A week had gone by since Mr. Knight's visit when my boss called me with some shocking news.

"I have to close the restaurant!" he told me. "Business hasn't been what I expected. The economy is plunging, and I can't pay the bills, Courtney! If I want a loan, my bank is requiring me to be chipped."

"What? Out here, nobody's chipped! Are you going to get one?"

He sobbed. "I don't know. Owning a restaurant has been my lifelong dream. I'd hate to let them stick those things in me, but to be honest, it would make my life a lot easier. Unfortunately, at least for now, I can't keep the place open. I'm sorry, Courtney!"

"It's okay, Frankie. It's going to be okay. Just let me know if there's any way I can help."

"Got a million pins?" He laughed. "Aw, you're a good soul, Courtney... and you sing like an angel." More sobs.

"Frankie, you *will* get back up from this."

"That's not why I'm cryin'! It's my cousin. His fiancée broke off the wedding that I hired you to sing at. Mamma Mia! I'm destroying all your dreams! You must hate me." The sobbing intensified.

I sucked a deep breath in. "No! No, I could never hate you!" I told him, which was completely true. "Besides, my life is great! I just got a few other singing gigs, so I'm good!" That part wasn't so true. "You don't need to worry about me. Just live by your own mantra, Frankie: *When life throws tomatoes at you, make marinara!*"

Honk. Frankie blew his wide Vinosian nose through the phone. *Honk.* "You're right … you're right. Make Momma's marinara and meatballs!"

"That's the spirit!" I cheered.

"Courtney. I'm so sorry. I can't even pay you for the past few days you worked. I hope the tips were good."

"Yes! The tips were great." Another white lie. "See? It all works out."

I got off the phone, and a minute later it rang again. This time it was Laurel.

"Mom, it looks like my college is requiring us to get the implant chips next year, and word on the street is they are going to start using the patrol drones here. I'm thinking of doing college online next year since online students don't have to be chipped."

"Wow! That's great! I would love that. You have no idea how lonely this place is lately."

"Oh, yay! I wasn't sure how you'd take the news," she said. "I'm glad you're okay with that plan. I know Nick would hate me if I got the chip."

"I'm more than okay with it. It is the happiest news I've had in a long time, honey! You still coming home for summer break in a few weeks?"

"Yep, and then I need to get a job."

"That makes two of us," I said.

"What? I thought you had a job. At a new Vinosian restaurant."

I sighed. "I did until, like, two minutes ago. Just got off the phone with my boss. The restaurant isn't making enough to stay open. On top of that, I'm not even singing at his cousin's wedding now. They're no longer getting married. It has just been one fine day."

I thought about telling her about the job interview at Ranfurly Manor but decided that could wait when she said she needed to finish her homework. We said our goodbyes.

My girl was coming home! At least I'd have Laurel back. I was sad that Nick wouldn't be home all summer. He'd landed an internship in The Capital working for PAX. I wondered how he would manage not getting chipped while working for them.

Once again, I was out of a job. The questions went through my mind: *Is it a sign? Am I supposed to take the job at the manor? Laurel will be home in a few short weeks to take care of the house and animals. I wouldn't be too far from her, and I could see her on weekends. But what will I do with the animals in the meantime? Hmm.*

I plopped into my teal armchair and puffed out my cheeks, then slowly blew out air, making a sound like a rocket ship launching. My shoulders felt tight and sore. *A man with strong hands would be nice right about now. Mr. Knight had strong-looking hands. I wonder if he gives good massages.* I stared out my back window.

Ring. Ring.

I jumped out of my teal armchair, wiping drool from my chin. Apparently, I had dozed off, and the red landline phone woke me.

I looked up at heaven. *If it's Ms. Stern, I'll take it as a sure sign I need to accept the job.* "Hello?"

"Mrs. Drake, this is Ms. Stern, Household Manager of the Ranfurly Manor."

"Yes, hello." I looked up at heaven again, lifting an eyebrow.

"Lord Ranfurly would like to offer you the position as his children's nanny."

"Your timing couldn't be better. I know I told Mr. Knight that I was not interested in the position. But just today I had a change of circumstance." Silence on the other end of the line. "Hello? Ms. Stern?"

"When did you tell Mr. Knight you were not interested?" she asked.

"Last week," I said, confused. "Didn't he tell you?"

Pause. "Mr. Knight has been missing for seven days. The police found Lord Ranfurly's Royal Rodney abandoned on a logging road in the Wildwoods Forest."

"Missing?" *When was he at my house? Oh wait! … The flip calendar quote!* I flipped the pages until I saw the quote. *Seven days ago.* "You're sure he went missing seven days ago?"

"Of course, I'm sure."

"But … seven days ago he was here. … Did he return after he left my house?"

"… He did not inform anyone that he was going to see you." She paused for a beat. "What was he *doing* at your house, Mrs. Drake?"

Now I was the one who had nothing to say. *What could have happened to the charming Mr. Knight?*

Ms. Stern heaved out a loud sigh. "Mrs. Drake, we need your decision."

"Oh. … Right. Okay. … Yes, I'll take it."

"Very good," Ms. Stern replied flatly.

"But on a few conditions," I quickly added.

"Conditions?" Ms. Stern was clearly thrown off, which, I must admit, made me beam on the inside.

"The first condition is that I never have to work weekends or holidays. The second is that if ever my own kids need me for anything, they get first dibs."

Again, silence on the other end of the line.

"Those are my conditions, otherwise I'm not interested. … And I will need everything in writing."

"One moment," Ms. Stern snapped. I heard clicking heels get fainter and fainter. A few moments later she was back on the line. "Ya, okay. Lord Ranfurly is drawing up a contract. Mr. Knight will be there to pick you up tomorrow at eight o'clock sharp."

Did she just say Mr. Knight? "Wait a second! You just said Mr. Knight was missing! Now you say he's picking me up. Is this a joke to you? Because I don't find it funny. In fact, I find it sick and twisted…"

"Mrs. Drake," A warm, baritone voice with an Uplandish accent broke through before I could finish my rant. "Hello. I'm Lord Robert Ranfurly. Sorry about the muddle. Mr. Knight, Sr. will be giving you a lift. You met the Jr. He only drives for me part-time, and his main job was taking care of the horses. Sadly, he's gone missing."

Like a tire, stuck in the mud, my mind was spinning but couldn't move forward.

The man went on. "The Jr. grew up here, you see. He was close to the other staff, and they are quite upset by his disappearance. Of course, my children don't understand all that has happened. But they've been asking after you."

My mind was still spinning in mud.

"Mrs. Drake? Are you still there?"

I managed to say, "Y-yes. I'm just … well, in shock, I suppose. I'm terribly sorry that your children are put in this situation." I didn't know how any words were forming and coming out of my mouth. "But I'm surprised to hear they are asking about me. They've only met me the one time."

"Ah, yes. Well, I was surprised as well. They don't typically like any of the nanny applicants. But, for some reason they're very keen on you."

"Oh! That's so sweet. I instantly liked them as well. But…"

"Yes? Is there a problem?"

"Possibly. Look, I'll be honest. I'm a bit of a rebel when it comes to structure. And Ms. Stern's schedule is not a mold I could ever fit into."

"*Ms. Stern's* schedule? Well, I can assure you, as my children's nanny, you'll be the one fully in charge of the schedule, Mrs. Drake."

"I will?" I sighed in some relief, although I had a feeling Ms. Stern was not going to be too fun to deal with if I worked there. "Is Ms. Stern aware?"

"If she's not, I'll make her aware."

"Oh." His voice was strong and commanding with a hint of playfulness. Very appealing. Then, it dawned on me. "Oh! My gosh, I don't know what I was thinking. I nearly forgot about my animals."

"Your animals?"

"Yea. I can't abandon them," I said.

"Well, what do you need for your animals? I'm happy to arrange something so we can make this work."

"Well … it would be a *big* ask."

"Name it."

"I would need about three hours daily to commute to feed and water my animals for the next few weeks until my daughter comes home. Unless you'd allow me to live at home? I don't mind commuting."

"I see. Unfortunately, frequent business trips take me away from home, so the nanny is needed here overnight. But my driver will take you home to feed your animals each day."

"I see. Well, I do have my own car so you wouldn't need to trouble your driver."

"I really must insist we leave your transportation in the hands of my driver."

Why would he insist on that? I wondered. "Well, can you please make sure to add the part about my animals to the contract? Also, can we maybe look at this as a one-month trial? It is a lot for me to leave my house and come to live there. I want to make sure that this is a good fit. On both sides."

There was a pause. "Very well. Anything else you wish to add?" he asked.

"No. I think that's it."

After we hung up, I hoped I hadn't come across as offensive by saying the last bit about a trial period. *Why do my words always come out not quite right?* But I couldn't envision myself working with Ms. Stern for very long. And to leave my comfortable little home was not something I looked forward to.

My mind flitted back to Mr. Knight, Jr. *Was there anything he said to me that day he was here that indicated where he might have been headed next? It was only a week ago. He'd been right here, playing my piano, singing songs, charming my animals. Beginning to charm me. Until I abruptly closed the curtain on that idea.*

How could he go missing? I couldn't see anyone kidnapping a man like him. He's probably around six feet two inches and in incredible physical shape.

But then, Keith was strong. He'd gone missing too. That turned out to be a PAX job.

Why would Mr. Knight's car be all the way in the Wildwoods on some remote road? That was four hours away from my house, in the far northwest corner of Cascadia. Did someone chase him off the road? If so, why?

Yes, I needed a job. But I also wanted to figure out why Mr. Knight had disappeared, and Ranfurly Manor might have the answers. I could kill two birds with one stone by working there.

LORD OF THE MANOR

THE NEXT MORNING
Mill Pond, Cascadia

The day started with a little blue in the sky. At long last, Cascadia was getting sunshine! I put on my yellow dress that looked and felt like spring, along with matching heels.

I ended up regretting the heels, which I never wore since I barely knew how to walk in them. Keith used to tease me about it and told me I shouldn't spend money on them. *Ugh. If I wasn't taking a job to work for a lord, I'd just throw on my scuffed-up white tennis shoes.*

When the Royal Rodney showed up in my driveway for the third time, the sky had darkened, and rain clouds were building up. *So much for a bright, sunshiny day. Welcome to Cascadia.*

This time it wasn't the dashing thirty-something Mr. Knight who stepped out of the automobile, but an older, bearded man with white hair. Maybe in his late sixties. The resemblance between Mr. Knight, Sr. and his son was unmistakable. I felt a lump form in my throat as he stepped out of the car. *Mr. Knight's father. He must be so worried.*

The father wore the identical uniform to the one his son had on that first morning I met him. He greeted me in a strong Highlandish brogue.

"G'day, Mrs. Drake. Lord Ranfurly bade me t'come fetch ya." He picked up my teal luggage that was sitting next to the front door and put them in the trunk of the Rodney, then opened the back door of the car and stood next to it.

"Thank you," I said, and got in the car. I could only imagine what a difficult time he was going through over his son's disappearance.

We drove in silence. I caught his reflection in the rearview mirror, and it seemed as if he was lost in his own musings. I was under the impression that he'd rather not be bothered with conversation.

Off and on, the rain flooded down so heavy it prevented me from seeing anything out of the windows. The rivers were higher than usual and water spilled into the two-lane road at one point.

My truck would handle this weather better than the Royal Rodney, I thought, feeling a bit resentful. Why was Lord Ranfurly so insistent on his own driver? I already felt suffocated, knowing I wouldn't have the freedom to just get in my car and come and go as I pleased.

We arrived at the manor. Mr. Knight, Sr. opened my car door for me. He looked straight ahead and avoided eye contact when I smiled at him in gratitude. I ran for cover beneath the awning that hung over the front doors, not escaping a dump of rain. Mr. Knight followed behind with my luggage at an even pace, as if the downpour had no effect on him. Fortunately, I managed to grab and put on my lightweight pink raincoat before I left my house, but without an umbrella my hair was drenched, and prickly goosebumps were forming on my bare legs.

Knock. Knock. Knock. I rapped on one of the huge doors.

Ms. Stern was the one who opened it. "Mrs. Drake. You look like a drowned, pink rat." She was dressed in the same grey she wore at the interview. Grey day. Grey manor. Grey Ms. Stern. My yellow dress, pink raincoat, and teal luggage couldn't have seemed more out of place. "Vait there vun minute!"

She slammed the front door, leaving us to wait out in the miserable, wet cold.

When Ms. Stern finally opened the door, she handed us towels. "I just had these floors vaxed. Dry off before you come in here dripping vet! Both of you! And Mr. Knight, off vith those shoes. You vill track mud!"

Note to self: Ms. Stern's accent really comes out when she's irritated.

Mr. Knight, Sr. grumbled something behind me. All I could make out from what he said was "…auld ugly witch."

Once we were sufficiently mopped up, Ms. Stern said, "Allow me to show you your room." She led me to the second floor, the same one I'd seen during my interview, where the classrooms were. We rounded a corner, and she opened a door that led to another flight of stairs.

On the third floor, she pointed to closed double doors down the hallway. "That is Lord Ranfurly's bedroom." She pointed to three doors down a hall to the left. "The children's bedrooms and their nursery are down that hall." Then she pointed to a closed door at the top of the stairs. "Here is your room, Mrs. Drake." I got the impression by her tone that she wasn't too happy about me staying in that room.

A beautifully furnished bedroom with a dark mahogany wood dresser, nightstand, and poster bed awaited us through the door. A white goose down comforter and paint the color of butter on the walls gave the room a cheery vibe, despite the dreary day. A vase on the dresser held a bouquet of fresh lavender. The large room had a walk-in fireplace with a white mantle, and double glass doors which led to a balcony.

"You have a valk-in closet there." She scowled as she pointed to a door with a full-length mirror hanging on it.

"Your vashroom and toilet, there." She pointed to a closed mahogany door in the far corner.

Mr. Knight, Sr. silently set down my luggage in the closet and slipped out.

"Once you are unpacked, Lord Ranfurly vishes to speak vith you in the parlor, downstairs. You remember how to get there?"

I nodded. "Yes, thank you."

A permanent frown on her face, Ms. Stern pivoted on her heels and was out the door. I got the impression she wasn't given a vote about who they hired as the nanny.

I hung up my raincoat and unpacked. Then I brushed through my wet hair and freshened up before I made my way back downstairs to the parlor.

The room was empty when I sat down on one of the wing-backed chairs. A minute later, the lovely Gretchen popped her head in and cheerfully said, "Hello again, Mrs. Drake. Here are scones. And coffee for you. Lord Ranfurly will be here shortly."

"You remembered that I like coffee! You're the best, Gretchen!"

She covered her mouth and giggled before she left the room.

Two cups of coffee and three scones-lathered-with-cream-and-marmalade later, Lord Ranfurly made his grand appearance.

Oh. … My.

Long dark hair was pulled back into a man bun. A trimmed beard framed his chiseled jaw. He wore white fencing pants and a white unbuttoned shirt that revealed the top half of his muscular bronze chest. And his eyes were green, like the foliage of a Hemlock, with flickers of gold when they would catch the light.

He wasn't like what I'd imagined. A stiff-necked snob with pointy features. Not at all. He was … beautiful.

This. This cannot be Lord Ranfurly.

"Mrs. Drake, nice to meet you. I'm Lord Robert." He held out a hand, and I noticed the scars. A *lot* of scars. I guess I expected his hands to look more manicured, being that he was a lord and all. *But by what he's wearing, he likes to fence. That must be how he got the scars.*

When our hands touched, it was like an electrical surge woke up my senses. His eyes trapped mine. "Forgive me for keeping you waiting. I had an urgent business call to deal with."

I was entranced.

Until I became aware that I hadn't replied. Then … I was awkward.

I managed to push through the feeling that my tongue was in knots, and sputtered out, "No worries, Gretchen brought me this amazing coffee and scones." I was sure I looked ridiculous, unable to wipe the smile off my face, and a little off balance in my high heels as I stood up to greet him.

He flashed a winsome smile that lit up every corner of the parlor. "Excellent. And did you enjoy your ride over with Mr. Knight, Sr.?" He shook my hand and held onto it. "It wasn't so bad having a chauffeur, was it?" I caught the glimmer in his eyes.

"Well … not *too* terrible." I tilted my head to the side and laughed. Like a dumbstruck schoolgirl.

I originally had what I was going to say all planned out. But now I couldn't recall what it was. Something about having my own car? Telling him that I had claustrophobia in back seats and car sickness? It wasn't *exactly* true. But I did feel trapped without my own car.

His stunning eyes seemed to be reading my every move. "And is your bedroom going to be sufficient for you?" The sound of his velvety voice was like a shot of bourbon in a bubble bath.

"Yes, it's perfect. Thank you."

"Good. I asked Ms. Stern to be sure to put fresh roses from the flower garden in your room. But she said they haven't bloomed yet; too cold, wet, and dark this year. Lavender was not my first choice."

Did he know roses were one of my favorite flowers? That would be flattering. But also, kind of sinister.

"Oh, lavender works just as good. I like it. Thank you."

He was still holding onto my hand. "The children are looking forward to getting to know you better, Mrs. Drake. But first, I have a few questions to ask you." Letting go of my hand, he sat in the chair opposite.

"Mmhmm?" I breathed out. It took some serious resistance to keep from melting into a puddle on the floor. I sat back in my chair, and straightened up, as proper and lady-like as possible. It wasn't easy. I was never the poised and graceful type. Even when I used to dance and cheer, if my moves weren't well rehearsed, I was a total klutz.

I averted my eyes from resting on his irresistible exposed chest.

"It's about my driver, Mr. Knight, Jr. You say he came to see you a week ago?"

The reminder of Mr. Knight immediately sobered me.

"Y-yes. He did."

"Would you mind telling me why he was there to see you? This information could be helpful in locating his whereabouts."

"I—well, yes. Of course. He was there to ask me if I was going to accept the job to work for you. I thought you sent him."

"No. I did not send him. In fact, Mr. Knight did not inform me he would be taking my car out that day. At that point, I hadn't made up my mind about who I would hire for the nanny position. My interims were still filling in sufficiently."

"Well, uh … I don't know why he came to see me then." I trailed off. *Why did he lie to me and tell me I had the job? What was the purpose in him coming over?*

"Mrs. Drake." He leaned in closer. "Please try to remember everything that Mr. Knight said to you when you saw him. Perhaps something he said will give us a clue to what might have happened to him. Did he mention where he would be going after he left your house?"

I shook my head. "No."

"Do you recall what he was wearing that day?"

I slowly nodded. "Yes. I do remember finding it surprising that he wasn't in the same uniform he'd worn the first time he picked me up. He was in a black business suit and jacket."

"Hmm. Interesting. Could be helpful. Is there anything else?"

I shook my head. "He just said his reason for coming was to offer me the position here. He was very upset when I turned it down." I was baffled as to why he lied to me.

Lord Ranfurly lifted an eyebrow. "He was upset?" He looked confused. "When you turned it down?"

I nodded.

"He was upset at you for turning down the position that he very well knew you hadn't been offered yet?" he asked.

Again, I nodded. When he put it *that* way, I realized how ridiculous I must sound.

Lord Ranfurly got up and walked to the fireplace, then leaned against the mantle. I couldn't help but admire his powerful frame. I followed his gaze as he looked out of the room's huge windows. There was a lovely view of a checkered lawn and a willow tree.

"So, you're saying that last week you had already made up your mind to turn down the position here? And what were your reasons for not wanting to work for me, Mrs. Drake?" He turned to me with an expectant look on his face.

I was surprised by the way he changed the subject. At first, I wasn't exactly sure I should give him an honest answer. I played with my coffee cup.

"Go on, I would like to know. Why didn't you want to work for me, exactly? Did I not offer a large enough salary?"

"No. The salary is fine," I said hesitantly. "Very good, actually."

"Well, what then? Do you not like the work environment? What is it that doesn't please you, Mrs. Drake?"

I squeezed my lips together, as a reminder to myself not to say anything stupid.

"I do hope it wasn't something the children did," he said.

"No! It wasn't the children! Not at all! There's nothing wrong with *them*."

"Not with *them*? Aha!" He pointed his finger in the air as if he'd scored a point. "But there is *something* you find wrong. Go on, then. Do tell me what it is."

I bit into my lip harder.

"Please, I insist."

I opened my mouth, and this is what came out. "Actually, with all due respect ... it was *you,* Lord Ranfurly."

"Me? But what did I do? I wasn't even here."

"Exactly. The fact that you weren't here for the interview. I felt like that was..."

"Was ... what?"

"Well, if the tables were turned and I were interviewing a caregiver for my kids, I would certainly want to meet them."

"Ah."

That's it? That's all he has to say?

He laughed. Laughed! Then shook his head and started pacing around the room. I watched him, wondering what he might do or say next. It was like watching a mesmerizing flame flicker. *Flames, at any moment, can burst into a raging fire,* I reminded myself.

"But the main reason I turned the job down, was because I have my animals and ten acres to deal with," I added quickly.

He stopped pacing to look at me. "Yes, well, I do believe I already told you that I'm willing to make an exception for you to take care of your animals."

Something about me that can be a problem: once I open my mouth, I don't always know when or how to close it.

"But I didn't know that a week ago when Mr. Knight supposedly offered me the job. Also, the way you had Ms. Stern call on a phone number I never give out to anyone. At an unreasonable hour. I never even agreed to the interview; you just sent your driver to pick me up."

Too late to turn back. It was already out there.

I needed to stand up. To breathe. Also, to feel taller. And my tongue just wouldn't stop wagging. "I'm used to working for employers who allow me my freedom and *treat me as an equal, Lord Ranfurly.*"

What is wrong with me? Please, just tell your driver to take me home so I can hide under my covers and never face anyone. Ever again.

Those green eyes seemed to devour me. "I see. Well. You certainly have a terrible impression of me, don't you, Mrs. Drake?" He held my gaze.

My breaths were uneven. Did he notice?

He continued. "But before you carry out a verdict on me, would you allow me to act as my own defense?"

"I-I suppose."

He flashed a winsome smile, gently put his hand on the small of my back, *oh my,* and gestured for me to sit down again. "Have a seat."

I obeyed.

He took his seat across from me. "More coffee?"

"I'm good."

"Right, then. Well, for my opening statement, I believe my employees will testify that I'm not one to generally micromanage. Everyone is free to do as they like. But … when it comes to matters involving my children, I have the highest of standards. Which is why I had an extensive background check done." He moved his chair closer to mine and leaned in, so our eyes were level. In a near whisper, he said, "My children are my highest priority, and I will go to the greatest measures to keep them safe. Would you do any less for your own children, Mrs. Drake?"

I shook my head. A whiff of his alluring cologne captivated my senses. I had a sudden urge to inhale his neck.

He went on. "You would expect a school to do a background check, yes? I just happen to have resources to do extensive background checks on people who want to work for me. Put yourself in my shoes. Would you use every resource you had available to keep your children safe?"

"Of course," I admitted.

"As for the late calls by Ms. Stern, I *am* sorry. I have no control over that woman. However, she is a solid employee. She's been at the manor long before I came along. I know. … She has a bit of an abrasive side. But she does a fine job in managing the household."

He had a certain kind of humility about him – a down-to-earth side. At first, I didn't see it. But it was starting to shine through, and I was starting to feel more at ease.

"But the schedule she has your children on is so … military! Do you want them to have that kind of pressure? They're only five, after all."

He tilted his head to the side. "Funny. You're the first one to bring this to my attention. No wonder they dislike Ms. Stern so much, poor tykes. I'll have to take a closer look at this schedule you're talking about."

"I'm surprised nobody's brought it to your attention before now," I said.

"Yes. Well, perhaps they were afraid that Ms. Stern might, I don't know, do them harm. She is a bit foreboding; *I* even feel frightened of her sometimes." His lips curled up on one side.

I laughed out loud. Too loud. Immediately, I covered a hand over my mouth, wishing I could take it back. *He must think I was born in a barn.*

To my relief, he laughed easily. I relaxed. Maybe a little too much. Because the next thing I knew, I was flirting.

"Yes, well, it is a bit surprising to hear that Ms. Stern frightens a strong man like *you*," I teased.

"Do I look strong to you, Mrs. Drake?" He held up an arm and flexed his muscles. "I'm flattered you think so."

I bit my lip, trapping in another loud laugh.

His eyes were smiling when they met mine. We both sat there, quiet for a moment. It was as if he was searching for something inside me.

I felt my cheeks grow warm.

"Listen," he said. "I grant you full authority over Elizabeth's and Luke's schedule. Except for whenever I'm home. Then I like to spend all my time with them. You'll still receive the same pay during those times. But those may be days when you'll wish to return to your animals."

I decided to ask the question that had repeatedly burned in my mind for so long. "Lord Ranfurly, why do you want me to work for you?"

A half smile crossed his lips. "Please, call me Robert. Lord Ranfurly was my father." He waited a minute before he answered my question. "I know your son Nick."

My jaw fell.

He clearly took pleasure in shocking me. "An impressive young man you raised. He has a sincere desire to make a difference in this world. He once told me you lived not too far from me, and it's been my desire to make your acquaintance for quite some time now."

He paused and poured two glasses of water. His fingers brushed mine for a moment when he handed me my glass.

A flutter went through me. *Was I the only one who felt that?*

"It wasn't long after I met Nick," he continued, "when your name came through as a job applicant for the nanny here. You can imagine my surprise."

"Really? That's an amazing coincidence," I said.

Lord Ranfurly lifted his eyebrows. "Coincidence? Or some would argue Providence. Either way, it was worth paying attention to. Mrs.

Drake, my children are not fond of having a nanny. In truth, they wish for a mother."

I almost choked on my sip of water. He didn't seem to notice but looked out the window and continued. "But that is not something I can make happen. My wife was my world. Finding someone to replace her would be impossible."

I felt the weight of his pain when he said that last part. "I'm so sorry for your loss. I understand the pain well," I whispered.

His eyes found mine. "Yes, I know you do. Nick told me about his father. I'm terribly sorry for your loss, as well."

I closed my eyes and nodded.

"Having an empathetic nanny is in my children's best interest, don't you think?" He twirled a curl of a loose hair with his finger.

I nodded.

"Also, it's becoming more difficult to find someone who isn't chipped these days."

"Too true," I said. "But, eventually won't everyone have to be chipped?"

"Perhaps. But for now, my employees are all without them and I should like it to remain this way for as long as possible." He stared into his glass of water. "We don't have drones here. In fact, we are so off grid and remote, I imagine Ranfurly Manor should be one of the last places drones will patrol."

"I hope you're right." I said without thinking. I was letting my guard down. What if he actually worked for PAX? PAX narcs were something to worry about, and from what I'd read, most of the royals had transferred their allegiances to the new regime. If he reported me, they would label me *Offender* for speaking against PAX. I needed to be more cautious, I reminded myself.

He broke into my fears. "It hasn't been easy to find someone. Most of the younger applicants I interviewed refused to give up their cell phones. The older ones can't keep up with my children. Then some simply can't hack the work environment here. As you can see, we have a unique dynamic at the manor."

"That's a way to describe it." I smiled into my own glass of water.

"You're the only interviewee who my children have asked after." He shook his head. "A day hasn't passed when they haven't asked if you will be their new nanny. It gives me hope."

"Hope?" I whispered.

Then the strangest thing happened. Our eyes met, and it was like we were transported somewhere. Were we in water? Space? A beautiful meadow? I'm not sure. But I had this feeling that time was non-existent in that place.

I had never experienced anything quite like that before. Not even with Keith.

He looked away and broke the connection. Then he stood, walked over to his desk, and picked up a sheet of paper. His tone was suddenly solid and professional.

"The contract, as promised. Read it, and you'll find everything you requested. The only item that is not included is your request to drive your car here. I ask you to wait a bit on that for this reason: I thoroughly vet everyone who comes here, and those I allow in very rarely are permitted to bring in their own vehicles. Special deliveries are made to a post office thirty minutes from here in the town of North Ireland. You may consider this over-cautious, but I assure you, I have my reasons." He paused for a moment.

How could anyone keep their place completely off grid with AI as advanced as it was? With satellites in space? Surely it would be impossible to keep a place like Ranfurly Manor hidden, I wondered as he went on.

"Oh, and I have one last defense to make. You ask, why wasn't I here on the day of your interview? Well, I originally planned on being here, of course. However, something urgent came up just before your interview. A matter of life or death, and I had to leave before you arrived. I received a full report of your interview from Ms. Stern … and from my children."

Hearing this, I felt terrible for giving him a hard time about not being there. "I'm sorry, I didn't know. Did everything turn out alright? Or…?" I sat stiffly on the edge of my chair. *I'm such an idiot for assuming.*

He stole a glance at me. "You can relax. Nobody died."

I sighed. "Thank God."

He was looking at a miniature statue of a raven that sat on a nearby shelf. I wondered if I'd imagined that magical connection between us. If only he'd make eye contact again, maybe I'd find out.

"Well then, what do you determine is the verdict now, Mrs. Drake?"

I lifted my eyebrows. "Not guilty."

He laughed. "Ah, wonderful. I can sleep at night." He studied my face a moment, then said, "You know, I see the resemblance. Your son favors you. … Perhaps you may help raise my children to grow up to be as fine as your son."

I felt the heat rise to my cheeks. "Well, I can't take all the credit. His father had a hand in it. How did you meet my son, anyway? Does he know I applied to work for you?"

He smiled. "I met him at a conference in Capital City. We sat at the same table and spoke for quite some time. He would be an excellent lawyer, and I told him so. You must be very proud. … And no, he does not know you applied to work for me."

"I see. And yes, I am incredibly proud of him. Thank you."

I was intently watching him, hoping he would look into my eyes again.

Then, at last he did. But no connection that time. *Too bad. It was just my ridiculous imagination.*

"Of course, I understand this will be a trial period for us both," he said. "Per your request. And that makes perfect sense. One should court before they wed, yes?" He smiled.

At his simile, I giggled a bit awkwardly. "Right. Exactly. Yes."

"Well, Mrs. Drake, today is going to be a day for the children to get to know you a little better. You don't mind if I tag along, do you?"

I struggled to swallow. "That's fine. Of course." In all honesty, I was nervous. *What if I mess up and do something stupid on the first day of the job? In front of him?*

"We will lunch, and then you'll get a tour of the manor and grounds. But first, I need to change out of my fencing knickers. I recommend you change out of that lovely dress into something more comfortable."

"Oh. Alright."

"Did you bring mud boots? It will likely be mucky outside."

"Yes, I brought mud boots."

"Good. Meet me in the hallway of our bedrooms at noon."

"Alrighty, then!" I clapped my hands together. "Thank you, Mr.-er–
Lord Ranfurly."

"No need to be so formal. Call me Robert. And do you mind if I call
you Courtney?"

"Yes, of course. I mean no, of course not. I don't mind." I bit my lip,
wishing I had a hole to crawl into.

He laughed lightly. "Very well, see you shortly." He opened the parlor
door for me. I started up the stairs. He was behind me.

Once I was on the second floor, I'd forgotten where the next flight of
stairs was. I stopped, unsure which way to go.

He laughed. "Allow me." I took in a whiff of his delicious scent as he
passed.

Now I was behind him. I shamelessly admired his gait.

"There you are." He opened the door to my room.

"Thank you," I said. *Wait … dear heavens, he's a lord. Am I supposed to
bow?* I attempted to curtsey.

He smiled and bent forward, then took my hand. When he kissed it,
I nearly stumbled into him. "Remember what I said?" he breathed. "I'm
simply Robert. No formalities are necessary between us, Courtney."

As soon as he left, I closed the door and swooned onto the bed. *Lord
Ranfurly! Oh my! I had no idea he would be so … so wow.* I sighed and got
lost in a little fantasy.

Wait. What are you doing? A loud voice came into my head. A mixture between Keith's and my own. *Remember the reason you are here! Mr.
Knight is missing! Only a week ago you were being charmed by him. What is
wrong with you, woman? Pull yourself together!*

I'd been thrown off my mission. *Lord Robert … He might as well be
the devil, distracting me like that!*

Back to Mr. Knight, Jr. Now, why did he really *come to see me that day?*
I tried to think of a reason. *Could it be that he was attracted to me? No. No!*

... But what other reason could there have been for him to drive all the way out and see me? After he'd stolen a car! What was that all about? Who might know something? Mr. Knight, Sr.?

Mr. Knight, Sr. looked like he would be a tough can of worms to crack open.

I knew if I asked the right questions to the right people, I might have a shot at learning something. But what were the right questions? And who were the right people?

UNDISCLOSED

SAME DAY ~ NOON

Ranfurly Manor

The new nanny. Courtney. Lord Robert smiled, recalling when he walked into the parlor and saw her. Like a ray of long-awaited sunshine, she lit up the room in her yellow dress, which revealed shapely legs and a delicious hourglass figure.

It couldn't be coincidence that she came across the job opening just a few months after he met her son. *Providence works in mysterious ways.*

SIX MONTHS AGO

CAPE Headquarters, Capital City

The young man stood out at six feet and three inches tall. He had a confident air about him as he gave his speech. He wasn't like the other nineteen-year-olds when he shared his experience of losing his father in The Day of Cleansing, and his strategy of how PAX could be stopped. Lord Robert understood why Peter Williams spoke so highly of him.

Peter had arranged it so that Nick would be seated next to Lord Robert at the dinner table. He wanted to introduce them.

Nick wore a black business suit, like all the other guests, but his yellow tie and matching yellow button with a circle and slash through the word PAX made him stand out.

"Your speech was rather good, wasn't it?" Robert said as Nick took his seat.

"Oh. Was it?" Nick asked.

Robert chuckled to himself. Nick wasn't used to the way a person from The Green Isles spoke. "It was spot on," Robert clarified.

"Thank you. I'm Nick Drake." Nick held out a hand.

Robert firmly shook it. "Robert Ranfurly."

"Oh! You're not … Lord Ranfurly?"

"Last time I checked I was," Robert said.

"No way! Great to finally meet you. Justice Williams told me about you. He said you live in Cascadia. That's where I'm from!"

"Oh. Whereabouts?"

"A little town called Mill Pond. About an hour south of Mt. Ziwa, on the edge of the Ziwa Forest. We're two hours from Emer Aude."

"Ah, yes, I know exactly where Mill Pond is. I'm sixty miles north of there, as a crow flies," Lord Robert said.

"So, Justice Williams told me you're a lawyer. Do you have any feedback regarding my speech?"

"It was convicting and persuasive. If I were an instructor, I'd give it top marks."

"Thank you. That means a lot coming from you," Nick said.

Robert was discerning, and he liked Nick instantly. In the young man's blue-grey eyes, he saw a purity and sincerity that he found refreshing.

Nick went on. "It felt great to speak freely here about what I believe. I didn't have to hold back, knowing I'm with likeminded people who all want the same thing. To bring down PAX."

Lord Robert nodded. "Peter explained the CAPE team's mission, then?"

"Yes. And I'm ready for it. I feel like being a part of this team is what I was made for."

Lord Robert saw a fire behind the young man's eyes that reminded him of himself.

Peter had never been wrong about who he recruited into CAPE. All the members shared the same drive and determination to stop the tyrannical government.

A dark man with a silvery black afro approached their table. "Aha! I see you two have met." The man's voice was deep and commanding.

Lord Robert stood and gave the man a bear hug. "Peter! Good to see you! Yes, I was just getting to know this fine young man, here."

"Did Nick tell you what he'll be doing?" Peter asked.

Lord Robert gave Nick a curious look.

"I'm studying Political Science at school, learning all about our new government," Nick said. "And I just got chosen to be an intern at PAX Headquarters."

"You got him on the inside, then, Peter? But how will you get around the implants they require?"

"PAX realized the chip implants had some sort of defect after a malfunctioning series of drones accidentally killed over thirty of their own workers. They decided to waive chips for their own employees until they can fix the issues. So, right now is the best time to get as many people on the inside as we can."

"You really don't do much, do you ole chap," Robert said. He turned to Nick, "That's a risky job, though, Nick. Let's hope you can blag it."

Nick laughed good-naturedly. "Actually, I played lead in a couple of high school plays, so I've got a little experience. My mom passed down her acting genes to me."

"Ah, very good. But you might lose the button."

Nick raised an eyebrow. "I don't know. I thought it might be fun to see the look on the head of PAX Intel's face when I go to their student conference next week."

"Careful, son. Your sense of humor could land you on an island," Peter warned.

"I know, my mom tells me I should tone down the humor," Nick said. "But with all due respect, sir, life is too depressing to survive without a sense of humor."

"Fair enough," Peter said.

"Does your mum know you are with The Resistance?" Lord Robert asked Nick.

"No. She'd kill me if she found out." Nick made a silly face. "Don't get me wrong. She's on our side. She hates PAX. But she thinks people in The Resistance are … you know." He spun a finger around next to his temple. "Wacko. … She's just afraid.

"Did your mum get the chip?" Robert asked.

"No, and neither did my sister, thanks to me convincing them. I'm determined to tear down everything PAX stands for."

"But PAX stands for peace, Nick." An attractive brunette, also about nineteen years old, bumped shoulders with him.

"Hey, Jocelyn! This is Lord Robert Ranfurly. He lives in Cascadia, where I'm from. This is my friend from school, and a fellow Poli Sci student, Jocelyn."

"Nice to meet you," Jocelyn said, imitating Lord Robert's accent. Nick laughed.

Robert maintained a serious face. "Where are you from, Jocelyn? I can't quite place the accent."

"Really? But I thought it was so obvious, Your Grace. I am from that village down the street from yours. It's been so long since I've been there, I forgot the name. Something or othershire."

Lord Robert played along. "Oh, you must mean Poppycockshire."

"Yes! That's the one! How are all my village people getting along these days?"

"Oh, you haven't heard? The entire place burned down."

"Oh dear!" Jocelyn put the back of her hand to her forehead, as if distressed.

"So, are you two an item?" He wagged his finger at Jocelyn and Nick.

Nick and Jocelyn turned bright shades of purple. At the same time, they protested, "No, no, we're just friends! Just friends!"

PRESENT

Lord Robert laughed out loud as he pondered the memory.

His thoughts returned to Courtney. How would she handle it if she knew her son was risking his life as a member of the Resistance? He was glad she wasn't chipped and wasn't a fan of PAX. How could she be, after what they'd done to her husband?

Robert's mind wandered back to when he looked into her eyes. He couldn't explain it, the strange connection he felt, the desire to know her deeply. Did he feel that way with Desiree? He couldn't remember if he did.

Desiree was the love of his life. Intense passion flared up for her and devoured him like a wildfire. Their relationship had been tumultuous. He had insane bouts of jealousy. If Robert was honest with himself, his hunger to be with her was to the point that it was unhealthy.

Courtney was nothing like Desiree, and what he'd just encountered was … different. He couldn't pinpoint exactly how, but it was.

He hadn't been interested in another woman before Desiree, nor after her. He had an ambitious, focused mind, and it took a unique type to attract his attention. After Desiree's death, he'd lost all desire for sex and love was the furthest thing from his mind.

After she passed, his two closest friends, Raymond and Simon, had tried to coax him to "just go out and have a good time. Spend a night with a woman. Make sure everything still works down there." But the thought of sleeping with a stranger repulsed him.

Then he moved to Cascadia. Fighting crime in the streets of Emer Aude became his coping method. When PAX took over and Peter asked him to join CAPE, it was an easy decision.

As for falling in love with someone, his kids filled all the space left in his heart. The last thing he wanted, or needed, was another woman in his life.

One of the most difficult things about his secret escapades was having to go without seeing his children for sometimes days at a time. But he reminded himself the reason he had to sacrifice time with his children was ultimately for their sake. They needed a safer, better world.

Elizabeth had recently asked him. "Why don't we have a mother?"

Robert wondered what had triggered the question. He wasn't prepared for it. He wanted to give his children so much more than he was able. He had grown up with a loving nanny, but they didn't even have that now that Peggy had died.

The best he could do for them now was find them a caring nanny.

He was almost one hundred percent back to good health, and as much as he wanted to spend all his time with his children, he couldn't. He had a CAPE job to do after they went to bed.

Time was of the essence. A few days ago, CAPE gave him a location that was believed to be used by a trafficking ring. It was close to Robert's property, across the river, only a thirty-minute boat ride from the manor. Robert needed to scope it out and, if possible, break up the operation.

But now, he would spend the afternoon with his favorite people: his children. And he would get to know Courtney Drake a little better.

V.I.P. TOUR

I was getting the V.I.P. tour. It was raining, so we stayed indoors, and planned to go outside later if it cleared up.

It's obvious the twins worship their daddy, I thought, seeing the look on their faces. Elizabeth held onto his hand, and Luke sat on his shoulders. *And he clearly adores them.*

"And this is the Grand Ballroom," Lord Robert explained. "Ranfurly the First built it for his wife in 2100. The ballroom and library were the last rooms to be added on during that period. Ranfurly the Second built the theater much later, in 2182, and added an indoor swimming pool and cabanas."

"Where is it? The swimming pool?" I asked.

"Out past the garages. Unfortunately, the pool is inoperable now. We most likely won't get that far today, though, with all there is to see. The castle I grew up in, Ranfurly Castle, is large. It's where Ranfurly the First grew up as well. But he built this place four times the size of Ranfurly Castle."

"So Ranfurly the First was also a lord, then? I'm not real up to speed when it comes to order of nobility," I admitted. "Is a baron higher than a lord?"

"A lord and lady rank beneath a baron and baroness. However, the proper way to address a baron is to address him as lord." He shrugged and laughed. "I didn't make up the rules."

"Oh. So, what are you, then? A lord or a baron?"

"Neither. My title is viscount, higher than baron or lord, but it comes with more responsibility. The Ranfurlys ruled over Knoxfordshire, before PAX dissolved the monarchy."

"So, were you pretty close to the throne?"

"Perhaps I could have been if the monarch didn't have ten children and eighty grandchildren."

I laughed.

"Doesn't matter now, though, any of it. Our beautiful history has been vandalized and torn down in riots. PAX convinced them to revolt against the monarchy. Just as they convinced people here to revolt against your leaders. Now PAX is in control. Brilliant way to steal power."

"Was your castle destroyed by vandals?" I asked.

"Don't know. Haven't been back since before all the riots. Since before PAX took over."

"Really? Your staff made it sound like you traveled back often."

"No. I mostly travel to The Capital for work these days."

He gestured to the grand room before us. "As I was saying, this room was built for Ranfurly the First's wife. Back when hosting a ball was fashionable."

"Let's pretend we're at a ball, Daddy!" Elizabeth pulled on her father's hand. Lord Robert played along and spun her around. Luke still on his shoulders, grasped his father's neck and laughed hysterically. Lord Robert stopped short and Luke held on for dear life while Elizabeth fell backwards onto her bottom, giggling.

Lord Robert held his side, as if he was winded. After he'd caught his breath, he cried, "But wait! We have no music! Maestro!" Standing up straight, he clapped his hands twice. As curtains closed automatically the room darkened. For a moment we were in complete darkness. Then music started to play, and an elaborate show of lights moved in sync.

"Oh my!" I covered my mouth in surprise as a disco ball began rotating above us and holograms of dancing couples floated around us like ghosts.

"Oh, Daddy! Let me down! Let me down!" Luke cried.

Lord Robert gently set his son down, and Luke walked around like a drunk midget. We all laughed at him.

Once he was able to stand still, Luke asked me, "Do you have any pets?"

"Yes, as a matter of fact, I do!" I replied, smiling.

Elizabeth asked me, in a very grownup manner, "Really? What kind of pets, Mrs. Drake?"

"Let's see … I have two dogs. Big scary Shays." I made a scary face at Luke.

He giggled. "I love dogs! What are their names?"

"Thor and Loki. And I have three cats. Fiona, Chadwick, and Glum. I also have two ducks and a whole lot of chickens. Which is why I need to go home every day. To feed them."

"Oh! I would like to meet your animals!" Luke cried. "Especially your dragon."

"Dragon?" Lord Robert eyed me. "What's this about a dragon?"

"Well, I don't like to tell people about it. But you wouldn't try to harm a dragon, would you?"

"My daddy would never do that!" Luke cried.

When the kids were out of earshot, Lord Robert said, "So, this dragon. You're not serious?"

"Actually, I *am* serious."

"Hmm. You do keep a straight face. I almost want to believe you. And Luke is right. I'd never harm a dragon. Unless it was threatening the life of my children. Or you, Mrs. Drake." He smiled at me, and I felt my face grow a bit warm.

"Well, that's good to know," I said.

"I should like to hear more about this dragon. Does it live on your property?" Lord Robert asked.

"I think it might, but I'm not sure. I've seen it come up from where there is an old mine that was boarded up long ago. So far, I've only seen it twice though. It's orange and is a flyer."

Lord Robert froze.

"Is something wrong?" I asked him.

It looked as if his mind completely trailed off when he didn't answer me at first.

"Lord Robert?"

He took in a deep breath. "I'm sorry, what?"

"Did something I say bother you? I mentioned the dragon and lost you for a minute…"

"No. No. It's just that … Well, my mother once told me she'd also seen an orange dragon. A flyer. She was a child living in La Belle Terre when she saw it. Never saw it again after that."

"Really? That is quite a coincidence. Who knows, maybe it's the same dragon. I've read that they can live to be hundreds of years old if they aren't killed by poachers."

"That would be something. You know, I thought I saw a dragon flying over Cascadia once. Not very long ago," Robert said.

"Was it orange?"

"It was too dark to be certain."

"Maybe it was my dragon that you saw."

He chuckled softly. "You are being serious, aren't you?"

I nodded.

"Hmm. Well, perhaps the children could go with you to feed your animals sometime? Would you be agreeable to that idea?"

The children had come over to where we were talking and had overheard that last bit.

"Oh, please say yes!" cried Luke. Elizabeth maintained her reserved manner, but I noticed a hint of a smile come over her face when her father mentioned this idea.

"Well, yes! I think that would be fun and I'd love for you both to meet my pets!"

Luke jumped up and down and clapped. Elizabeth looked away, but I saw her smile.

"But Luke," Lord Robert turned to his little son, "you can't go traipsing through Mrs. Drake's forest looking for dragons. Dragons aren't tame animals."

"That's right," I agreed. "And also, the mine is very dangerous. My husband's brother died in that mine."

"Okay." Luke stuck out his lower lip and stooped over, showing he was disappointed. A beat later, he popped back up. "Would you like to meet *my* pets now?"

"Of course I would!" I smiled.

Elizabeth and her father exchanged a wide-eyed look.

"Luke, I'm not sure if Mrs. Drake will be a fan of your pets," his father said.

"None of the nannies ever like Luke's pets," Elizabeth said matter-of-factly.

"Oh my," I said.

We went into the Conservatory next. It was massive, like a museum. Different plant species were everywhere, gold labels stating the scientific names.

"Do you want to watch me feed it?" Luke was pointing to a Venus flytrap. "We keep the flies here." He pulled a live fly out of a little container and dropped it into the plant. We watched it snap closed.

"Very impressive! So, this is your pet? What's its name?" I was so relieved it wasn't as frightful a thing as I imagined it might be.

"His name is Monster," said Luke. "But that's not my only pet. Wait til you meet Elsie and Alfred."

"Ah," I said, as Luke led the way through varieties of plants and flowers. "This is an amazing conservatory."

"It is. It was designed by the Ranfurly the First when he built the place. He had a passion for botany," explained Lord Robert.

We were across the room now, facing an eight-by-five-foot vivarium. Inside was a hefty boa constrictor. "That's Elsie!" Luke said excitedly. "Would you like to hold her?"

"Elsie, huh?" I recalled Mr. Knight, Jr. mentioning Elsie. "Is she friendly?"

"Of course, she's friendly!" Luke exclaimed.

"Unless she thinks you are a threat. She's very protective," warned Elizabeth.

"It's alright. She has only strangled three nannies out of … nearly twenty," Lord Robert said seriously.

"Oh. Fair odds," I said.

Elsie slithered to Luke as he reached into her habitat. She wound herself around his arms and over his shoulders, and he laughed. "Hi there, Elsie! This is Mrs. Drake."

"Let us know if we can trust her, Elsie," hissed Elizabeth. I lifted a brow at her.

"You can call me Courtney, Elsie," I said to the boa. I was glad that I had no fear of snakes. In fact, I thought some were even cute. If they weren't poisonous.

"Would you like to hold her?" Luke offered.

"Sure, why not?" I leaned down so he could put the snake on me.

Elsie slithered up my arm and over my shoulders. She wound her long, thick body around my neck several times. Once she stopped coiling herself, she slowly began to squeeze, and I felt myself being choked slightly.

Maybe they weren't joking about those nannies after all.

Lord Robert must have seen my alarmed expression. He stroked Elsie and said, "It's common for her to behave this way when she meets someone new. Just relax and she'll release her hold."

I let out a long breath and did my best to communicate with her through my body language that I came in peace. Just as Lord Robert promised, Elsie unwound herself from my neck.

"Does this mean we're friends now, Elsie?" I asked the snake.

"I believe you passed the test," Lord Robert said, with a half grin.

"Oh goodie," I said.

"Now come and meet Alfred!" Luke cried.

Lord Robert put Elsie back into her vivarium and we headed to a new area of the conservatory. In a smaller glass case was a hairy tarantula.

"He's probably hungry. Want to feed him?" Luke looked up at me, with pure elation on his face. I was quickly learning what the child's passions were.

God help me. I detest spiders.

But I wasn't about to let on that I had a severe case of arachnophobia. Oh no. I could not let those devilish people know that. I had to pass the second test. I calmed my breath and tried to do a mental flip to change my perspective of the spider. *It is a cute and friendly little furry fellow. We will be good friends, little Alfred and me. We will.*

Luke pulled a live grasshopper out of a small nearby container. "Here. You can feed him. It's okay. He loves these."

I pinched the grasshopper's body and dropped it into the tarantula's cage. We watched the creepy guy devour its lunch.

Lord Robert must have read my discomfort because he said, "Well, the skies have finally cleared. Mrs. Drake, would you like to see the stables?"

"Yes, that would be lovely! Thank you, Lord Robert." *My rescuer!*

"Aww, but Alfred wants to come out and play!" whined Luke.

"Another time, Luke. Let's go check on your four-legged pet now," his father said cheerily.

We went out through double glass doors onto a balcony that overlooked a few acres of green pasture and forested landscape beyond it. The children ran ahead of us and down steps that led to the barn.

Lord Robert lagged. "You did well with the snake, but you aren't a fan of Alfred, are you?" he asked me.

"Was I that obvious?" I asked him.

"I think I was the only one who caught on. But you certainly did better with Luke's pets than any of the other nannies we've had."

"Well, Luke doesn't exactly hang with the easiest friend crowd," I pointed out.

"I suppose that's true. But do you know what an even greater deterrent of nannies has been?" Lord Robert asked.

"Wait … let me guess. Could it be the bad fairies?" I asked.

He stopped and looked at me, a twisted smile on his face. Then he laughed. "You are quite charming, Courtney. The bad fairies?" He laughed harder.

"Your daughter made a point to mention them in the letter she wrote me. Apparently, they like to eat nannies." I brought my voice to a whisper and added, "And they look like spiders with wings."

Lord Robert looked in the direction of where his children were, a twinkle in his beautiful green eyes. We could hear them playing in the distance. He smiled and turned back to me, "Yes, we keep those bad fairies well-nurtured on a steady diet of nannies."

Now I had to laugh. "Well, this nanny has come prepared. I wear a special fragrance that deters them. Also, I eat certain herbs that they despise the taste of."

"Oh! Very good, you are most certainly the cleverest of all nannies," he said. I thought we were going to start walking, but he gently grabbed my wrist and stopped me. "Courtney."

"Yes?" I turned back and looked at him.

"I'm—my children—we're glad you're here. I think you will do an excellent job. But … I want to be sure you are clear on the rules."

"Which rules are you referring to?"

"No electronics. No cell phones. We don't have Wi-Fi. Most of the nannies have had a difficult time with those rules."

"Well, to be honest, can you blame them? It doesn't exactly seem normal in this world to not use our phones for everything. And I'd like to talk to my own kids every day. It'll be an inconvenience to have your driver take me down to North Ireland to get cell reception every day."

"I understand it isn't a normal rule to ask someone to follow. That's why I'm counting on you to NOT be normal, Courtney."

"Well, I'm definitely NOT normal!" *Wait … why did I say that? He's the one who's not normal!*

The barn and horse stables were immense, just like everything else about the manor. We walked past three well-groomed Thoroughbreds with silky manes and shiny coats. Lord Robert stopped to pet each of them.

We came to the fourth stall, and in it was a much smaller white horse, maybe half the size of the Thoroughbreds.

"This is Lady Rose. Lady Rose, meet Mrs. Drake," Elizabeth said in her very grownup manner.

"How do you do, Lady Rose." I curtsied to the horse.

Elizabeth lifted an eyebrow at my clumsy, off-balance curtsy. "You don't actually have to bow to her, you know."

"Well, she is a lady, isn't she? Besides, horses are all noble creatures," I corrected her, mimicking her grown up and matter of fact tone. Elizabeth looked at her father for some backup.

"Mrs. Drake is absolutely right, Elizabeth," he said.

Thank you for taking my side over your five-year-old know it all, I thought.

"However, Mrs. Drake," he continued, "this is not a horse. This is an Upland Pony."

"Oh," I said.

Elizabeth shot me a look as if to say, "So there."

"Still, she is a lady, and one should always bow to a lady, Elizabeth," Lord Robert instructed his daughter.

"You might want to work on your curtsies, though." Elizabeth advised me, then flashed a bratty smile.

"I will count on you to show me how to do them properly." *I'll win your heart, little stinker. You won't even see me coming.*

Luke was waiting by his horse's stall. "This is Sir Edgar, *my* horse!"

"Is that a miniature horse?" I asked. I had limited experience with them, other than visiting a miniature horse ranch in The Goldens when my kids were young.

"Yes, he's the perfect little horse for Luke. The right size, and they both have plenty of energy," said Lord Robert.

"And they're both extremely stupid," Elizabeth blurted.

"We are not! You're stupid! And you have a dumb pony! She's not even a real horse! Sir Edgar is way smarter than your dumb girl-pony!"

"Alright! That is quite enough," interrupted Lord Robert, looking from one little freckled face to the other. "How would you both like your animals to be donated to the foster children in Emer Aude?"

Elizabeth and Luke both shook their heads fiercely. Lord Robert went on, "Well, that is exactly what I will do with them if you two continue to argue and insult one another. Elizabeth, you started it. What do you have to say to Luke and Sir Edgar?"

The child's eyes were glacier-ice green, her lips pursed tightly.

"Elizabeth?" Lord Robert's commanding tone was enough to make even me straighten up.

"Sorry," Elizabeth finally said, her eyes fixed on the door of her pony's stall.

"Luke?" said Lord Robert.

"Sorry, Elizabeth and Lady Rose," Luke said, sounding more sincere than his sister.

"That's better." Lord Robert was quiet for a minute, as if he was contemplating. The children each busied themselves with their horses. I went over to the stall of a horse named Xavier and held my hand out flat to let him sniff it. He took a whiff but then moved to the further part of his stall, as if he didn't care for what he smelled.

Lord Robert said, "Listen, I'm sorry to say I have to leave tonight for another business trip."

The kids let out sad moans.

"When are you coming home?" Luke asked.

"I'm not sure yet. It might be tomorrow, or it may last a few days. But when I get home, I look forward to hearing nothing but marvelous praises from Mrs. Drake about how you both behaved. Is that clear?"

You're leaving us? My heart sank. I was just getting used to having him around. It wasn't normal for me to warm up to people quickly, but with him it had been surprisingly easy.

His children were heartbroken.

Elizabeth ran into Lady Rose's stall and whispered into her horse's ear, petting her and ignoring us.

Luke grabbed his dad's hand and pleaded, "Please don't go, Daddy. Please don't go! We'll be good! We won't fight."

Lord Ranfurly squatted so he was eye to eye with Luke, and his tone was gentle. "Luke, you do understand that I'm not leaving because you and your sister had a tiff. I made the plans long before today to go on my business trip. One day you'll be a grown up and you'll have a job, and then you'll understand better."

"Okay," Luke said in his high-pitched small voice.

"We will spend more time together as soon as I get home. Alright?" Luke nodded. Lord Robert pulled Luke into his chest and hugged him.

"Okay, Daddy," Luke said, sniffling. "I promise to be really nice to Elizabeth when you're gone."

Aww. Talk about yanking my heart strings.

"Luke, why don't you show Mrs. Drake how you exercise Sir Edgar now?" Lord Ranfurly stood up. He turned to me. "Edgar needs to get out of his stall every day, Mrs. Drake. He doesn't like to be cooped up. Luke will show you his horse's routine." Then, in a hushed tone, he said, "I need a private word with Elizabeth."

"Of course," I said. Luke and I went out to give Sir Edgar a good run. After about twenty minutes, Lord Ranfurly came out of the stable, leading Elizabeth on her pony. Her face was puffy and pale, like she'd been crying.

After spending some time with Sir Edgar and Lady Rose, the children's spirits were lifted. We helped them put their animals back in their stalls, then walked more of the grounds.

"Is that electric fence over there where your property ends?" I pointed across the vast span of green pasture, where a chain-link, electric fence divided it from the tall firs and cedars beyond.

"No. The Ranfurly estate sits on thirty thousand acres. An equivalent of forty-five miles. Those tall cedars and firs on the other side of the electric fence are inside what is known as Ranfurly Park. Ranfurly the First opened it up to the public as a campground and hiking location, but his grandson, Ranfurly the Second, let it go wild and shut it up."

"Really? Funny that Ranfurly the First decided to open it up to the public out here in the middle of nowhere. Who would come out here? The town of North Ireland is a good thirty minutes away, and there's only a population of what? Less than two hundred people in it?"

"Back when Ranfurly the First built the manor, there was a thriving mining town next to North Ireland. When the miners moved out, the dam was lifted, and the old town was flooded. Now it is known as Lake Ireland."

"So there is a ghost town at the bottom of the lake?"

"That's right."

"Have you been inside Ranfurly Park? Anything interesting to see in it?"

Robert laughed. "Yes, I have been inside it, and it's being taken over by wild berries and wild beasts. Who knows, maybe even dragons live in there."

He led us through the staff quarters, which was a very nice, updated apartment building. "Each staff member has an apartment of their own, and they share an indoor swimming pool that is operational year-round. You're welcome to use it."

We walked almost a mile down a lovely path that led to a massive ten-car, two-story garage. "This is where Ranfurly the Second kept all his motor cars."

"Now they belong to you?" I asked.

Lord Robert's expression was meek. "Yes, for which I am grateful. ... The second floor is the home of Mr. Knight, Sr."

"He gets a big home. Must be about ... what? Four-thousand square feet upstairs?"

"Five thousand. Yes, he was a favorite employee of Ranfurly the Second. Mr. Knight, Sr. isn't too fond of me, though."

"Really? How could he not be fond of you?" I asked. I was being sincere.

He laughed, and his bronze skin deepened to a shade of red.

"I'm sure it wasn't easy for the staff to lose my cousin Theo. I never met him, but I've heard enough about him to know I can't compete."

"Well, I never knew Theo. But I can't imagine a man like you ever needing to worry about competing with anyone," I said truthfully.

He laughed again. "That's very kind of you to say, Mrs. Drake."

I was a little baffled. He could easily wield his power, parade his wealth and position, yet I hadn't seen him do it with his staff. On the contrary, he seemed uncomfortable with all of it. I wondered if he had imposter syndrome.

He led us into a beautiful courtyard: perfectly trimmed boxwoods surrounded rose bushes which hadn't bloomed yet. Cobblestone paths met in the center, where a large sculpture of a raven stood. In the four corners were fountains, and in several locations, there were benches. Beyond the garden, laurel trees formed into thick walls that formed a labyrinth.

"Wow, breathtaking!" I cried.

"Yes. This is one of my favorite places."

I studied his face. He seemed more peaceful. "I can see that," I said, unable to take my eyes off him.

He met my gaze and locked into it. It was as if we each had magnets sewn into our garments, as we moved closer to each other. I felt the brush of his fingertips against mine. My breaths quickened.

Gretchen's laughter distracted me.

She was at the edge of the hedge labyrinth, speaking with one of the gardeners who was hunched over clipping.

"How many gardeners does it take to maintain all of this?" I asked.

"We have three full-time gardeners who maintain the property," he explained. "Curtis and his brother are my main gardeners. They grew up in North Ireland. A little warning about those two, they can get a little rowdy and crass. You'll meet them along with the rest of the staff soon. Now we'll be heading up those steps there, which lead back into the house through the kitchen. On our way, I'll show you the kitchen garden where we grow all our vegetables and herbs."

As we were heading up the steps to the kitchen garden, we heard a woman scream. "Help! Someone, help!" It was one of the staff members. She was standing outside the staff quarters.

"Stay here with the children!" Lord Ranfurly ordered. As he turned and ran, I admired his powerful, muscular movements.

He reached the woman who had screamed, and she spoke to him in a frenzy. Gretchen made her way over to them as well, and they listened to the woman's story. They were out of ear shot so the children and I had no idea what she was saying.

A strawberry-haired woman in her thirties, petite with a boyish figure, built like a gymnast, walked up behind me. She wore her hair shaved on one side, bangs cut to her cheekbones on the other, but short in the back. "What's going on?" she asked me.

"I-I have no idea," I replied, wondering who the woman was. She must have read my expression.

"Sorry to sneak up on you like that. I'm Marie Roth. I work here. And you must be the new nanny."

"Yes, Courtney Drake." I extended a hand to shake.

"Courtney Drake. Yes. I've heard *all* about you," she said, holding onto my hand, her hazel eyes dancing.

"You have? How?"

"Oh, we'll definitely have to chat about that later." She gave me a pat on the back. "I better go see what this is all about." She darted over to the others.

I watched them, wondering what might have happened. After a moment, Gretchen put her face in her hands as if crying. Lord Ranfurly pulled her into his chest, and held her for a moment, then cupped her face and said something to her. She nodded, and the three women went into the house, arms wrapped around each other.

Lord Ranfurly ran back to us. "Please take the children to their rooms, Mrs. Drake. We have a situation that needs my immediate attention."

14

MURDER AMONG US

Today was not going as planned.

He shuddered. *A murder. Right here on my premises. Why would anyone want to do in old Jake, a gardener who worked here for thirty years? And how did they get past my security system?*

Unless they were already inside?

His mind raced through the members of his staff: *The brash gardeners, Curtis Butters and his younger brother, what was his name? Did they get angry with old Jake and strangle him in a fight?* Robert wouldn't put it past them to get in a bar brawl. But to harm old Jake, a soft-spoken man, a peacemaker by nature. He couldn't see the Butters brothers doing anything to hurt him.

Who else would have a motive to kill old Jake? Obviously, it wasn't Eleanor. She was beside herself at finding his body.

And it certainly wasn't sweet, young Gretchen.

And I'm sure it wasn't the Roths. They were Robert's favorites. Kind-hearted, good people.

What about Davey Reed? Mid-twenties, and strong enough to strangle anyone. But if it was him, what motive did he have?

Robert turned his thoughts to some of the women on staff.

Mrs. Pemberley? He laughed and shook his head.

He certainly couldn't see Marie, the Roth's daughter, murdering the old man. Nor could he see the other maid, Jasmine, doing such a thing.

What about Mr. Knight, Sr.? What motive would he have to kill the old man? Robert knew that after one too many whiskies, the chauffeur could turn nasty. *Hmm. It could have been him.*

Or Ms. Stern? Robert tried to picture Ms. Stern strangling old Jake, then laughed. *Oh, I wouldn't put it past her. But, then again, she would be the obvious choice.*

He wondered if Mr. Knight's son, who had mysteriously disappeared a week ago might somehow be related to the murder. *Odd, the timing of both things happening so close together.*

Robert knew Sean grew up at the manor with his father until he went into the military after high school. Then, in his mid-twenties, he moved to Highland. That was all before Robert inherited the place. But a year ago, Sean returned to the manor, where Robert vetted him before hiring him.

Did someone kill Sean? If so, why? And could it have been the same person who murdered old Jake?

Or … is Sean still alive? If he is, he has the passcode to get through the front gate. But why would he want murder old Jake? Unless old Jake confronted Sean about something, knew Sean was doing something he shouldn't be doing. That would be enough reason for some people to commit a murder.

I'd best set a reminder to have all the passcodes changed.

Robert wanted to kick himself for not replacing the security cameras at the front gate. He kept putting it off, believing he didn't really need them since he already had the best alarm system in the world installed around his entire thirty-thousand-acre property.

But now, having camera footage could have made all the difference.

Robert shook his head. None of the pieces connected. *Why did Sean steal the car? And why did he go to Courtney's house? Why did he want Courtney to work here? Did he already know Courtney, before she applied? That didn't seem likely since Sean didn't live close to Mill Pond.*

Could Courtney have something to do with Sean's disappearance, or Jake's death?

His mind flitted back to her. Something about that woman brought out feelings that he thought had been dead and buried with his wife Desiree. Even a woman as enticing as Jasmine had no effect on him. Oh, sure, he noticed her, and appreciated her beauty and form. But he felt nothing.

So, why does Courtney have such an effect on me? He'd done a thorough background check on her, knew a little bit about her from Nick.

When Robert looked into her eyes, it was almost as if he'd always known her. As if their souls had been long and well-acquainted. *He shook his head. No. I just can't believe Courtney had anything to do with Sean's disappearance, or with this murder.*

Another voice in his head argued, *Or is it that you don't want to believe she has anything to do with it?*

As he wrung his hands over the situation, a reality suddenly slammed into him. *I've been a fool! To think I could banish evil from my home, my children. While I've been out there fighting in Emer Aude, evil slipped in right here ... into my own home. Now my children's lives could be in danger.*

Lord Robert felt overwhelmed, knowing that he now had to deal with another matter. It was the night he would move in on the traffic ring operation that was near Ranfurly Manor. He hated having to leave. Now, when he should be home, with his children. Protecting them. A gnawing, self-loathing ate away at him.

But I can't put it off. It must be dealt with. Tonight.

❧ *Courtney* ❧

I stayed with the children that afternoon. They wouldn't stop guessing at what Eleanor could have been screaming about.

"I wonder if someone stole something from her?" Elizabeth surmised.

"I bet she saw a ghost. Or a bad fairy." Luke's eyes shone with excitement.

"Isn't it time to do your chores?" I smiled, acting like it was a super fun idea.

"But today is special! We don't have to do chores!" Luke said.

Elizabeth nodded. "It's true. Daddy told us today was a field trip because we're being your tour guides. A field trip is something they do at *real* school. Daddy lets us do them whenever he is home."

"Hmm … Well, in that case, perhaps you two would like to show me some more of the house."

"Yes! Yes! I think that is a great idea!" Luke gleefully jumped up and down.

As for Elizabeth, she seemed to be trying her best not to like me. "I guess."

As we walked, they brought up the screaming housekeeper again. And I did my best to get their minds off it. "What about the swimming pool? Do you know where it is? I'd love to see it!"

"Yes, we do know where that is. But there isn't any water in the pool. It doesn't work," Elizabeth explained.

"That's okay. Let's just explore a little. This house is like a castle! And you," I pointed to Elizabeth, "are a princess. And you," I tapped Luke's head, "are a prince."

Luke liked this.

Elizabeth lifted an eyebrow. "Then what are you…?" she asked.

"I am … an evil witch! Who wants to eat you!" I made my best scary face and reached out my hands to grab her. The children screamed and ran out the nearest door. It led out to the Kitchen Garden. I chased them down the steps, cackling in my best witch voice.

Then I realized, to my horror, that they were headed straight for the labyrinth of hedges.

Oh no. "Come back here, my pretties!" I said in the witchy voice. But in no time at all, the two little pickles managed to disappear into the labyrinth. Out of sight.

It dawned on me that playing the witch card and chasing them wasn't the brightest idea I'd come up with. *Brilliant. I've already managed to lose them within the first hour.*

I walked through the entrance to the labyrinth. I could hear giggling. Quietly peering around corners, I hoped to surprise the little munchkins.

Then one of them jumped out from behind a wall of laurels and growled. "Grr!"

Luke. I tried to grab him, but he was off and running again. Too fast for me.

I followed the path between hedges, deeper into the labyrinth. Just like everything else at Ranfurly Manor, it was colossal and felt endless. *How am I going to find those kids? I may not even be able to find my own way out!*

Suddenly, it grew quiet. Too quiet. No giggling. No sound of little feet running.

I was starting to panic. *How far into this labyrinth am I? What if I really did lose them? What if one of them falls and gets hurt? Or what if a cougar prowls into the maze and drags one of them off?*

I turned another corner, and another.

What have I done? Dear God, help!

I turned more corners around towering hedges. Until I crashed into something. ... No. *Someone.* A gardener.

I must have startled him because he dropped his shears and they hit the ground next to my foot, missing it by an inch.

He was hunched over, with what appeared to be a hump on his back. "Pardon me, Miss." He pointed past me while he bent over to pick up his shears. "The children are back that way," he practically whispered.

His voice, it reminded me of ... I wasn't sure. His hat shaded his face, but I noticed his long, grey beard. He turned his back to me and went on shearing hedges.

"Thank you," I said, as I trotted in the direction he had pointed.

A minute later I crashed into the children. This time, I managed to grab them both.

"There you two are! I've got you now!" I said in my witch voice. They both screamed. "But wait ... The labyrinth has magical powers to turn me into a beautiful fairy." I swirled a hand over my head in the air, magic-like. Then I changed my voice, so I sounded regal, like Lord Robert. "Now I am destined to protect you both, your highnesses!"

"You talk like Daddy now!" Luke laughed.

"Not exactly. Your accent sounds … weirder." Elizabeth scrunched up her nose.

"That's because it's a Goldupish accent," I said.

"That's not a thing," Elizabeth said.

"It most definitely is a very radical, awesome thing," I said.

"No, it isn't," she shot back.

"Yes, it is. I swear on the grave of my first pet cockatiel. It's, like, the best accent ever. Like, I can teach it to you. Like, you know? In fact, we can use our own words that nobody else will know but us."

"You mean, like have code words?" asked Elizabeth, her eyes lighting up.

"Exactly, that's what I mean, your most radical awesome highness." The children both laughed.

"The first code is *Royally Gag Me with Spaghetti* and it means *Meet me in the Kiddie Bistro Loft*. Now you make one up." I looked at Elizabeth.

"*Pixie Hairs* means *Ms. Stern is coming*!" Elizabeth said, her eyes wide. She giggled.

"*Blarney Barney*!" cried Luke. We all laughed.

"I like it! But what does it mean?" I asked.

Luke kept grinning and looked at us, trying to think of what it could mean.

"I know! It means *Elsie escaped*!" Elizabeth said. More giggling.

We carried on, making up words like this all the way to the swimming pool. By the end of the day, I felt it had been quite successful. I tucked them into their little beds and read them each a story.

After the story, Luke wrapped his tiny hands around my neck, pulled me into a hug, and whispered into my ear, "I hope we can keep you."

When I left his room, I suddenly found myself fighting the onset of tears. An overwhelming flood of memories of Nick and Laurel swept over me. I missed the moments like these when they were little. I went to my room, lost in thoughts of my own children, now adults! I wondered how they were. If only I could simply call them. *These ridiculous rules about using phones.*

My thoughts shifted to Mr. Knight. I was trying to think up ways I could learn something more about his disappearance when someone knocked on my door.

I jumped. I wasn't used to my new surroundings, and at night, the room felt eerier than it had earlier.

I opened the door to a distraught-looking Gretchen.

"Hi, Mrs. Drake. Can I come in?" Her eyes were puffy, as if she'd had a good long cry.

"Of course! Please sit." I gestured to a chair in my room and took a seat in the chair opposite. "By the way, please call me Courtney."

She nodded. "Okay." She paused.

I waited.

At last, she quietly asked, "Did you hear about what happened today, by any chance?"

"No, I didn't. I've certainly been wondering though. You look upset. Is everything alright?"

She shook her head violently. "Everything is not at all alright. Old Jake died! He was one of our gardeners who has been here forever. Since before I was born. My mother is beside herself."

"Your mother? Who is your mother?" I asked.

Gretchen covered her mouth, as if she didn't mean for that to come out. "I forgot … you're new here. Well, if you stick around long enough you will probably find out anyway … just don't mention that you know, or that I told you. My mother doesn't like to tell the nannies we are related."

I raised my right hand. "I solemnly swear on my favorite pet duck not to repeat a word of anything you tell me."

Gretchen laughed, and I saw her face relax for a moment. "Favorite pet duck?"

"Oh, yes. I have my own petting zoo back home. Anyhow, you were saying, about your mother?"

Gretchen sucked on her lip a few seconds and looked at her feet. Then she said, "Ms. Stern is my mother."

"Oh! My! Ms. Stern … is your … wow. I wouldn't have seen that one coming," I blurted. "So, how did old Jake die?"

"He was strangled. Eleanor found him inside of Mr. Knight's room."

"Strangled? Woah! But in Mr. Knight's room? Doesn't Mr. Knight live above the garage?" I asked.

"No, the other Mr. Knight. The one who went missing," she explained. "Sean," she added. Her eyes welled up. "Lord Ranfurly gave him an apartment of his own in the Staff Quarters when he came back here a year ago, so he wouldn't have to live with his father."

Sean. So that was his first name. It was a bit strange to think that we hadn't been on a first name basis. Then I realized this might be a good opportunity to finally ask some questions about him.

"Really? But his dad's place is so huge. You'd think he would just live there with him," I said.

"Sean told me that he and his dad are like two rams locking horns." Gretchen shrugged.

"Oh. But why would old Jake be in Mr. Knight's, er, Sean's room, I wonder?" I asked.

"My guess is he was looking for something. Sean used to work with the horses, and Jake was filling in on the job until Lord Ranfurly could find someone permanent. Or until Sean returns. Maybe Jake needed something for the horses that was in Sean's room?"

"Do you know Sean well?" I asked her.

I noticed a flushed look come over her. "Yes," she replied, then started pulling her fingers through her long blond hair. She was a lovely young woman. And by the way she was acting, I was almost certain her feelings for Sean went far beyond friendship.

"Did you and Mr. Knight … were you two close, Gretchen?" I asked.

She looked down at her hands. "It sounds strange when you call him Mr. Knight. That's what I call his father." She smiled and looked up at me. "Sean and I had just started dating before he disappeared."

I knew it. Sean was a player. Flirting with me while he was toying around with a cute little blond that looks like the same age as my own daughter. And Sean must have been in his thirties.

Gretchen looked around the room, and toward my balcony doors, and changed her tone. "This is a lovely room, isn't it?"

"Yes, it is. That reminds me, Gretchen. Your mom didn't seem all too thrilled about letting me have this room. Do you know why she would have an issue with me in here?"

"Hmm." Gretchen frowned. "No. I can't imagine why she wouldn't want you to stay in here. I mean … it isn't the usual room the nanny would stay in. Maybe that bothered her. She likes things to be a certain way, you know."

"Where does the nanny usually stay?" I asked her.

"The staff quarters, where all the workers live."

"Who usually stays in this room, then?" I asked.

"Nobody," she said. "It originally belonged to the wife of Ranfurly the First. When she died, Ranfurly the First's daughter took it. Her son was Mr. Ranfurly."

"Who was Mr. Ranfurly's father?" I asked.

Gretchen opened her eyes wide, and a look of fascination came across her face. "Nobody knows," she whispered. "His mother never married. It was a huge scandal back in those days. The daughter of Ranfurly the First single and pregnant. The father of her child a big secret."

"Wow, maybe it was a servant who lived here!" I said.

"Nobody's ever learned who the father was," Gretchen went on, "and Mr. Ranfurly, just like his mother, never married. But he had many lovers. And after his mother died, this is the room they would sleep in. He was quite a ladies' man. I remember his last girlfriend before they died in the plane crash. He was in his sixties, and she was in her early twenties. A gorgeous model. They say this room is haunted by her ghost."

"Lovely. Now I'll have a murderer and a ghost to keep me awake at night." I laughed. But I didn't really find it funny. "By the way, what was the maid who found Jake doing in Sean's room?"

"Oh, Eleanor was cleaning," Gretchen said matter-of-factly. "My mother instructed her to dust his room regularly; in case he turns up again." Gretchen sighed. "I hope he does."

"Hmm. Me too. ... Do you have any ideas about what might have happened to Sean?"

I watched her reaction closely. Was she hiding something? Her face seemed flushed.

"I-I wonder if someone might have been after him and chased him off the road?" she said.

"Yes, I've wondered the same thing. But why? Was he a criminal, do you think?" I prodded.

"Oh no!" she replied, defensively. "I'm sure he wasn't. If anything, he was the opposite!"

Okay, then. It was certainly obvious Gretchen had some rock-star worship for Sean.

With those big, bright blue eyes, she looked at me, a picture of innocence.

"I'm so sorry, Gretchen. He was your boyfriend, and this must be very difficult for you." I patted her small, soft hand.

"It is. I think I love him, Courtney." Her eyes widened. "But poor old Jake. It's scary to think a murderer is running around somewhere." Gretchen's eyes shifted around the room and settled on the balcony doors again. She was creeping me out. The blood had drained from her cheeks, and her pale face made her look ghastly. "Courtney ... you haven't seen..."

"Seen what?" I asked her.

"You haven't seen ... anything out of the ordinary, have you?" she asked me.

"I don't know. I mean, this whole place is out of the ordinary for someone like me," I said. That was an understatement.

"What about people who don't look like they belong here?" she asked.

"I'm probably the only person who doesn't look like I belong here, Gretchen. But I promise, I didn't kill old Jake. I can barely stand to see a fish die on a hook, let alone kill someone. Besides, I have an alibi," I said.

"Yes, you were with Lord Ranfurly, I know. I saw you," she said. "But were you with him the entire day?"

"I was with his children the entire day," I said, a little defensive. *Was she trying to accuse me?*

She quickly explained. "Well, what I mean is, could Lord Ranfurly have been the one to…" She stopped herself and looked at me. "I'm sorry. I shouldn't have said that."

"Wait … Lord Ranfurly? You suspect him of murdering the gardener? Why would you think that? Is there something about him I should know?"

"It's just that he…" A knock at my door interrupted her. She jumped.

I got up and cracked the door open. It was Lord Robert. His hair was down, and fell past his shoulders, and his shirt was unbuttoned at the top, revealing a bit of his muscular chest. He had a strained look on his face.

"Hi, I'm just checking in to see how it went today with the children?" he asked.

"I think it went well. Your children are lovely, and I really enjoyed spending time with them," I said honestly.

He exhaled, relieved. But there was still a crease above his eyebrows. "I'm afraid we had an incident today. The reason Eleanor, the maid, screamed…" he started to say.

"Ahem. Well, I should get going." Gretchen got up and excused herself.

"Oh, Gretchen. I didn't see that you were in here as well. How are you? Feeling better now?" Lord Robert asked her.

"I-I'm pretty worn out. It's been a rough week with Sean … and now this," she said. She turned to me, "It was nice to chat with you, Courtney. I'm glad you're here." Once she was behind Lord Robert's back, she widened her eyes as if warning me to watch out.

Lord Ranfurly waited for Gretchen to head down the stairs. When she was completely out of sight he asked, "Did Gretchen tell you what happened?"

I nodded. "She told me your gardener was strangled to death," I said, searching his face, wondering if he could be guilty, as Gretchen seemed to suggest.

"Yes, he was. It's been … hectic, to say the least."

"But you knew that he'd been murdered when you left me with your children. Why didn't you tell me then?"

"The last thing I wanted was for my children to hear about it," he said defensively.

"Well, you could have pulled me aside and told me that there was a murderer on the loose. At least then I would have been warned so I would know to protect the kids. But instead, I ran around the grounds with your kids today, not having any inkling that there was a murderer out there somewhere. I even lost them in the labyrinth at one point! Then I ran into a scary hunchback gardener who nearly cut my foot *off with his shears!" Oops. I shouldn't have mentioned that.*

"Scary hunchback gardener who tried to cut off your foot?" he repeated slowly. His green eyes suddenly turned dangerous.

"Yes. … I mean, no. He didn't *try* to cut off my foot. But I accidentally ran into him, which caused him to drop his gardening shears which nearly landed on my foot." I sucked in air, frustrated. "The point is, you should have told me so I would have been more cautious. I certainly wouldn't have been running around outside with your kids, had I known about the murder."

He pulled his hair back from his hairline with a hand and rested his other hand on his hip. "You're right, Courtney. I should have told you. I realize that now." He turned as if he were about to leave, but he didn't.

I couldn't take my eyes off his profile. He was the most beautiful man I'd ever laid eyes on. His long hair, clenched jaw, square shoulders. Shoulders that looked like they carried the weight of the world.

An urge to reach out and squeeze the tension out of those shoulders came over me. Of course, I didn't. That would have been completely inappropriate. But oh, how I wanted to.

He turned to look at me. "Courtney, I'm sorry about all this. You're probably regretting taking the job right about now, aren't you?"

I took in a deep breath, unable to hide the truth. "Well…"

"I understand," he said, not moving.

"I won't bail on your kids right now, if that is what you're worried about."

He turned to look at me. "That means more to me than you can know. Thank you," he whispered, his eyes grew watery.

It was strange, but I could feel the weight of the stress that crushed him, and all I wanted was to relieve it. "Are you alright?" I asked him.

He shook his head. "People on my staff don't ever ask me that."

I forgot that he was my employer at that moment, forgot he was a lord, forgot he was the wealthiest person I'd ever met. "Well, I'm asking. So, are you?"

"Well, since you asked … I-I'm feeling a bit overwhelmed. You see, I have an urgent matter at work. I wish I could get out of it, but I can't. I must leave tonight, and I'm not certain I can get home by tomorrow."

"Right. You mentioned that earlier today. So, is it really that urgent? Your work won't understand that you have an even more urgent thing going on here?" I asked him.

"No. I don't use the word urgent lightly. When I say it is urgent, I mean it is a life and death situation."

"Oh," I said. I recalled his reason he didn't show up at the job interview was a life and death situation at work, as well. *What exactly does he do for a living?*

"In case I can't get back tomorrow, I've stationed guards at each end of the hall on this floor, and at the bottom of the stairs. Stay on this floor with the children while I'm away. The maids will bring your meals up here until I return. Sorry to confine you to this floor, but I want you to be safe."

I nodded slowly. He put a strong, warm hand on my arm. "And Courtney … I don't have a gardener who has a hump on his back."

KILLING SNAKES

MIDNIGHT

Courtney's story about the hunchback gardener was biting away at his mind as he headed to the traffic ring location. The only thing he could take comfort in was knowing his security guards were keeping watch. The sooner he could break up the ring, the sooner he could get home. He only prayed he could avoid getting another injury. Dillard and Baca sent him "a new and improved suit." *Tonight's excursion will be a good test to see how it performs.*

Robert's tip on the trafficking ring had come from CAPE member Kila Jeffries. She sent him the coordinates of an abandoned warehouse in the wilderness.

The only access to the off-grid warehouse was by boat or by way of an old logging road. Hikers, fisherman, and four-wheel adventurists might have seen the place, but not too many people ever came out there, especially in wet or snowy months. The river was high, and it was still very wet. Normal for Cascadian weather in spring.

The river on his property was a chute off the main river, and Robert's security system went across it by way of a small dam, keeping intruders from getting in by waterway. For Robert to get to the bottom of the dam by boat, there was a lift he could drive his boat onto. It then drained water out of it and lowered him and his boat down to the river outside of his property. From there, he continued to the main river.

Once he reached the warehouse, he left the boat in a nearby inlet, out of sight of the warehouse but close enough that it was accessible by foot.

Robert crept silently to a dark location under the dock. From there, he had visibility to scope out the warehouse entrance. Kila warned him to watch for a black van.

He scoped the area. A man, armed with a gun, was sitting by the entrance door. He waited to see if any others came out of the building.

There was no movement. Nothing but a fish occasionally jumping in the river, and the sound of rain hitting the leaves on the forest trees. A searing pain shot through him from where he'd been stabbed. It had scabbed over, but the damp cold aggravated it.

"God, be my guide and my strength tonight."

Praying wasn't a thing he'd always done. For most of his life, he'd denied the existence of God. Then he met Desiree, who had turned his world upside down. Her death had impacted him even more than her life, causing him to leave everything he'd ever known behind and start over on the other side of the world.

The memory of her hurt more than the stabbing pain in his side. She was … everything.

To this day, her murderer was out there. Somewhere. Free to run the streets, to mutilate more innocent victims. Every time Robert caught a killer, he wondered if it was the murderer of his wife.

She'd been stolen away from him. The young and beautiful mother of his children, robbed of the full life she could have had.

In those months after Desiree's murder, a moment came when Robert needed a miracle. God answered. He revealed Himself in such a way that Robert would have been a fool to ignore Him. After that, he'd taken solace in the Scriptures, and found himself talking to the God he once didn't believe in.

But there were plenty of missions where Robert bypassed asking for God's help. The night he'd been stabbed was one of those.

Perhaps You allowed me to get jabbed by that knife to teach me a little lesson. I certainly wouldn't put it past You.

A cold wind blew, and the trees creaked. It almost sounded like laughter. *I hear You chuckling. It's a great comfort to know You're amused by my suffering.*

He waited for a sign to make his move on the warehouse. *At least this suit keeps me dry and warm.* He remembered the days when he was soaked on the soggy streets of Emer Aude, wearing only black sweatpants and a sweatshirt. Before CAPE Tech made him a suit.

Gone were the days of concealing a gun in the pocket of a black hoodie. He had a mega upgrade.

Dillard and Baca weren't the ones who came up with the original design. Caleb and his wife, Emilie, were world renowned fashion designers. They served PAX's elite ten leaders while secretly contributing their talents to help CAPE's agents by creating brilliant suits.

A reflection shone on the water. A light came on in the warehouse. The guard who'd been sitting outside the front door entrance stood up, holding a radio to his lips, handgun in a side holster.

Headlights lit up the nearby trees. Robert heard the low rumbling of an engine driving over rocks. Seconds later, a black van approached and parked near the warehouse entrance. Two men got out, armed with handguns. They disappeared into the building.

There was still a man standing guard outside. Robert snuck up behind him and knocked him unconscious with the butt of his gun. He placed a cuff on the wrist of the passed-out guard, drug him down to the dock, and attached the other cuff to a boat pull ring bolted into the dock. He pocketed the guard's gun in his suit jacket.

He crept to the entrance of the warehouse and slipped into the dark building.

A man who looked like an angry gorilla stood in his way.

Like a raging bull, Robert ran at the man headfirst, knocking him to the ground. He kicked a foot into Angry Gorilla's abdomen.

Angry Gorilla grabbed onto Robert's calf and pulled him down.

Robert was pinned.

Angry Gorilla grabbed him by the throat.

Robert was losing air.

Choking, Robert attempted to jab Angry Gorilla in the throat with the side of his forearm. He missed.

Angry Gorilla slammed his knee into Robert's belly.

Robert was in a triangle choke. But his hands were still free.

He pulled out a knife hidden in his suit and jabbed it into Angry Gorilla's ear.

Angry Gorilla screamed in pain and released his hold. Blood was squirting everywhere.

Robert pulled a taser out of his suit and shocked Angry Gorilla until he passed out.

"What's going on down there, Petra?" A voice shouted from upstairs.

Robert disguised his accent and yelled, "Stubbed a toe. I'm fine!"

He slowed his breath and wiped away some blood that had splattered on his face. He pressed a button in his suit to turn on two small head-lamps that were built into the dragon mask, just above where the slits for his eyes were.

He peered around the large warehouse room, checking every corner to make sure nobody else was there. Joint wrappers and beer cans littered the floor. It smelled sickly, like skunk, cheap beer, and cigarettes. Other than that, the room was empty.

The one who had yelled down at him was talking to somebody up-stairs. He turned off the headlamps and backed into a dark corner to listen.

"…move them tonight. Somebody *** nabbed Jared's phone back in The Capital. Stupid Jared. Might have given our *location away*. Hurry up and get them into the van."

Robert heard heavy footsteps coming down the stairs. An enormous figure stopped at the bottom of the steps, looking like a big Blob in the dark room. Keys jingled. The Blob was trying to open a door.

A man upstairs yelled, "Goliath, tell Petra to get his *** up here and help me carry this *** load to the van!"

Something heavy was being dragged around on the floor above.

If the guy I just knocked out was Petra, Robert thought, *then Goliath must be the Blob.*

Goliath was now coming his way. He was a slow-moving giant.

The man upstairs yelled down, "Goliath! Where the *** are you goin'? Get the girls out of the basement first, moron! Put them in the van and tell Bruce to start her up. And tell him to *** turn on the seat warmers this time, I'm freezin' my *** off!"

Keys were jingling again. Goliath was fumbling, trying to open the basement door in the dark. The door opened and Goliath's balky form disappeared. After a few minutes, two smaller dark silhouettes emerged out of the basement. Next, a smaller silhouette emerged. Goliath came out last.

"Move it! Moo!" Goliath's deep bass voice rattled the windows.

The silhouettes passed. Two teenage girls and a younger child. It wrung his insides to hear the child's sobs.

Goliath stalked behind the girls.

Robert quietly slipped behind him.

Once the girls were outside, Robert pushed the barrel of one of his guns into Goliath's back and grabbed him in a chokehold with his free arm.

That's one thick, unbreakable neck.

Goliath wrenched back fiercely.

Robert was forced to release his hold.

Goliath knocked Robert's gun out with one sweep of a huge arm.

He attempted to wrestle the giant, but the giant's strength was unlike anything he had ever been up against.

Goliath pinned him against a wall. The giant smiled as Robert struggled to break free.

Robert quit struggling and went limp.

Goliath fell for it and loosened his grip.

Robert kneed the giant in the groin.

Goliath groaned and let go of him.

Robert pulled one of his guns out of a holster and shot the giant in the chest.

Any other man would have gone down. But the giant kept clawing at him.

Robert took a second shot.

The man was unstoppable, still fighting with the same strength! He grabbed Robert's arm and twisted it so hard it was about to break off.

A deafening sound exploded like a cannon and shook the ground. Robert felt it in his face. His diaphragm. His lungs. A ringing in his ears left him feeling disoriented.

The mountain of a man seemed to fall in slow motion and crashed onto the ground.

Robert looked into the eyes of the shooter who had just saved his life. *The little one.*

She dropped the gun she'd used to kill the giant. Tears spilled out of her eyes. She was shaking.

"Thank you." He said to the child who had saved him. "I came to get you out of here. But we need to hurry!"

The two teenagers stood gaping at him, looking confused.

Everything went black.

He heard men's voices and tried to open his eyes. *Ow. My head.* It throbbed like a hammer was hitting a nail inside his brain. He could make out nothing but blurry shapes. His hands and feet were bound.

Once his vision cleared, he saw the man he'd tasered. He had returned to consciousness and was hurrying to get the girls into the van.

He spotted Goliath's gun. It was in the same spot where he'd sent it flying earlier. *Not too far from me, if I could just free my hands and feet.*

He worked quickly, moving his elbows in and wriggling his wrists. The rope stretched and he used his teeth to loosen the knots.

Once he freed his hands, he was able to reach his hidden knife. Caleb had designed a flap for it, camouflaged on the outside of his boot. He cut the ropes that bound his feet and inched over until he was able to nab Goliath's gun.

He ran outside. The van was already heading down the gravel road.

Robert shot one rear tire. Then the other. The van came to a halt.

A slender man stepped out of the driver side of the van. Gangly arms, a long neck, a small, flat nose with nostrils that looked more like slits, and beady eyes. With his hairstyle puffed up on each side of his center part, it gave him a snake-head shape.

Simultaneously, the man Robert had tasered earlier came out of the van's sliding door.

"Petra, shoot the mother ***!" Snake yelled at the man.

Petra shot at Robert.

Robert dodged into the warehouse for cover. He fired his gun back at Petra. A few shots were exchanged.

It finally grew quiet. Robert's shot had hit its mark. Petra was dead.

Meanwhile, Snake used the diversion to drag the little child out of the van. He had her by her hair, and she was screaming. He pointed a gun to her head.

"I remember you, Dragon," Snake said. "You're the *** hole who chased me a week ago in Emer Aude." He grinned. "How's that knife wound I gave you?"

So, Snake is the Ninja.

"Dragons are immune to poisonous blades, Snake."

Snake laughed. A hideous, creepy sound. "Why do you waste your *** time fighting us anyway? We work for PAX now. Law-abiding citizens."

"I follow laws that outrank PAX."

"Oh. You're with the Resistance. Which group do you work for? There are so many. But they never last long, do they?"

"I work for *them*." Robert looked toward the girls in the van.

"Them? They can't pay you. In fact, one of them was sold to us by her own *** father."

Robert's voice was low and steady. "Seeing oppressors like you punished for harming the innocent is my reward, Snake."

"Who's the innocent? These filthy girls? They aren't innocent. They eagerly went with the young men who coaxed them. They swallowed the pills we gave them and begged for another hit when they crashed."

"You preyed on their naivety and used it to ensnare them. Then forced them into addiction."

The snake smirked. "I simply showed them what they were missing. They're getting free ****** drugs! An upgrade from the poverty they came from. You really should find a new battle to fight, Dragon. If you're smart, you'll switch sides. The Resistance has no hope of winning."

"Oh, trust me Snake, you'll be the one wishing you had switched sides."

Snake bared his teeth. "I know you came all the way out here hoping to get some *** excitement. I'd hate to disappoint, so I'll let you watch me as I blow this little thing's brains out."

The child wailed, as Snake yanked her hair.

Robert's heart quickened. He had to think fast. *God, help me!*

Without killing Snake, he could see only one option. But there would be no room for error.

He aimed for Snake's hand that held the gun.

The child screamed as the gun shot blasted and the bullet whizzed past her to hit its target.

Blood squirted out of Snake's hand onto the child. Snake swore profusely and pressed his hand into his stomach to slow the blood flow. He darted off into the forest.

Robert would have gone after him … but the child.

She was screaming. Terror-stricken. He had to look after her. Kneeling, he pulled her into an embrace. She sobbed into his suit jacket.

"Shh. There now. You're alright. I've got you. Will you let me carry you out of here?"

She nodded and wrapped her tiny arms around his neck. Robert swooped her up, and she buried her head against him.

He scanned the area around them. Snake was nowhere in sight. The teenage girls were peering out of the van, looking dumbfounded.

Poor girls. They look strung out.

Carrying the child, Robert hurried to get the two older girls out of the van. The girls cowered, and it was then that Robert realized the black dragon mask must look frightening to them. He pulled it up so they could see his face. "I won't hurt you. I have a boat hidden close by. Follow me."

Robert pulled the mask down again, in case Snake came back.

He led the girls away from the van. They passed by the guard who was handcuffed to the dock, Bruce. He was just coming to. As he saw them walk past, he shouted profanities after them.

Robert led the girls to his boat. As they set off up the river, he scanned the forest for a sign of Snake. Nothing.

They reached the dam and he used his Digi-watch to open the security door to the boat lift. They drove inside the lift, the door closed behind them. Light flooded into the lift.

That was when Robert caught sight of the serpent earrings on the teenagers.

"Can I see those earrings you're wearing?" he asked one of the girls. He kept his tone gentle. The poor girl had been through enough trauma. The last thing he wanted was to add to it.

The girl handed him an earring.

Sapphire eyes, not rubies. He scanned it with his Digi-watch and found the tracking device. *Sapphire eyes. Trackers, girls are alive. Ruby eyes. No trackers but girls are always dead. Thus far, the pattern has been consistent.*

He coaxed the girls to give him the other earrings. Opening the security door, he chucked the two pairs of earrings into the river.

Now that he knew the girls were free of trackers, he closed the security door once again. They were lifted to his private waterway, and he drove them to the dock at Ranfurly Park.

He took the girls into his hangar, where warmth and comfort awaited them. Once inside, he set the child on a couch and took off his mask.

"See? I'm not so scary, now, am I? I promise I won't hurt you." He smiled.

She had stopped crying and now sat, shivering.

"Are you cold?"

Wrapping her arms around herself, she stared at him.

Probably too frightened to speak.

He went into the next compartment, where Vivienne was parked. "Hello, Vivienne. How are you?"

"I'm bored stiff, wondering why you ditched me tonight for a minging boat."

"Your frame is a little too large for some of the places I needed to access tonight, Viv."

"Rude! I take offense to that, Lord Robert."

"You shouldn't, my girl. You're a fine, slender shape, and you fit in lots of snug places. But they didn't build you for rivers."

A closet in her compartment held a stack of blankets. He pulled them out and went back into the room with the girls. The older girls had already conked out on comfortable leather couches. He covered them up, then wrapped a blanket around the little girl.

"Those two need to sleep off whatever drugs the bad men gave them," he told her.

Shivering under the blanket, she kept a watchful eye on him.

Robert smiled warmly at her as he dialed Peter's number. "I'll be over there, not far away," he whispered to the child as he walked into a corner of the large hangar out of the child's earshot, but where she could still see him.

"I found three girls. Two of the captors are dead. The little child shot one in his head, a dead shot."

"A child? How old?"

"Seven or eight, maybe."

Peter whistled. "Sounds like a miracle, if you ask me."

"Hmm. But their leader got away. On foot. I would have stayed out there to track him, but getting the girls to safety was my priority. I saw the one who got away, though."

"Did you find anything else in that warehouse? Kila said they were supposed to have four hundred bricks of coke."

"I heard them dragging something around upstairs. They might have loaded it into the van when I was unconscious. I didn't have time to check. I also left a man handcuffed to the dock. But I won't be able to go back to the warehouse and take care of all the loose ends. You'll have to send someone else from CAPE to do it."

"Why?"

"One of my gardeners was murdered. And another staff member disappeared a week ago. My own children are my main concern now."

"Doesn't sound like you'll be getting too much sleep, does it?" Peter said. "Okay, I'll send people to handle the cleanup out there and send a couple of CAPE trackers to hunt the man that got away. But Robert … why isn't Winnie with you tonight?"

"Winnie?" Robert had completely forgotten about Winnie. But he couldn't admit that to her Uncle Peter. "Well … because I needed her back at the house, what with the murder that just happened."

"You should have taken her along tonight, should have had backup. You might not have a guy on the loose if she'd have gone," Peter said.

"Or you might have lost your niece. And then I wouldn't be able to live with myself."

"I told you not to underestimate her," Peter said. "Have a little more faith in my judgment."

"Or you could have a little more faith in mine," Robert said.

An uncomfortable silence passed between them.

Robert finally said, "Look, I'm tired, Peter. I'm anxious to get home and check on my own children." Robert looked at the sleeping girls, and the little one who sat shivering under a blanket. He couldn't help but dread the thought of this happening to his own children.

"I understand. McGregor and Kila are on their way. They'll get the girls to a safe house where my wife will look after them until we reconcile them with their families."

"Oh … that reminds me. I learned that one of these teens was sold to the traffickers by her own father. Make sure to vet the families thoroughly before sending the girls back to wherever they came from."

"Man, that breaks my heart," Peter said.

"I know. Oh … you should also know that the man who got away tonight was the same man from Purgatory. The Ninja with a poisonous blade. These two teens were wearing serpent earrings with sapphires."

Robert explained to Peter about the pattern he'd noticed with the earrings.

"Strange. Do you know whether the jewels in the earrings are genuine?"

"Yes. They are."

"Then why are they leaving them on the corpses?" Peter asked.

"Haven't the foggiest."

"…And you're certain the ones with rubies don't have trackers?" Peter asked.

"So far, they don't. It's the first thing I check for. … But the person wearing them is always dead."

"Hmm. Well, I don't like that the guy got away. Now he's running free in your neck of the woods. Hopefully my hunters can find him," Peter said.

"My property is thirty miles away from that warehouse, and even if he reached it on foot, he'd never get past my security perimeter."

"That's good. Oh … Nina is here and says hello. She also says she expects you to take good care of our Winnie."

"Tell Nina I say hello and assure her I'll not let harm come to a hair on Winnie's head. And tell her she's a saint for putting up with you."

Peter chuckled. "I tell my wife she is a goddess every day, without fail."

Robert smiled. Then, more seriously, he added, "Please don't mention anything to anyone except Nina about the murder at the manor."

"You know better than to have to say that to me, bro."

They ended their call.

Robert thought about Peter's wife, Nina. The woman was a force. She had a brother who was a criminal. She never stopped hoping to reform him and had made it her life's mission to help rehabilitate prisoners once they were released.

But now, criminals weren't charged. They were recruited by PAX. Her field of study no longer seemed relevant. But Nina wasn't the type to give up fighting. Using her insight to help trap criminals, she worked alongside Peter to lead CAPE.

The little girl was watching him curiously as he crossed back over to her.

"Hungry?" he asked.

Her eyes grew wide.

He pointed to the refrigerator. "In there, I have sodas, waters, chocolate puddings, apples, and cheese sticks. And there are treats in the drawer next to the fridge."

She shifted her gaze to the refrigerator.

Lord Robert smiled. "You can go pick out whatever you like."

The girl shook her head.

"No? Would you rather I go get you something?" He headed to the fridge and pulled out some goodies.

He set a root beer, a chocolate pudding, and a box of *Milky Duddies* next to her on the couch. "My stash," he whispered, with a finger to his lips. "Don't tell anybody."

She looked at the treats. A light had come into her eyes.

He handed her the box of *Milky Duddies*.

She took the box, and carefully opened it with her tiny, shaking fingers. She popped a dud into her mouth and worked hard at chewing the sticky candy.

Robert lifted his eyebrows and pointed his chin at the candy. "Those are my favorite."

She smiled, showing caramel and chocolate covered teeth.

"Can I show you something?" he asked her.

She nodded.

"I have two children of my own. Twins. A boy and a girl." He flipped through his photos on his phone and showed her pictures of his kids. She seemed fascinated as she studied the pictures.

"How old?" she asked, her mouth full of candy.

"Five. But that one," he pointed to a picture of Elizabeth, "is five going on thirty-five."

Outside Balcony Doors

The first night at Ranfurly Manor was turning out to be … not promising. I fidgeted with my toiletries and tidied up my drawers in my new bedroom, all the while wondering what I had just gotten myself into by taking the new job.

The original plan was that I could go home the next day to feed my animals. But now that there was a murder investigation underway, would I even be able to leave? *And Lord Robert is on some business trip? Grr. Why does a murder have to happen right when I show up? Just my luck.*

And on top of everything else, a ghost of a model might be sharing my residence.

I shrugged it off. Ghosts were the last of my worries.

Still, I would have *liked my big dogs with me. Hmm. I wonder if I could persuade Lord Robert to allow my animals to live at the manor. There's certainly plenty of space. It would certainly save us the drive every day. … Although, it wouldn't surprise me if he's as picky as Keith was about dogs in the house.*

The sound of rain drumming against the balcony doors interrupted my thoughts. *The way Gretchen kept shifting her gaze to those doors when we spoke earlier creeped me out. I'm four stories off the ground. I shouldn't be worried about a murderer lurking out there on my balcony. Should I? Plus, there are guards on my floor, so that should make me feel a little better. Shouldn't it?*

I thumbed through the books I'd brought along to read.

"Let's see," I spoke out loud, in case the ghost was interested. "*Thirteen Wrong Answers.* I just love me a nice Cotter Daniels murder mystery, but now that I'm living in one ... maybe not. *Werewolf Apocalypse* by D.M. Howell ... *I don't think so.*"

I looked over at the desk in the room. There were a few books on it. I scanned titles:

"*Fashionistas.* Fashion's definitely not my thing. *Living with Ghosts.* Oh, please! No! *Myths About Dragons. Hmm.*"

That last one caught my interest. Book in hand, I flipped through pages until my eyelids grew heavy.

I awoke to drool running down my chin. The book was lying open on my chest. The wind was howling outside, and the light next to my bed had been turned off.

"That's strange. I don't recall turning off my light."

The balcony doors flew open.

That's a very strong wind.

Now the doors appeared to be slowly closing. *Am I imagining this?*

A shadowy figure was coming toward me.

If I wasn't convinced ghosts were real before, I was fast becoming a believer. I pulled my blankets up over my face and came close to wetting the bed.

"Mrs. Drake?" A familiar man's voice broke into the darkness.

I was too afraid to speak. Or peek.

"Don't be alarmed, Mrs. Drake. It's just me, the driver from last week. Mr. Knight. I'm not here to hurt you."

"Mr. Knight?" I said under the bed covers. "Are you a-a ghost?"

Mr. Knight pulled the covers off me. "No, I'm not a ghost. May I?" He gestured to my bed.

My jaw dropped. "Shame on you, Mr. Knight!" I gave him a scolding look.

"What? You think I'm trying to rape you? Hardly. I'd just like to sit and explain why I'm in your room. Is that a problem?"

"Oh." *I must be dreaming.*

He sat on the edge of my bed and turned on my light. "Hello again."

"Hi?" Everything appeared fuzzy. *This is the strangest dream.*

"So, you took the job after all, I see," he said.

"Yes. I did, Mr. Knight."

He laughed. "Call me Sean, please. Mr. Knight sounds like you're addressing my father."

"Right. Okay. Nice to know you're not dead, Sean," I said. "By the way, why did you turn off my light?"

"You mean, why did I turn *on* your light?" he asked me.

"No. I meant earlier. You must have been the one who turned it off. You're the only one in here." *I'm sure it was on when I fell asleep reading.*

"No. I just came into your room, and it was turned off. I never touched your light, until just now." He got up and thoroughly checked every inch of my room, my closet, under the bed, behind the curtains, inside the bathroom. He even checked the bathtub. "All clear, it might have been the wind," he whispered.

I lifted an eyebrow. "The wind? Blew out a light bulb?"

"You probably turned it out and don't remember … or there really is a ghost in this room, as rumor has it." Sean's lip curled into a half grin.

He returned to where he was sitting on the edge of my bed. Only this time, it was a little too close. I could smell the fragrance of mint and earth on his clothing. "Courtney, listen. I'm here on assignment."

"On assignment? So, what are you? A spy?"

"If I told you who I worked for, I'd have to kill you."

"Oh right. Like I've never heard that line before," I said, thinking he must be joking.

"I'm dead serious," he said. He didn't seem to be in a joking mood.

I shifted in the bed, uncomfortable.

"There's been a murder here. And the people I work for suspect Ranfurly. It doesn't look good for him, Courtney."

"Um. But Lord Robert has an alibi. *Me.* He was with me when the murder happened," I said.

"Was he, though?"

"Yes! We were together from morning until the body was found."

"The entire time? You were together before lunchtime?"

"Well, um, there was maybe a thirty-minute window before lunch when I didn't see him."

"Enough time to strangle old Jake."

"Why would he want to kill his gardener?" I asked.

"We're still looking into a motive. When I was working here, I was doing my best to keep an eye on him. He has a dirty past, Courtney. My assignment was to watch him. To be honest, for a long time, I thought it was a pointless assignment. But then, last week, I was chased into the Wildwood Forest." by someone on a motorcycle."

"Okay. So?"

"Ranfurly rides a motorcycle."

"You were chased by a motorcycle the day you did your disappearing act?"

"Yes."

"You came to see me that day. To convince me to work at Ranfurly Manor. Lord Robert hadn't even decided to hire me yet, but you lied and said he offered me a job here. Why did you do that?"

Sean sucked in air and his broad chest expanded. "I didn't tell you that he hired you. I just said I was sure he *would* hire you."

"Hmph. Well, you sure made it sound like he had already hired me. I was under the impression he had sent you to offer me the job." I crossed my arms. "Why *did* you come to see me that day, anyway?"

"I know I wasn't making much sense that day I came to your house, Courtney. It's just that–well…" He drew in a deep breath. "Truth be told, it was a pathetic excuse."

"Excuse for what?"

Sean laughed and said in a soft, husky tone, "It isn't obvious? Courtney, I wanted to see *you* again."

I swallowed too loudly. The room suddenly felt smaller, as Sean moved in closer. I scooted farther toward the middle of the bed, to make some space between us.

"Surely the connection I feel for you can't be one-sided," Sean said.

"How did you get out of the Wildwoods?"

"Hitchhiked to a place where I finally had cell service. Then I called someone I work with, and they dropped me off here earlier this morning. I've been hiding out on the property ever since.

"Hiding out where?"

A mischievous smile crossed his lips. "… The gardener with the hunchback."

"That was *you*? You almost sliced off my foot with those shears!"

"I was so surprised by you crashing into me out there. I mean, surprised in the best way. You're welcome to crash into me, anytime. But that was the first time I learnt you were here." He met my gaze. "I wondered if I'd ever see you again."

Poor Gretchen. She was in love with the cad. Told me they were a couple. Come to think of it, I'd seen her laughing with the "hunched gardener."

"Does *Gretchen* know you're alive?" I asked him.

"Gretchen?" He studied my face, inquisitively.

"You do know Gretchen, don't you?"

"Em, yes. We're well acquainted."

I smiled and nodded. "Are you, now? I thought I saw her speaking with you when you wore that—costume—in the garden."

"Yes. I made a little joke in a disguised voice. Was glad she didn't seem to recognize me. … Absolutely nobody else can know I'm here, Mrs. Drake."

"Not even your own father?" I asked.

"Too risky."

"Yet you trust me? Even though you barely know me?" I asked.

"Crazy, right?" His sugary eyes searched mine. "I can trust you, can't I?"

"As I recall, you came close to amputating my foot today. It seems I should be asking you that question."

"Right. Clearly didn't score any points for me, did it? But I promise, I won't try to kill you or amputate anything on accident the next time we meet."

"Not on accident? You'll try to kill me on purpose, then?"

Sean's lips curled into a half smile. Then he changed to a serious expression. "Listen … may I call you by your first name?"

"I don't know. Depends on whether you're a murderer or not."

"Listen, Courtney. Be careful around Ranfurly," he warned.

I didn't know what to believe. *Lord Ranfurly, a bad guy? Or Sean a bad guy?*

"And also … I could use your help with something." He stood up.

"What?"

He extended a hand, as if he expected me to take it. "You want me to get out of bed and follow you somewhere? *Now?*"

"There's a secret passageway behind that fireplace," he pointed to it, "into Lord Ranfurly's room."

Now I was really creeped out. At the same time, I was intrigued.

He went on. "I overheard my father telling old Jake about it when I was in my teens. Our former employer, Mr. Theodore Ranfurly, was a playboy. Always had women staying in this room.

Once after a trip, when my father was putting luggage away in Mr. Ranfurly's closet, a woman popped in through a wall panel. Stark naked!" He gave me a sly look and chuckled. "My father loved telling old Jake that part of the story. Of course, out of curiosity, when the coast was clear my father snuck through the wall panel to see where it led. That's when he discovered it came out in here, *your* room."

Sean was standing in front of the fireplace and lifted the bottom of a portrait that hung above the mantle. The entire wall moved.

With that mischievous half grin, he held out his hand and beckoned me to join him.

I hesitated. *This is so wrong, Courtney! Lord Ranfurly's your boss! You can't sneak into his bedroom!*

But my curiosity had been piqued. I was dying to see the passageway. I took Sean's hand and let him lead me down the dark corridor. We reached the end and pushed the wall open.

There we were, inside Lord Robert's enormous, and glorious, closet!

"Would you look at all those expensive shoes and ties the man has," Sean said.

"Impressive," I breathed. I would have *killed* for that closet.

Sean peeked through the closet door, which was cracked open, into Lord Ranfurly's bedroom. "He's not here," he whispered. We returned down the secret corridor, back to my room. As Sean pushed the fireplace wall closed, I wondered how many more secret passageways a massive house like that might have.

"Courtney, you won't mind if I come through your room occasionally so I can make use of the passage?"

"Sean ... of course I would mind. That is *so* wrong. No!"

"Courtney, don't you understand the gravity of the situation? A man's been murdered." Sean grabbed my shoulders and looked me square in the eyes. "Don't you want to do whatever is within your power to stop the murderer before he strikes again?"

"Yes, of course. But..."

"I'm not asking you to spy on him. I'm just asking for you to allow me in here, so I can do my job."

"Well, when you put it like that ... I-I don't know."

"Courtney, you seem to me like the kind of person who would want to do the right thing."

"Sean, I *do* want to do the right thing! But I'm not so sure that *this is* the right thing."

"Look, all I'm just asking is that you help me by being my eyes and ears on Ranfurly."

"You just said you weren't going to ask me to spy on him!"

"Not spy, just report things to me..."

"Sean. That's exactly what spying is! Besides, I'm not really a good spy-type. I can't tell a lie to save my life."

"But if the lie could save someone else's, could you then?"

"…And what if he's innocent?" I asked.

"Well, then you will help *prove* his innocence, won't you? Either way, you're doing the right thing, Courtney. Don't you see?" He squeezed my shoulders. "If you can help, we may be able to solve Jake's murder and prevent others from being harmed."

He had a point. I might be able to prove Lord Robert was innocent if I helped.

"Okay … Okay. But for the record, I don't believe he murdered Jake. I mean, unless you have evidence, then…"

Sean stared at me.

"What's that look?" I asked him. "You don't actually have evidence, do you?"

"I told you. He has a dirty past."

I didn't know if I wanted to hear it.

"How much of it is fact, and how much is rumor, Sean?" I asked.

"We're talking documented facts, Courtney. … You remember when I told you that Ranfurly's wife bled to death during childbirth?"

I nodded, feeling ill at the thought.

"The truth is, she was murdered. Only a couple months after her twins were born. She was mutilated in her bed."

I put a hand over my mouth and turned away from him. "Oh, awful. Sean. I don't know that I want to hear this…"

"And Ranfurly was accused of the murder," he said.

"No!"

"He was tried and eventually got off as innocent. But many people believe he covered it up. He would have the means and power to do so. A high-ranking member of the House of Lords," Sean explained.

Could he really have done such a thing? I watched him with his children. Looked into his eyes. Those couldn't possibly be the eyes of a monster.

Sean continued. "He left behind a bad reputation in Upland and fled here under a false identity. In fact, he led people in Upland to believe he was dead. Does that sound like something an innocent man would do?"

"Awful," was all I could say.

Sean nodded. Then he continued, "Courtney, you don't need to go out of your way. I'm not asking you to risk anything. You never have to go near that secret passage. I'll be the only one making use of it. All you have to do is act normal, and report anything that catches your attention as *off*."

I didn't want Lord Ranfurly to be a murderer.

But perhaps Sean was right: I might be able to help prove his innocence.

And if he's guilty? I didn't even want to think about that.

"Alright. If I notice something that is *off*, I'll let you know."

Sean's caramel-colored eyes danced. "I knew I could count on you. ... You have no idea how good it is to see you again." He took my hands in his and held on to them. "You're like a sweet summer day in this somber place."

It was like I was in a crazy dream meets nightmare meets fantasy meets twilight zone.

He stepped in closer to me and said in a hushed whisper, "Courtney, I don't want to put you in any danger. I'll be back as often as possible to check in on you. Just act normal, okay?"

I nodded.

He stayed there a moment, looking into my eyes. Then he whispered, "Sweet dreams, beautiful." He kissed his finger and gently placed it to my lips.

I stood motionless, not really believing any of it was happening.

He left the same way he'd come in, through the balcony doors.

After he'd left and I had a few minutes to shake myself out of the daze I was in, I played what all had just happened out in my head.

That was surreal. Mr. Knight, Jr. ... Alive and well. And was just in my bedroom!

Is he a secret agent? If he is, that would mean he is working for PAX. And if he's working for PAX, that would mean he can't be trusted.

If he's not working for PAX, then who is he working for?

Is he lying about Lord Robert?

I don't know what to believe!

I locked the balcony doors, shut the curtains, and crawled back in bed. Glancing over at my lamp, a chill went through me as I wondered if perhaps there was a ghost in the room, after all. I picked up the dragon book and read until I eventually managed to fall asleep.

Note of Consequence

THE NEXT MORNING
Ranfurly Manor

Robert stayed awake another four hours, waiting with the three sleeping girls at the hangar. It was nearly five o'clock in the morning when McGregor and Kila finally called to let him know they were coming in for a landing on his private runway.

After sending the girls off with them, Robert left the boat docked at Ranfurly Park and had Vivienne fly him back to the cavern. He headed up to the hidden cellar rooms and crashed on the bed. He passed out as soon as his head hit the pillow.

When he finally awoke and saw the time, he jumped out of bed and splashed water on his face. *Ten o'clock. I slept longer than planned.*

He showered in the hideout's bathroom, where he had a stack of clean clothes at-the-ready. He put on blue jeans and a black turtleneck, then quickly fastened his hair into a manbun.

A grumbling in his belly reminded him he needed protein. He opened the fridge. *Empty.* All he could find in the hideout's kitchen was a spotted banana and a granola bar. He munched them down, then bounded up to the loft above the Kiddie Bistro.

The room was vacant when he peered out over the rail. He slid down the fireman's pole and was on his way to see his children when he collided with Spencer Lee, the music teacher, who was headed toward the music room.

"Pardon me, Lord Robert!" Pages of sheet music dropped and scattered everywhere. Flustered, Spencer bent over to collect all the loose pages.

"No, I'm sorry. My fault!" Robert bent over to help. "Your music pages are all out of whack now, aren't they?" He noticed a handwritten note among them. His quick eye saw it was addressed to someone called *Thirteen* and signed by someone called *Ten*.

It was none of his business, but it was a strange note. "This one here doesn't even look like music." Robert held up the note for Spencer to see.

"What? Oh, hmm. Wonder how that got in there?" Spencer said absently.

"Is it yours?"

Spencer shook his head. "Nope. Never seen it before."

Robert read the note out loud.

Thirteen,

Confirmed diagnosis: Zygopetalum Blooms Indoors 642. Did necessary weed removal. A south hole is a good place to plant seeds at midnight.

-Ten

"What's this about, I wonder?" Robert asked, studying Spencer's face.

"I have no idea." Spencer shrugged. "Sounds like plant talk. I have no knowledge of plants. I'd ask one of the gardeners if they wrote it."

"Right. Hmm. Good idea." Robert handed the music pages to Spencer. He held on to the note. "Well, I'm sure you're anxious to get on with your rehearsing."

Spencer took the music pages and said, "Yes, I'm feeling a bit pressured for time. I've got to memorize this piece for a gig in Emer Aude in less than a week."

"Ah. It certainly is a long piece, isn't it? I have complete confidence in your ability to master it. You always do." It wasn't just flattery. Spencer was the best pianist Robert knew.

"Thank you, Lord Robert." Spencer smiled and bowed his head, then hurried off to the music room.

A moment later, Robert spotted Simon. He was hurrying down the hall, looking agitated, eyes darting about. "Lord Robert, there you are! The whole household is going crazy. Everyone is on edge about the murder."

"Yes. It's been difficult. Old Jake worked here longer than anyone. He was close with most of the staff."

"Oh, no Monsieur. I'm talking about *today's* murder. Marie Roth. She was found in the staff common room. Have you not heard?"

"What? Marie? I just saw Spencer, and he didn't mention anything about it." Lord Robert combed his hand through his hair.

"I was just on my way to tell him," Simon said.

"Her poor family. Do her parents know?" asked Robert.

Simon shrugged. "I don't know if they've heard yet. Maybe. News travels fast in this little manor." *Little* was a funny word to describe the humongous estate.

"You say this just happened? How do you know?" Robert asked.

"She was seen alive less than an hour ago."

Lord Robert sighed and shook his head, unable to believe it. *What is going on in my own house, right under my nose?* "I'd best check on the rest of the staff. Thank you for letting me know, Simon."

"Of course. You don't happen to know where Spencer ran off to, do you?"

"Music Room!" Robert called over his shoulder, already on his way downstairs to the staff common room.

When Robert got to the Staff Commons, Gretchen and Mr. Knight, Sr. were over Marie's corpse. Ms. Stern was lecturing them. "And someone needs to tell Lord Robert!" she was saying, a hand on her hip.

"I'm already aware." Lord Robert startled them as he broke into her lecture. "Simon just informed me. Everyone, clear the room, please. I need to have a look."

Before Ms. Stern whisked out of the room, she said, "I ordered the staff to refrain from touching the body or anything else in the room."

"Very good, Ms. Stern." He looked at Marie's body. "Our murderer has now struck twice. And by the look of it, both times the murderer used strangulation as the method."

"Yes," Ms. Stern agreed.

"But why them? Marie? Old Jake?" Lord Robert looked Ms. Stern in the eyes, trying to interpret her expression. He thought he read something in them. Fear?

"And who will be next?" Ms. Stern was pale as she asked the question. Robert noticed how white her knuckles were, as she clutched her black skirt.

"Yes. Ms. Stern, that is my main concern as well. We can't allow the murderer to take another life here. No doubt you worry about your own daughter, sweet Gretchen."

"Ya. Her head is full of flowers and fluff. It is hard not to worry about her," Ms. Stern said.

"Has anyone informed Marie's parents yet?"

"Ya," Ms. Stern sighed. "They are not taking it well."

Robert nodded, sadly. "I will check on them. But first I need to check on my children." *And Courtney.*

He left the staff common room and headed up to the third floor, mind reeling.

Out of the entire staff, he trusted the Roths, Simon, Spencer, and Sophie more than anyone else who worked for him. The latter three were friends he'd met through Desiree.

Robert remembered once feeling jealous of Spencer, who was a brilliant musician. Desiree had refused to marry Robert unless Spencer played at the wedding. Later, after one of Desiree's stage performances, Robert walked backstage only to find her arms wrapped around Spencer's neck while he played the piano. Robert was furious.

"Desiree, is this the kind of performing you do behind the scenes?" he'd asked her.

Desiree had laughed at him, which made him even angrier. "No! You have it all wrong! Spencer isn't into *women*!" She laughed.

After a little time, Robert grew to like Spencer.

Then there was Sophie, the Language Instructor from La Belle Terre. Robert recalled the time Desiree said to him, "I despise all women. The only tolerable female on the planet is Sophie."

Over time, Sophie had proven herself to be a true and loyal friend, to both.

And there was Simon, Desiree's choreographer and personal trainer. Robert had been jealous of Simon at first, too, until it was clear he had no reason to be. Eventually Robert hired Simon to become his own personal trainer, and the men became close friends. They had fitness and fencing in common. To some extent, Robert even confided in Simon. Of course, he never told him about CAPE, or about his secret escapades.

Before Desiree died, she told Robert she wanted her children to be taught music by Spencer, and she wanted Sophie to teach the children Bellais. To honor Desiree's wishes, Robert offered Sophie and Spencer their positions. That was one year back, just after Peggy died and the kids were four, the right age to begin lessons.

Even though they already had his trust, he did routine background checks on Sophie and Spencer, and made sure they were not chipped, before offering them employment at Ranfurly Manor.

It was a huge step for Robert. He'd managed to keep the fact he was alive, living in Cascadia, from everyone he knew in The Green Isles. They were the first ones to find out.

Now, it was a comfort to know they were there.

About three months ago, Sophie had encouraged Robert to contact Simon, who was living in La Belle Terre. That's when Robert offered Simon his position.

Of course, none of them were aware of Robert's secret escapades. As their employer, he'd simply tell them, "I'll be out on business for some time." and no questions were asked.

The three of them certainly had no motive for killing Marie, a kitchen staff member, or Jake, a gardener. They lived in the East Wing of the house, were paid more than anyone else in his employment. Treated like royalty, as Desiree would have wanted it.

Robert pondered over the details of Jake's murder. *What was the murderer doing in Sean Knight's room?*

And then there was Sean's suspicious disappearance. *His behavior just before he went missing was odd. Could he be dead? Or was he still alive? If alive, he could be a suspect in Jake's death.*

And if he was alive, it would be possible for him to have come back to the manor. He had the front gate code. What if Sean came back and went into his own room. Disguised as a hunched back gardener? Did Jake come into his room and recognize him? Did Sean not want to be recognized, so he killed Jake? Could he have been seen by Marie this morning, so he killed her as well?

I need to ask Dillard and Baca to see what they can dig up about Sean Knight.

DIVERSION

Ranfurly Manor

Robert was anxious to see if his children were alright. *I wonder how they are getting along with their new nanny.*

As he passed the guard at the bottom of the stairs that led to the third floor, he asked him, "Good morning. Have you had any trouble?"

"Good morning, sir. All quiet since my shift started at four o'clock."

"Did you hear about the murder that just happened?"

"Not until a minute ago, sir. It just came over my radio."

"Splendid way to start off a day, isn't it? What about the guard last night? Did he report anything I need to know about?"

"No, sir."

"Alright. Carry on." Robert reached the third floor. Courtney's door was closed.

He knocked.

No answer.

He waited a minute and knocked again. When there was still no answer, he turned toward the guard that stood at the top of the stairs. "Did the nanny come out of her room this morning?"

"Yes, sir. She's been with your children since seven. They're safe in your daughter's room."

"Excellent, thank you." Robert headed to Elizabeth's room and peeked in.

When he caught sight of Courtney, he had to catch his breath. She was wearing one of the pirate costumes that was in the children's dress-up closet. She had on a laced-up bodice that accentuated her small waist and full breasts.

Elizabeth and Luke had bandanas around their heads and had blacked out some teeth.

"Here is some of that treasure! Aargh!" Courtney dangled a bag of golden wrapped chocolate coins.

The children ran to her, and she handed each of them a chocolate piece.

He found the diversion pleasant. It was more confirmation that his selection in a nanny had been the right one. *At last.* In fact, she exceeded his expectations. A part of him wished he could enter their innocent world and stay there. *If only real life was this simple.*

What a contrasting reality he just came from down river. Three young girls, kidnapped, drugged, beaten. He didn't want to think of any of it when he was with his own children. It was his custom to detach his mind from the darkness he saw on CAPE missions once he got home. Home was his haven, where nothing could touch him, or his kids. He'd done everything in his power to make sure nothing could touch them.

Until now.

"Daddy!" Elizabeth had spotted him. She squealed and ran to him.

"Argh!" Luke said and showed off his blacked-out teeth, now covered in chocolate.

Courtney stammered, "W-what are you doing here? I-I thought you were on a business trip?"

Robert was expert at reading people, and he could have sworn the look he read on her face was … a guilty look. As if she'd done something wrong and he had caught her. But why? *Is she embarrassed that I walked in on her playing with my children? If she only knew what seeing her like this does to me.*

"It ended sooner than I expected," he said. "Found some treasure?" He smiled at her reassuringly.

She returned the smile, showing she also had blacked-out teeth.

"And the children showed you their costume collection, I see," he said.

"Why yes. Do you like my hat?" she held her hand on top of it and struck a pose.

"You make a fine buccaneer in it. And the eye patch completes the look perfectly."

"I lost the eye in a fight with a terrifying sea creature that had razor sharp claws," she said.

"Yes, indeed-y, matey!" Elizabeth showed off her blacked-out front tooth.

"My word. The three of you need to see a dentist," Robert said. "You two mateys keep looking for more treasure. I need to speak to your pirate queen for a moment. Argh!" His hand guided Courtney by the waist and led her out under the threshold.

Once they were out of earshot of anyone else, he stepped close to her ear and whispered, "Thank you for taking care of the children today. I'm delighted to see them so happy."

Courtney matched his tone. "Oh, good. You aren't upset that I let the children dress up and fed them chocolate before lunch, are you?"

Ah. That's what the guilty look is about. He chuckled softly and whispered in her ear. "On the contrary. I love that you've connected with them. Watching you with them reminds me of their mother. She would have loved getting to play pirates with them. She was a talented actress..." He trailed off. *Why am I telling her this?* "How has everything gone since I left you last night?" His fingertips brushed against hers.

"It's been ... fine. No problems."

Why does she seem frightened? Then it dawned on him. *But of course, it must be terrifying for her, a murderer lurking somewhere. Living in this huge house. She isn't used to a place like Ranfurly Manor. And now I'm about to break the news about Marie. Another staff member killed, this time a woman her same age. She has good reason to be afraid.*

It suddenly occurred to him that Courtney could be the next victim. He instinctively wrapped his arms around her.

"Courtney, I know this has all been a frightening experience. I promise I won't let any harm come to you." His lips brushed against her soft hair that smelled like strawberries. "But you should know, there was another murder in the staff quarters."

Lifting the patch, she stepped back so she could look up at him. "What? Who was murdered?"

"Marie Roth, a member of the kitchen staff. Like Jake, she was strangled to death."

Courtney's face paled.

"Are you alright?" he asked her, tightening his grip around her waist.

His eyes shifted to her throat as she swallowed. Her heaving chest was hard not to be aware of in the laced-up bodice.

"I'm doing my best to act fine in front of the kids," she said. "But knowing there's a murderer here … I worry about them. I feel so helpless. If someone were to try to hurt them, I don't know what I'd do."

"I'm sorry, Courtney. All this happening right when you get here." He had an overwhelming desire to kiss her pink cheek, to make every fear disappear. *That would be crossing some lines, wouldn't it old chap? What on earth has gotten into me?* He removed his hand from her waist and took a step back. "My guards are here to protect the three of you. I won't let anything happen to you."

She made a sound, as if she wanted to say something.

"What is it?" he asked her.

She took in a deep breath.

"It's alright. Do you need something?"

"I-I'm also worried about … my animals. It sounds so petty after hearing about the murders, I know. But they haven't been fed today, and I thought I'd be able to go home and…"

"Oh, no! Your animals. They completely slipped my mind." Robert put a hand through his hair, thinking. He had given his word to her. He'd even put it in a written contract.

Lord, she must hate this job, he thought. *She asked for a one-month trial. She must already be thinking of quitting. What person in their right mind would want to work here now?*

But I can't lose her.

"Is it still alright for me to go feed them?" Her ocean blue eyes were pleading.

Robert didn't feel it would be safe for her to leave. Not with a murderer lurking about. It was *the absolute worst* timing.

Her big blues were looking up at him expectantly.

Dear lord, here's a woman I don't think I could ever refuse.

"Courtney, how about I send Mr. Knight to take care of your animals instead?"

"Mr. Knight?" Courtney gasped as if she were frightened by the idea.

"My driver," he reminded her, wondering why she was so jumpy at the mention of him.

"Oh! Right. Mr. Knight, Sr." She exhaled. "Well … he won't know where I keep their food. My dogs might even show aggression to him – a stranger. They need *me*. All my animals need *me*."

Those pleading eyes. He felt horrible. He couldn't disappoint her. He had to think of something. "Courtney, will you give me a minute?"

She bit her lip and nodded. His gaze lingered on her lips for a moment. Then he snapped out of it and remembered what he was going to do. "I'll be right back."

He left her with his kids, and headed into his bedroom, where he paced for a few minutes to think.

Perhaps I could have Mr. Knight, Sr. drive Courtney home to feed her animals. … But wait. What am I thinking? Can I be sure he isn't the murderer? No, I can't. And if he is the murderer, allowing him to drive off with Courtney would be like handing him his next victim on a silver platter.

Then, an idea occurred to him.

He'd already told his staff that there would be no PAX interference in the murder investigation. It was one thing the staff agreed on. None of them trusted the new government.

But a *private* investigator, that would make sense.

He pulled his CAPE phone, hidden inside a compartment in his closet, and dialed up Peter's number.

"We've had another murder this morning," Robert told him. "Another member of my staff."

"You've got to be kidding." Peter made a low, rumbly sound. "What can I do to help?"

"How are your acting skills?" Robert asked him.

Peter laughed. "You've got to be kidding, Robert. I haven't acted since my university days when I played a judge in mock trials. Which wasn't exactly acting."

"Ah. Well, how do you feel about the role of P.I. Peter Williams?"

"Oh boy. You and your ideas, Robert. Let me run it by the boss – my wife."

"Ask her if you can fly out immediately."

Peter sighed. "Hang on, she's right here. … Nina, Robert needs me. He says it's urgent."

"Well, if Lord Robert says it's urgent, you better go then!" Nina said in the background. "And tell him he better be taking good care of our Winnie."

"Tell Nina thank you from me," Robert said. "And Winnie is doing just fine." A guilty pang shot through him. He'd completely forgotten about Winnie.

He hung up and went back to Elizabeth's room. "Excuse me again, mateys. I need to borrow your beautiful pirate queen once more."

The children giggled.

Courtney's cheeks turned a deep pink.

Every time he was near her, he lost all sense of reason. The urge to touch her was so strong, his hands tingled with longing. His fingers gently touched her hip to nudge her back out into the hallway. When they stopped to face each other, his hand rested on her hip and refused to budge from its spot. He clenched the other hand into a fist and forced it to remain at his side.

"Alright, I've arranged it. I will personally *take* you to your home to feed your animals today."

Anxiety was wiped from her face. He loved the way her eyes sparked with joy, and he had that feeling he got when shooting an arrow and hitting the bull's eye.

"You don't mind if we bring the children along?" he asked.

She beamed. "No, of course not."

"Good. But before we leave, I need to have a mandatory staff meeting. You'll need to be there."

"Of course. But who will watch your children during the meeting?" Courtney asked.

"They can come. It'll be brief."

He hated having to say this next part.

"But Courtney, I'm afraid the only solution moving forward is that we hire someone to stay at your house to take care of your animals."

"Oh, no, Lord Robert, please! I don't know anyone I could trust to do that."

Robert inhaled her scent. Urges were taking over his body … it had been so long since he'd felt that way. He longed to win her affection. Her trust.

Quickly, he thought up a different idea that he was sure would please her. "What if we just bring all of your animals here?"

Oh, the elation he felt as he saw her face light up. Another bull's eye.

"Are you serious?" she asked.

"It's the only solution that makes sense, isn't it?" he grinned. That other hand found its way to her waist. "And by the way, you're still calling me Lord Robert. It's just Robert."

"Oh," She breathed. "Robert."

"I like to hear my name coming from your lips," he whispered.

She seemed to lose her balance. Robert tightened his grip to steady her.

She broke free and stepped back, putting distance between them. "Lord Robert, I'm sorry. I-I…" she said.

He felt like a fool. *Damn. I came on far too strong. Now I've scared her.* "Why? You've nothing to apologize for."

"But it's just that I … I forgot to mention that I have two large dogs, three cats, plus several chickens and ducks."

This struck Robert as incredibly funny. "Oh! No. You never mentioned that." He kept a straight face. "That's it. Deal's off."

Courtney's face fell.

He took immense pleasure in teasing her. But it pleasured him more to please her. "I suppose the chickens could go in the old hen house."

Courtney's eyes widened in surprise.

"…And we would need to buy the ducks a little house of their own and put it next to the pond. Will your cats and dogs mind the barn? What do you think?"

Courtney jumped up and threw her arms around his neck. "Thank you, Lord Robert! Thank you so much! This means the world to me!"

Her response took Robert off guard, but he loved it. *The way to this woman's heart is through her animals,* he thought. Seizing the opportunity to do that thing he'd been aching to, he tightly pulled her toward him, leaving no space between them, and brushed his lips against her ear.

"I'm glad you like the idea," he whispered. Electricity flared. His pulse sped. Rational thought was conquered. His lips found hers and savored their honey-sweet flavor.

For the second time, Courtney broke the connection.

"I'm sorry. I…" Robert stammered. He'd lost his mind for a minute. "I know … I shouldn't have…" There was an awkward distance between them now. He turned to leave, then stopped. He clenched his hand into a fist and dug his nails into his palm. "I just want you to feel at home here. I know this has all been difficult for you." He started to head downstairs. *Robert, you're an idiot.*

"Lord Robert," she whispered behind him.

He turned. Hoping she would call him back; hoping she didn't hate him for being so forward.

"I-I really appreciate everything. I hope you know that."

Gah! She's so beautiful. "I just want to make you happy."

She smiled.

His head spun. It was painful, wanting her. But she had made it clear she didn't want him in the same way. "It's almost lunch time," he said. "I'll have Gretchen bring up some food for the three of you."

He started down the stairs.

"Robert?" Courtney interrupted him again.

He spun half around, his heart beating faster. "Yes?"

"I-I was wondering…"

"Yes?" he turned completely, so he could behold her. She met his gaze.

And there it was again. That strange, beautiful connection. For a moment, neither of them spoke.

He was tempted to climb up the few steps that separated them and close the distance, but would she reject him a third time?

She finally said, "Would it be too much for me to ask if my dogs would be allowed to come inside the house and sleep in my room?"

The question was so absurd that Robert burst out in laughter. *This woman really does have a thing for her animals.*

She smiled and laughed lightly.

It was a welcome relief, after the awkwardness.

Once the laughter dissipated, Robert put on a straight face. "Don't push your luck," he said.

❧ *Courtney* ❧

I held my breath in until Lord Robert had reached the landing and disappeared around a corner. Once he was out of sight, I could finally exhale.

What had just happened? My lips still tingled with the sensation of his warm mouth on them. It felt like a flower bomb firework exploded inside me. Sparks were shooting out throughout my entire body. I'd never felt so alive.

Why did I push him away? It isn't like I didn't enjoy it and want it to last forever. It was that I wanted it too much. *Way* too much. So much that I couldn't think straight.

I was being watched. The guard had seen it all. *He sure got an eyeful of entertainment. That whole ... whatever that was that just happened between us.* I headed back into the bedroom and rejoined the two little pirates on their treasure hunt. But I had a tough time engaging with them, as I replayed the scene over repeatedly in my head.

While I was eating lunch with the kids in the Kiddie Bistro, Robert popped in to see his children. The fuzziness after the kiss still lingered. Seeing him, all I could do was blush and stammer. I seized the moment to excuse myself so I could change and get ready to go get my animals.

In my bedroom, thoughts and questions bombarded my mind:

Did I do something to start whatever that was between us? Was I acting inappropriately toward him? ... He's my boss! This is so wrong!

Then ... there was Sean, who had asked me to spy on Robert. *How could I possibly do that?*

What a mess.

I don't want him to be a murderer. Please, don't let it be him!

A voice in my head whispered: *But Gretchen seemed to think he could be one.*

But a second voice said: *Gretchen could be under the influence of Sean. She clearly worships him.*

My thoughts shifted to the staff member who'd been found dead that morning. Marie Roth.

Could Robert really be a murderer? If he was the murderer, he had to have a reason to kill both Jake and Marie. What reason could he possibly have?

So far, the only person I'd met at Ranfurly Manor who I could imagine being a murderer was Ms. Stern.

MOTLEY CREW

AFTER LUNCH
Ranfurly Manor

It was a good thing I brought these along. I did a spin around in the mirror. *Good thing I lost those twenty pounds so I could wear these jeans again.* People always told me they were the jeans that best showed off my "assets". I pulled on my favorite off-the-shoulder blue shirt, zipped on my brown boots, then braided my hair into one long tail.

There was a rap on my bedroom door. "Courtney, our staff meeting begins in ten minutes in the parlor." It was Lord Robert. The sound of his voice sent a rush of dopamine through me. "We'll leave to feed your animals as soon as it's over."

I opened the door and smiled. "I'm ready."

He gave me a look over. "So you are." I read approval in his eyes.

As we walked down to the parlor, I decided to try my luck once more about getting my own vehicle. "So … Is your plan to load all my animals into the Royal Rodney?"

A half grin crossed his lips. "You're still really making a play to get your own car here, aren't you?"

I smiled.

"Because I do have other cars besides the Royal Rodney, you know. I'm actually a bit embarrassed to admit how many. But I can assure you, there's at least one truck in there."

"Yes. But I wouldn't want to mess up any of your cars or trucks. My ducks and chickens are no respecter of cars."

He laughed. "Very well, Courtney. Whatever you wish."

I couldn't believe it! That was too easy.

"Wait … really? So, you're okay with me following you back in my own truck?" I felt less suffocated at the thought of having my own vehicle with me.

"As long as you aren't planning on ditching me." He looked at me sideways.

I laughed.

Sean's voice popped into my head. *You might need to ditch fast if he's a murderer, Courtney.* I deleted the thought immediately. The dopamine rush Lord Robert was giving me felt too good for me to entertain that suspicion. "Thank you, Lord Robert."

"It's just Robert," he said softly. "And bear in mind, you're the *only* exception to the rule."

Downstairs in the parlor, I had a feeling Ms. Stern had a hand in how the room was set up.

The staff were assembled like a cast of characters in a play. Hanging above their chairs were their names and staff positions.

Lord Robert directed me to sit between a man and a woman, both I'd never met. There were no signs over *our* chairs.

Looking around the room, I recognized Ms. Stern, Gretchen, Eleanor (the maid who had found Jake dead), Mrs. Pemberley (the sour faced woman who I'd met at my first interview), and Winnie Williams, whom I'd met briefly when she brought snacks up to us earlier that day.

Winnie had just arrived a few days before me. She was a tall, dark, and athletic beauty with a radiating confidence. She didn't strike me as someone who would choose to work as a maid, but more like someone who would give motivational speeches.

Another person who struck me as a bit out of place: Jasmine Lopez. She was a maid but looked like she belonged on a movie set. In fact, it was hard to peel my eyes away from her. Drop-dead gorgeous. Captivating mocha-brown eyes with lush, long lashes. Her curvaceous figure was impossible to conceal in the teensy maid's uniform, the plump of her breasts spilled out of them. I envied her deep bronze, flawless skin. Her shapely legs were exposed all the way up to the top of her thighs in the miniskirt.

I was disappointed in Lord Robert for having the maids wear outfits like that.

Questions began to race through my head. *Is he a womanizer? One of those billionaires who treats his staff as if they were his harem?*

Next to Jasmine sat Davey Reed, a tall, dark, handsome, twenty-something man. He was staring at Jasmine. Who could blame him?

Next to Davey were Curtis and Ben Butters, the gardeners. Both the Butters had chestnut curly hair and scruffy beards. They reminded me of dwarves, but taller. They were maybe in their thirties, and they too, couldn't take their eyes off Jasmine.

I stole a glance at Lord Robert, wondering if he, like the rest of us, had his eyes glued to Jasmine.

To my surprise, I caught him staring at me.

I quickly looked away.

Next to the Butters brothers were Mr. and Mrs. Roth, the parents of Marie. They looked like a sweet couple, and my heart broke for them.

Who here looks like they just knocked off two people? I looked from face to face, at each person's eyes. *The eye should tell me everything. Eyes are the windows to the soul, after all.*

After studying every face in the room, and trying to read what was behind their eyes, I decided I would have been a terrible detective. I didn't have a single clue which one of the people in that room might be guilty.

The man sitting next to me interrupted my thoughts. His slanted, ebony eyes were kind and inquisitive. He had a streak of blue woven through his otherwise jet-black hair, an earring in one ear, and a large tattoo of a musical staff etched into his forearm. "You're the new nanny, aren't you?" he asked in an Uplandish Common accent. It wasn't Uplandish Proper, like Lord Robert's.

"Yes, Courtney Drake." I smiled and extended a hand.

"Spencer Lee. I teach the children music lessons."

I noticed another tattoo on his wrist when he shook my hand. It said *Desi* and was surrounded by a diamond.

He went on. "This is Sophie Batiste, the foreign language instructor, and this is Simon DuPont, the gymnastics instructor." He pronounced the latter the way the Bellais would say it, See-mow Doo Paw.

"Nice to meet you," I said to them.

Sophie was poised and pristine, every hair in her short, straight bob smoothly in place. I guessed by her dark features and olive skin that she was likely from the south tip of La Belle Terre. Her feline-like eyes were the color of midnight. "This is turning out to be a weekend of horror, isn't it?"

"No kidding," Spencer said in low tones, shaking his head. "Brings back too many memories for me of Desi."

"Desi?" I asked him.

"The children's mother," Sophie whispered, looking over at the twins. They were coloring in a corner of the room, out of earshot.

"She was my best friend." Spencer said, also in a lowered voice. "The way she was killed … sheer brutality. It took me three years of therapy to stop having nightmares."

"I still have nightmares," Sophie whispered.

"I'm going to need to see my therapist again after all this," Spencer said.

"It seems as if murder follows poor Lord Robert wherever he goes," Simon whispered. He looked like he might also be from the southern tip of La Belle Terre. He was a disarming dish: bright green eyes that reminded me of a cat's; short, dark, curly hair; an amazing physique. His accent was as thick as Sophie's. I wondered if they were siblings.

Lord Robert's commanding voice interrupted our discussion. "Thank you for attending the meeting. It appears that everyone is here now, so we'll begin. You are all aware that we've had a series of unfortunate occurrences over the past week, beginning with the disappearance of the equestrian instructor and caretaker of the horses, Sean Knight."

Murmurs and sad sighs could be heard throughout the room.

"Then yesterday," he continued, "old Jake Smith was found in Sean Knight's room, strangled to death. Now today, Marie Roth was found strangled to death in the Staff Common Room."

The poor Roths. I looked over at them, and my motherly heart ached as I watched the way they held each other and wept.

Lord Robert went on. "You all know how I feel about having PAX get involved with anything here at the manor, and I know you all feel the same. They will not be informed of the murders. But I do believe this situation requires outside assistance, which is why I've called a friend of mine who is a private detective. He is looking into the disappearance of Sean Knight and will be investigating the murders. He will arrive later this afternoon. Until that time, you will all need to stay in your rooms. For your own safety. I have posted my guards to be on watch."

The room broke into unrest.

Lord Robert raised his voice above the complaints. "Understand, a murderer is at large. None of you are safe to roam freely around the house until the killer is caught. All are at risk. The safest place for you to remain is in your rooms." He went on. "After this meeting, you are to pick up a boxed meal for dinner." He gestured to a table with neatly lined up boxes. "Take your meal and go directly to your rooms. Please do not make any stops along the way."

"Go directly to jail. Do not pass go," Simon whispered to us behind a cupped hand.

Sophie rolled her eyes.

As the grumbling staff got up to leave, Lord Robert made his way over to the four of us. "I'm sorry to inconvenience you all. I *really* am," he said. "Spencer, you may stay locked in the Music Room during the afternoon so you can rehearse," He turned to Sophie and Simon. "However, I'm afraid you'll both have to stay in your rooms."

"You do realize I have a date with a gorgeous blonde this evening in Emer Aude?" Simon said. His bright green eyes flashed like an irritated cat's.

"Oh, poor Simon. The whole world revolves around Simon!" Sophie said and huffed off dramatically, her hips swinging from side to side.

Simon huffed off in a different direction, making an equally dramatic exit.

He moved in a strong, masculine, smooth way. She, the same, only the feminine counterpart. Like two beautiful panthers. Again, I wondered if they were related.

He's certainly a ladies' man, I thought. *But not my type at all.* Still, I knew plenty of women who would consider him the creamy foam on a latte.

"Don't mind those two. They have an off and on relationship. Today, it's apparently off," Spencer said to me, rolling his eyes.

"Oh!" I said, surprised to hear that. *I guess they aren't siblings after all.*

"Thank you for locking me in the Music Room, Lord Robert," Spencer said. "I would've locked myself in there anyway. The love of my life is my music," he said to me, smiling in a sad way.

I smiled and nodded.

What a motley household this is turning out to be.

Monster in the Shire

AFTERNOON

Mill Pond, Cascadia

The children were as thrilled as I was to go for a day trip to visit my house. Lord Robert even seemed more at ease as soon as we'd crossed the bridge that separated us from the river island where the Ranfurly Estate was located.

The day started off foggy, but the further away we drove from the house of murder, the clearer it became, until the sky was a brilliant blueish purple. White clouds formed into shapes overhead.

"That looks like a dinosaur!" said Luke pointing at a cloud shape.

"I think it looks more like a dragon," Elizabeth said.

"I'm seeing an elephant with wings," Lord Robert said.

"I see a very fat duck," I said.

Suddenly, a massive, snow-covered peak appeared. Mt. Ziwa had decided to come out in all its glory.

Reading my thoughts, Lord Robert said, "The mountain comes out to reveal itself once again."

"Yes, it always takes my breath away."

"So much of the time, the mountain is concealed by the clouds. Invisible to us. Yet it is there, all the same. Standing firm and strong, watching over the land," Lord Robert said.

"Like God," said Elizabeth.

Lord Robert said, "That's a very good simile, Elizabeth."

"But God is even more amazing than that mountain, because He created it," said Luke.

Lord Robert smiled. "My children are pretty smart for five-year-olds, aren't they?"

"Yes, they most certainly are," I said.

"Do you believe in God, Mrs. Drake?" Elizabeth asked.

"I-I suppose so." The question made me uncomfortable. "But we should be careful. PAX forbids talking about God."

"There are higher laws than PAX laws, Courtney," Lord Robert said. "And in my house, and in my vehicles, we are always allowed to talk about God."

I bit my lip. "Okay."

"If we give in to all of the demands that PAX throws at us, we will lose and they will win," he said.

I decided for the children's sake, not to say out loud the thought that popped into my head. *I already lost Keith. They've already won.*

We finally arrived at my house. My heart was overjoyed. I didn't realize how terribly homesick I was. I'd only been away from home one night, but it felt like weeks!

My dogs and cats ran up to the car to greet us.

I introduced them to everyone. "This is Thor, and that's Loki."

Luke petted the dogs. It was love at first sight.

Elizabeth picked up my chubby orange cat, Glum. "Oh, he's so fat!" she cried, laughing at him. Glum scowled.

"You might choose a different word to describe him, Elizabeth. He's the sensitive type," I advised.

My other cats, Fiona and Chadwick, rubbed up against my legs to greet me. I scooped them both up at the same time and said hello.

"What about the dragon? Where do you keep him?" Luke asked me.

"Well, remember how I told you that the dragon is wild and lives in a dangerous mine in my forest?"

Luke frowned and crossed his arms over his chest. "You aren't lying to me, are you?"

"I'm not. I really do have a dragon living in my forest. I promise I'm not lying."

"Alright!" Lord Robert clapped. "Let's feed all the animals, then we can get this farm loaded up into Courtney's truck!"

The children jumped up and down. "Yes! Yes! Yes!" they cried.

They followed me around and helped me feed the animals. "Would you two like to help me take care of my animals every day once they move into your house?" I asked them.

Elizabeth tilted her head and thought a minute. Then she said, "Well, they *are* much easier to take care of than horses."

Since it was a beautiful day, we hiked around some of my forest trails while the animals finished eating.

When we were back at the house, I said, "Well, since you're here, I may as well give you a tour inside my *grand* castle."

The children and Lord Robert laughed, seeing that it was more like a hobbit hole in comparison to Ranfurly Manor.

As I started to put my key into the front doorknob, I saw that the door was cracked open. "Oh no! Did I leave my front door open like this?"

Lord Robert looked at me. "Wait," he said. "Let me go in first."

I followed him in, and I knew immediately something, *or someone*, had been inside. A raccoon? They'd left everything in disarray. My teal, wingback chairs had been overturned. Kitchen cabinets were left open.

The couch had been knifed open.

Lord Robert must have been reading my mind. "A raccoon didn't do that," he said.

I felt dizzy and nauseated.

Lord Robert must have noticed because he put his hand against my back to steady me. "Are you alright, Courtney?"

"No, I'm not. Someone broke into my house. … Why? Why would anyone *do* this?"

"Does it look like anything is stolen?" Lord Robert asked.

I looked around the house to see if things were missing. First, in Nick's room. Books were knocked down off his large shelf and scattered all over the floor. Next, I went down the hall to Laurel's room. Items had been pulled out of drawers, her memory box pulled out from under her bed and dumped on the floor. Her pillows were slit open.

"I don't have anything of real value for them to steal. Other than our heirlooms and memories," I said. I could feel the sting in my eyes, and I fought hard to keep tears from escaping.

Then I remembered something. My husband's loaded Raven pistol along with our other weapons. When PAX came out with new antigun laws, Nick, Laurel, and I had built a hiding spot for them.

"I'll be right back. Wait here," I said to Lord Robert and the kids as I headed down the front hall and rounded a corner, then pushed open the wall panel that led to a walk-in safe. The safe was unhampered inside. The intruder hadn't found it. I pocketed the Raven pistol into the back of my pants and closed the safe.

Once I returned to Lord Robert and the kids, a loud thump made me jerk my head.

"Did you hear that?" Robert asked me.

I nodded. "It sounded like it came from the direction of the Master Bedroom."

Lord Robert held a finger to his lips and pulled the children and me out to the front porch. He closed the front door behind him. "Courtney, are those dogs trained to protect you?"

I nodded.

"Take my children and your dogs." He handed me his car keys. "Get in the driver's seat and keep your dogs with you inside the car. Be ready to drive on notice."

I hurried the children outside and put them in the Royal Rodney with the dogs. I told the kids to get down on the floor of the back seat.

The kids were impressively quiet and obedient.

My dogs were well-trained to protect on command.

I waited in the driver's seat.

Something didn't feel right. Here I was, the one with a gun. Someone was in my house who apparently had a knife by the way they cut up my furniture. Robert had no weapon to protect himself. *Why am I sitting here doing nothing? I should be in there!*

My dogs had already started to bond with Luke and Elizabeth. "Thor and Loki. Protect." They could do as good a job as I could at keeping the kids safe. Maybe even better.

I headed back inside the house to the Master Bedroom.

❧ *Lord Robert* ❧

Robert left Courtney and the children on the front porch and quietly went back inside the front door. He pulled out a handgun concealed in the inside pocket of his jacket. He used the walls as his cover until he was outside the entrance to Courtney's Master Bedroom, where they'd heard the sound. He held his gun ready as he entered the room.

Inside was a small alcove that led into the bedroom. A walk-in closet was on his right. A closed door was straight ahead of him.

He scanned the bedroom.

Clear.

He scanned the closet.

Clear.

He opened the closed door. A bathroom. He walked in, peering into the shower and toilet stall.

Clear.

Just as he was about to leave the bedroom, a person rounded the corner and faced him with a gun. His finger moved to the trigger, but then he realized – it was just Courtney. She was aiming a pistol at him.

They both lowered their weapons.

"What the devil? I could have shot you!" he said.

"I'm sorry! I had no idea you had a gun. I thought you were unarmed and might need…"

Feet knocked into Robert, who dominoed into Courtney.

Courtney's gun went off. The bullet just missed hitting Robert.

A person who had been hiding in the Master Bedroom crawl space had swung down on them. He or she was already out the front door and out of sight by the time Robert and Courtney realized what was happening.

Robert ran out front but saw no sign of the intruder. *Are they on foot?* He ran down the driveway.

Courtney's dogs were barking inside the Royal Rodney as he ran by them. He saw his kids were safe inside with the dogs. Then Robert heard a motorcycle engine start up in the forested area of the property, near the driveway entrance. A second later he saw the motorcycle. The rider wore all black, the helmet concealing his or her head. Robert shot after it, but it moved at high speed through the forest trails out onto the street and zoomed off.

"Bloody ****!" Robert roared. He whipped around and saw Courtney standing on the front porch of her house. "I told you to stay with my children! You almost got us both killed! And my children had nobody to look after them! Why didn't you do what I told you?"

Courtney narrowed her eyes at him and glared.

He went on. "The next time I tell you to do something, I expect you to follow orders," Robert shouted, fuming.

"Excuse me? This is *my* house!" Courtney shouted back at him. "My husband made sure I went through the training to learn how to protect myself and *my* property in case something ever happened to him. And something did happen to him and I sure the *** have a right to protect my own property. How dare you expect me to sit in a car while some intruder is in my house! I didn't know you had a gun! As far as I knew you went in there unarmed. I was trying to cover your ass!"

Robert laughed, mocking her. "A lot of good that did. You nearly got us both killed!"

The dogs were in a frenzy, barking in the car. Robert was pacing back and forth, trying to calm down. "Did you get a look at the person?"

"No. It was kind of hard to see anything when you fell on me," Courtney said coolly.

Robert scowled. "I think it was a man, but I can't be certain."

Courtney didn't say anything.

Robert couldn't understand why she had behaved so foolishly. "Courtney, I can't believe you didn't listen to me when I told you to stay with my kids. What were you thinking?"

Courtney was livid. She spoke through gritted teeth. "I was thinking you were worth sticking my neck out for. Apparently, I was wrong."

Lord Robert opened the back door of the car, and Thor growled at him. Loki ran down the driveway, barking.

He held out his arms for his children. "Are you alright?"

They nodded. Luke looked more excited than scared.

Elizabeth said, "I saw her."

"You saw … who?" Robert asked, surprised.

"The woman. She ran right by us."

"You're sure it was a woman?" Courtney asked, making her way toward them.

"Yeah, I'm sure," Elizabeth said.

"What was her hair color?" Robert asked.

"Black. With a patch of white in front," Elizabeth said.

"It was not a woman! It was a man with short spikey hair. He had a tattoo of the number thirteen on the side of his neck!" Luke shouted.

"Hmm. Okay, well, whatever pronouns the person uses, you both gave a very good description for us to go on. Good job, little Ranfurlys." Robert patted them on their curly red mops.

"Does this mean you will get us ice cream?" Luke asked.

❧ Courtney ❧

The man was infuriating! He was yelling at me for defending my own house. Ordering me to stay in the car! … I was pretty sure I was going to be fired after this. I didn't care. *Let him fire me! This is* my *house! I left his kids safe, in the best of hands, er ... paws. My dogs would have given their lives to protect them.*

How was I to know he was carrying around a handgun? He never let on that he was armed. Maybe Sean was right – maybe Lord Ranfurly is a murderer!

Sean asked me to let him know if anything seemed off about Lord Robert. Well, did I have news for him!

Then it occurred to me that Lord Robert might just tell me not to bother returning to Ranfurly Manor after all this. How was I supposed to share anything with Sean if I was fired? Would Sean come find me at my house?

"Are you going to fire our nanny, Daddy?" Elizabeth spoke what I was thinking.

"You won't fire her, will you? We want to keep her," Luke said.

"Her dogs saved our lives," Elizabeth added.

Lord Ranfurly looked at each of his children and sighed. "No, I'm not going to fire Mrs. Drake. I just want to make it clear to everyone," he directed this last part at me, "that in the future, my orders are to be followed. To the letter."

I was fuming. If only I was holding my cast iron frying pan, I would have fast pitched it at him! I wanted to quit right there and then.

"May we have a word? Alone?" I asked him, holding back the explosion that wanted to blast out, for the sake of the twins.

It was obvious he wasn't too pleased. But he followed me some distance away, so the children couldn't overhear us.

My jaw ached from how hard I clenched it. "I might have been *part* to blame for the person getting away. But *you* obviously didn't clear the room very well, did you? And I had no idea you were carrying a gun, so I felt it was my responsibility to go in my house, since I have mine. Besides, I barely know you, so why should I trust you to defend my property?"

For a minute, he seemed to be biting his tongue, holding back. Then he said, "You're right. We don't know each other well enough, do we?" He turned and walked off.

A few seconds later, he stopped.

He turned around and walked back toward me. He stopped just in front of me.

"Shall we start over?" he asked. He held out his hand to shake. "I'm Robert. I happen to carry a concealed weapon. At all times. And you are?"

"You know my name," I said with a hand on my hip.

"And do you carry a concealed weapon at all times, Mrs. Drake?"

"No. I do not."

"Ah. Well, maybe you should. Especially considering the way things have been going lately."

"Hmm." I crossed my arms. "I thought you said you never micromanage people. Seems to me like you get off on telling people what to do."

He tilted his head from side to side and frowned. "Perhaps. On occasion."

"Well, you might want to keep in mind that I am more inclined to rebel when someone patronizes me," I said.

"I can see this could be a problem for our relationship in the future," he said.

"It most definitely will be," I said.

"What would you propose we do about it?" he asked.

I stuck out my lower lip. "Not proposing we do anything."

"I see." He stared at me, and I stared back. Stony faces. Mean faces.

I was the first to break the silence. "I need to clean up the mess in my house."

"Very well." Lord Ranfurly stood frozen, now looking past me in the direction of Mt. Ziwa. "Should you decide to return, the manor can't be discovered by any navigation systems. ... I'll write down directions for you, along with the new code to get into the security gate. I'm *trusting* you won't share any of this with anyone."

I folded my arms and frowned.

He continued. "If you don't return by this evening at eight o'clock, I'll take that as your resignation." He turned and called to the children, who were playing with the dogs. "Come on, Elizabeth! Come on, Luke! Time to say goodbye!"

The children ran to me.

"But I thought Mrs. Drake and the animals were coming back with us! Aren't we going to load them in the truck?" Elizabeth asked.

I forced a smile. "Not right now. I need to clean up the mess that person made in my house."

"Can we at least bring Thor and Loki with us now? Look! They love me!" Luke said as Loki licked his face.

"They do love you! But I think I'll keep them here with me in case the crazy motorcyclist comes back around."

Robert was stiff. "I'm certain Mrs. Drake will be able to take care of herself if that should happen. Come on, kiddos. Back in the car." Lord Ranfurly rushed his kids into the Royal Rodney and sped off down my driveway.

Thor gave me a pathetic look. As if I was a bad human.

"What? What did I do? That man is impossible! I doubt any of you would like it at his house anyway. It's a horrible, horrible place!" I huffed and stormed back into my house.

21

UNWELCOME DESIRE

THE SAME NIGHT

Ranfurly Manor

Five minutes past eight. Robert paced across the floor of his bedroom. Courtney still hadn't returned.

After spending the rest of the day with his children, he had tried to get his mind off the war of words they'd exchanged back at her house in Mill Pond. But his children wouldn't stop talking about everything pertaining to Mrs. Drake: her amazing animals, her cute little house, her heroic dogs, how pretty she was, how she was the best nanny ever, blah, blah, blah.

God help me. Robert wanted to tear out the hair from his own head.

But later, once his temper cooled and he'd given it some afterthought, he felt only regret. *What is wrong with me? Of course, she had a right to defend what was hers. It was her home, after all.*

Now in his room, he was listening for her, constantly checking the time. *Why did I have to tell her to be back by eight o'clock or I'd take it as her resignation? Why give her an ultimatum? I'm such a fool to stoop to manipulation. I've probably lost her forever.*

Trying to control the situation had only backfired on him, and now he'd lost her. How would he explain it to his children?

He felt feverish. The woman was making him insane. He took off his shirt and used it to pat the sweat dripping down his chest, neck, and back.

He pulled the note that he'd found earlier out of the pocket in his jeans. Earlier, at the staff meeting, he'd asked the gardeners about it. It didn't belong to them, and they had no idea what it meant.

He sat at his desk. "Thirteen." Robert spoke out loud. "Hmm … Didn't Luke say the intruder had a tattoo of the number thirteen on his neck? The note was addressed to *Thirteen*. I wonder … could the person who broke into Courtney's home be the same *Thirteen* in the note? And was there a *Ten* running around somewhere with a tattoo of the number ten? Could it be that simple?" Robert slowly coiled his long strands of hair through his fingers, deep in thought.

"If the *Thirteen* in the note was the same *Thirteen* at Courtney's house, then the note and the break in are connected. But could the note be connected to the murders?"

The sound of light footsteps coming up the stairs broke his concentration. They stopped at Courtney's room. He immediately left the note on his desk and went out to see if it was her.

"Courtney," he said in a husky tone. She stopped before going into her room, avoiding his stare.

He stood still, devouring her profile. She was wearing the blue blouse he saw her in this morning, that exposed her shoulders and creamy white neck.

She wasn't a wild kind of beauty, like his Desiree had been.

Desiree's flaming red hair and bombastic nature drew everyone's eye. She had been famous, a sex symbol. Fully aware of her power over men, she'd often used it to her advantage. She justified lying if it benefited her. To find the real Desiree underneath her façade was nearly impossible.

Stay away from her, Robert's rational mind had warned him. But in the end, he had fallen for the actress.

Courtney, on the other hand, had an understated, quiet kind of beauty. Her bright turquoise eyes and pale skin contrasted by her dark auburn hair gave her a striking appearance that caused people to stop and stare.

She didn't flaunt her attractive shape, but he certainly took notice of every curve.

Unlike Desiree, she was down-to-earth, honest to a fault, and a bit awkward at times. She wasn't full of herself nor was she self-serving. But she did have a fiery temper, and a stubborn streak that could make a mule blush.

Yet it was what was behind her eyes … the depth of her ran deeper than anyone he'd ever met. He saw in them an endless ocean that he wanted to explore. A soul he *needed* to know, *needed* to understand.

I can't lose her.

"It's ten past eight," he said hoarsely.

She turned his way. Her eyes were defiant, but her voice was soft. "And?"

"And … you came back."

Her eyes shifted down to his shirtless chest. He noticed the way her lips slightly parted.

He slowly made his way to her, fixating on her creamy neck, her throat. The defiant look in her eyes became wild, like the unpredictable ocean.

He was tired of fighting. He just wanted to dive into that ocean and forget the rest of the mad world. He whispered into her ear, "And you're late."

"So, am I fired?" she asked, breathless.

He let his lips feel her. Just a light brush of her ear, then her cheek. "No. I am."

She wasn't breaking away. No. In fact she was leaning into him.

He kissed her neck, her shoulder.

She allowed it.

The fire inside stoked to full flame. He pressed himself against her and found her lips. This time he kissed her hard.

When they both took a breath, he asked, "Will you forgive me?"

She leaned back and searched his eyes. "Yes. But don't cheapen my forgiveness by behaving that way again."

It was as if she had seared him. Chastened him with a hot iron. "I wouldn't dare."

"Goodnight, *my lord*," Courtney said with a hint of sarcasm as she backed farther into her bedroom and closed the door behind her, leaving him to stare after her.

❧ *Courtney* ❧

Save me from myself! I didn't understand it. How did I have such intense desire for a man I absolutely loathed a minute ago? In a matter of seconds, I went from questioning whether he was capable of murder to feeling an overwhelming desire to throw myself into his arms.

What's wrong with me? I knew that if that man was to continue prancing around shirtless, I wouldn't be able to stop myself from letting things get out of control.

Think of Sean … What did he look like again? It was difficult to recall Sean at that moment. I still had the vivid picture of Lord Robert in my head. *Is he still standing on the other side of the door?* I swore he was. I could sense him.

❧ *Lord Robert* ❧

He stood there, glued to the floor. Only a door stood between him and the one he desired. He pulled his hair back with both hands and exhaled audibly. He was tempted to barge into her room and kiss her hard and fiercely.

But in the end, his mind won the battle over his urges.

He went back to his room. On the way, he noticed the night guard, standing at the top of the stairs, pretending not to have seen anything. Robert knew better.

In his room, he wondered, *Why her? Why now?*

He'd had opportunities to be with all types of women: models, actresses, princesses, lawyers. Beautiful, exceptional women. Yet he felt nothing for any of them. Not until Desiree.

When she died, desire was buried with her.

Then, Courtney Drake replied to an ad.

He'd researched her background: acted in community plays, sang, danced, was top student in her high school class. Raised as an only child by her parents, lived with them all throughout her childhood and teen years until she married. She was a cheerleader and fell in love with the quarterback. They married right out of high school. Typical dream couple from Cascadia.

Robert chuckled. He couldn't relate at all as a noble from Knoxfordshire who lost his mother as a boy and was raised in boarding schools.

They were worlds apart.

She'd had very little upper-level education, only a semester of community college and became a mother when she was eighteen.

None of that bothered him. Not really.

Then again … if he were honest with himself, maybe he had some preconceived ideas about her. Even though he'd heard wonderful things about her from Nick, Robert had conjured up an image of what she would be like in his mind.

She's probably a very kind woman, like my nanny had been. Common, not highly educated. But nurturing and motherly.

It had been ingrained in him, that there were the *Commoners*, and there were those born with a higher calling. But then he'd met Peter Williams, who challenged his elitist perspective.

Now that he had met Courtney Drake, his ideas were challenged even further. Courtney was anything but Common. She was the most extraordinary creature he'd ever met.

His body hummed as he imagined her in his arms. How he loved her childlike innocence, the way her head tilted to the side when she laughed, the chemistry she had with his children, the glisten of her silky hair, her delicious smell.

The taste of her lips.

The curve of her hips.

He sucked in air, feeling dizzy, achy. "I've been alone too long; that's all this is."

Back in his bedroom, he took a cold shower. As the freezing water met his skin, it gave him the sobering jolt he needed to focus on the matter at hand. The note. After the shower, he went to his desk to look at it.

"Hmm, strange. I know I left it right here on my desk," he said out loud, searching around the room to see if it had fallen somewhere.

It was nowhere to be found.

CRACKING CODES

MEANWHILE
Ranfurly Manor

"I see you've been busy with the lordy-lord while I've been away."

I jumped.

Still leaning against the door, lost in thought, trying to remember what Sean looked like, I was shocked when he appeared from behind the curtains.

"Do you have to sneak up on me like that?" I whispered. *Is Lord Robert still outside my door? Oh no!*

"Wait!" I made a stop motion with a hand and held a finger to my lips. Peeking out my bedroom door, I checked for a sign of Lord Robert in the hall. I could smell the lingering of his soapy scent, but he wasn't there. The night guard at the top of the stairs was looking the other way and didn't notice me looking out. I closed my bedroom door before he could turn around and locked it.

"You're awfully flushed, Courtney. Are you alright?"

"Yes, I'm fine. You just scared me to death, that's all!"

"You aren't falling for him, are you?" Sean looked at me sideways.

"Who? The security guard? Of course not!" I retorted.

"Not the guard, Courtney. You know who I mean." He contorted his eyebrows. "Lord High and Mighty."

"No! I just did what you asked me to do. My job! But it sure has been a heck of a day."

Sean plopped down into one of the armchairs in my room. "You went home today and brought your animals back. I know that much."

"How do you know that?"

"I went to check in on the horses, and was greeted in the barn by Thor and Loki, and that cat who loves me…"

"Fiona," I inserted.

"Yes, Fiona. And I saw a couple cats lying next to Fiona. One fat cat with a sour look on its face and a cute little orange cat."

I smiled. "Oh! The orange cat is Chadwick, and the fat sour puss is Glum. It makes me happy to have them here. … My chickens are here too! and the ducks."

"That's good. You'll be safer with your guard dogs here." Sean's caramel-colored eyes danced in the dimly lit room.

"Well, I don't know how much safer I'll be with them all locked up in the barn at night. But yes, at least they're here."

"Sit down and stay awhile." He patted the chair.

I laughed. "Gee, thanks. Considering this is *my* room." I sank into the chair next to him.

"So, anything to report to me about Ranfurly?"

I'd been waiting all day to tell him. "There was another murder today."

Sean looked alarmed. "What? Who?"

"Marie Roth. A kitchen maid."

"Marie?" Sean seemed rattled. Finally, he said, "That's terrible…"

"Did you know her?" I asked.

He nodded, looking sad. "We both grew up here."

"Did you and her, like, you know…"

He looked at me. "Did we go out? Yes. We dated when we were teenagers."

"Right, of course you did. Who haven't you dated, Sean?"

"Oh, lots of people! I've never dated Gretchen's mum. Never dated Marie's mum. Never dated a man before."

"Well, that rules out half the population here, at least!" I laughed.

Sean blew air through his lips and made a flapping noise.

I realized I wasn't being very sensitive. He had just learned that he lost someone he cared about. "I'm sorry, Sean. About Marie."

He nodded. "What else happened today?"

I recounted the events of the day as he relaxed into his chair listening intently, eyes closed. At one point I asked, "Sean? Are you sleeping?"

He opened his eyes. "No. This is how I take in detail. It's a thing."

"Oh. It's a thing, huh?"

"Yes. Go on."

I picked up where I left off. When I got to the part about what went down at my house, he opened his eyes and sat upright in his chair.

"A person with the number Thirteen?" he asked me. "Interesting." He pulled a note out of his pocket. "Take a look at this. I just found it on Ranfurly's desk."

"You were in his room? Just now?"

Sean flashed a cunning smile and read the note to me.

Thirteen,

Confirmed diagnosis: Zygopetalum Blooms Indoors 642. Did necessary weed removal. A south hole is a good place to plant seeds at midnight.

-Ten

"So, that person with the tattoo could have been *Thirteen*!" I was getting excited. Then my spirits sank as I realized, "but you found the note on Lord Robert's desk. Really?"

Sean nodded slowly.

"Do you think Lord Robert wrote the note, then? Could he be *Ten*?" I asked.

"It certainly looks that way, Courtney." Sean said.

I stood up and began pacing the room. I didn't want to believe it. *No. That would mean Robert was working with the person who destroyed my house. How could he do that? He clearly had no idea the person was even there.*

Unless he did know they were there. ... But that would make him a monster.

Sean stood up and grabbed me by the arms, putting a halt to my pacing. We locked eyes. "Courtney, why don't we look over the note and see if we can make out the rest of it?" he whispered.

I nodded.

We sat down again, and he scooted his chair closer to mine so we could look over the note together. "Zygopetalum is a type of orchid," Sean told me.

"Really? You just know that off the top of your head? Impressive."

"Coincidentally, my father is obsessed with orchids." He moved his eyebrows up and down funny-like. "So ... this note appears to have something to do with orchids."

"Orchids?" I asked, tapping my finger on my lip, thinking.

"This isn't the best climate for orchids. As the note says, they bloom indoors."

"Ah. Hmm. So, then, maybe the note has to do with your father?" I guessed.

"That seems highly unlikely." Sean scratched his five o'clock shadow. "My father only has three or four orchids in his apartment. Wait ... the Conservatory has a collection of them."

"I can check in the morning to see if this plant is in there. Can you check your father's apartment, to be sure he doesn't have one? But if we find one, then what? What are we looking for exactly?"

Sean threw his hands up. "I don't know! ... Let's look at the rest of it," he said.

We combed through the note again in silence.

Sean broke through my concentration when he stood and said, "Courtney, I want to show you something."

"Um ... okay."

"Meet me outside in the barn."

"When?"

"Now. I'll head down there my usual way … through the balcony. You go through the house. We can continue to brainstorm after I show you," Sean said.

"Alright, I guess." Luckily, I was still dressed to go back out. "I'll tell the guard I need to check on my animals, which is true."

Moments later, I was in the barn with my animals.

"Good evening!" Sean stepped out of the shadows doing an impression of a vampire.

"What is wrong with you? I'm pretty sure you get off on making me jump." I stuck my tongue out at him.

He laughed. "You're certainly right about that. Alright, time to come with me. We need to stay out of sight and be quiet out here."

"Sweet dreams, fur babies. I'll be back early in the morning to check on you," I told my pets, kissing each of them.

I followed Sean to a thicket not far from the garage. A light in a window above the garage went on. "Doesn't your dad live there?" I asked him.

"Yes. But he doesn't know I'm here. Shh…" Sean put a finger to his lips, then disappeared through the thicket. A second later, his hand popped out of the bushes, beckoning me to come with him. I grabbed his hand, and he pulled me through. I brushed off the feeling of spiderwebs and shuddered, hoping I didn't have creepies crawling on me.

Sean and I were now facing a steel door, camouflaged so it blended into its surroundings. He punched a code into a concealed keypad. The door opened. We climbed down stone steps toward a dim light.

At the bottom of the steps was another door. "Ladies first," Sean said.

"What is this place?" I asked.

"Another secret passage built into Ranfurly Manor. I found it when I was a child."

"Is this where you've been hiding?"

"Yup."

"I looked around the place. "How did you sneak stuff in here? Like that couch, for instance?" I imagined him carrying a couch through the thicket and down the stairs.

"The furnishings were always here. I just added my special touches. Like this…" He pointed to a small modern painting of a sax player and a pianist dressed in tuxedos. "And this…" He gestured to a roll of toilet paper in the bathroom. "And this…" He opened his refrigerator. There was nothing in it except a carton of eggs, a beer, and a pitcher of a green concoction.

"Wow. This place could use a woman's touch. Do you bring Gretchen here?" I asked him.

"No, and I'm trusting you won't share this secret with her or anyone else. Ever. Can you promise me that?"

I sighed. "More secrets. Ever since you came into my life, I'm forced to keep secrets."

He took me by the hand and sat me down next to him on the green couch. "I brought you here because I didn't want to risk someone over-hearing our meeting up in your room. I never meant to drag you into my insane world. … But those magnetic powers of yours, Courtney. You're hard to stay away from."

My inner guards crossed swords. He was coming on way too strong.

I stood up and walked over to his wall painting to put a distance between us. "Don't worry. I won't tell anyone about your little hideaway here."

"Thank you, Courtney. Okay. Let's have a look at this note again." He pulled it out of his pocket and read. I paced the room, listening.

"*Did necessary weed removal…*" I repeated.

Sean surmised. "*Weed removal*, planting seeds … all things that have to do with…"

"Gardening," I finished.

"Yes. Hmm." Sean drummed his fingers on his leg.

"Wait!" I pointed at him. "Jake was a gardener!" I said, excited.

"Yes. I thought of that too." Sean sat there, continuing to look over the note for a while.

I did a wall sit.

Neither of us said anything. Until suddenly, an idea popped into my head. "What if this note has nothing to do with gardening. *Zygopetalum*

Blooms Indoors. Do you see how those three words are capitalized? Maybe it's a code. If you take the first letter of each, what does that spell?"

"Z-B-I … ZBI!" Sean finished, raising his brows. "Zone B Intelligence. Could it be that simple? Let's see if that fits with the rest." He read the note, "*Confirmed diagnosis. Zone B Intelligence 642. Did necessary weed removal…*"

We looked at each other, both ignited by the new trail we were on. Sean was speaking quickly now, "Let's assume this means Ranfurly is *Ten*."

"And let's assume you are ZBI," I said.

He raised his eyebrows. "Let's assume Ranfurly assumes that I'm ZBI. But 642? What could that mean?"

"That *must* be your number. Like *Double Oh Six.*"

He shook his head. "Fiction, Courtney. ZBI doesn't have numbered agents."

"How do they keep track of all of you if you don't have numbers?"

"ZBI uses code names."

"Ha! So, you admit it! You *are* a Zone B Intelligence agent!"

"I admit nothing. And for the record, ZBI no longer exists. Not since PAX took over."

"Oh." I was deflated. "I didn't know. They dissolved it?"

"*Technically* they did. But really, they just changed their name. So, you might be onto something here."

"Could *642* refer to the time? 6:42?"

Sean shook his head. "I don't know. The rest fits, though. Jake must have discovered Ranfurly in my room. So, Jake was the *weed* that had to be *removed.*"

My heart was racing.

Sean went on, "But that last part. *A south hole is a good place to plant at midnight.* What could that mean?"

"To plant. … To plant a bomb?" I said, alarmed.

"Possibly. But a hole could also be referring to a place to bury something."

"Bury something. ... Like a treasure?" That seemed exciting. "Something stolen?" I was throwing pasta on the wall. "A body?"

"*The south hole* ... hmm. The manor has a South Wing. My guess is that Ranfurly is *Ten* and he'll be meeting *Thirteen* somewhere in the South Wing *at midnight*," Sean said.

"Sean, wait, what about motive? Jake wouldn't dare question Lord Robert for being in your room. He owns the place and would have every right to. What reason would he have for killing Jake?"

Sean raised his eyebrows. "Who knows? Maybe Jake saw Ranfurly doing something terrible."

I crossed my arms. "I don't know."

"Look, the fact is, I just snuck into Ranfurly's room while you were having your little whispery chat with him and found this note lying on his desk. Why would this note be on his desk if he isn't *Ten*?"

I couldn't come up with a reason.

"You want him to be innocent, don't you?" Sean asked me in a low voice.

"Of course!"

"Because you have *feelings* for him." Sean crossed his arms over his chest and scowled.

"Pff. Of course not. I want him to be innocent because his kids need him."

Sean was quiet. I could see he was holding something back. Finally, his words sliced through the silence, like a sharp blade. "Courtney, what if I told you that those kids might not even belong to Ranfurly?"

FAST KNIGHT

Sean's Hidden Bunker

"What do you mean, the kids might not be Lord Robert's?" I asked Sean.

"I was recently informed that Desiree, Ranfurly's dead wife, was a prostitute."

"Elizabeth and Luke's mother was … a prostitute?" *Lord Robert could have his pick of all the maidens in the land. Why would he marry a prostitute?*

Sean nodded. "Apparently, some of her *clients* were criminals. IRIS hired her to gather intel on the criminals."

"Iris? Who is she?"

"Not she. It's a nickname for ZAI. Short for Zone A Intelligence, in case you didn't know."

"Oh." I stared Sean down. "You certainly do know a lot about Intelligence for not being an agent."

He replied with a poker face.

"Well, does your source have any proof that Desiree was still sleeping with other men *after* she married Lord Robert?"

"Yes. She was still working when she was married to Lord Robert."

"By working, you mean sleeping with other men," I said.

He nodded.

My hackles were rising sky high. *How could she do that to him?* I despised her. And I refused to believe Elizabeth and Luke could be anyone else's kids. "I don't care what she was or who she slept with. I know they are *his* children. Elizabeth has his eyes."

"Ranfurly isn't the only person on the planet who has green eyes."

"Sean, do you realize the repercussions of what you're saying? If those kids were taken away from Lord Robert, their lives would be destroyed!"

"If Daddy's a murderer, do you really think the kids should be in his care?"

I crossed my arms and went back to pacing.

Neither of us spoke, both of us caught up in our own musings.

Then, a thought occurred to me. I stopped pacing. "Wait a second. If what you say is true, then that could prove Lord Robert was innocent of killing his wife!"

"How?" Sean looked at me doubtfully.

"Because there were others who would have had a motive for killing her. She was passing on secrets about criminals. If one of them were to discover that she was spying on them, they'd have a reason to want her dead."

Sean stood and raised the paper in his hand. "Then why did I find this note on Robert's desk, Courtney?"

That stupid note. "Well, that note might mean something else! Who knows? We just need to go to the South Hole tonight and find out for ourselves what that's all about," I said.

"We? Oh no, no, no." He got up and crossed over to me and put his hands on my waist.

Boundaries, buddy! I backed away from him.

By the look on his face, he thought I was playing hard to get. "You need to stay safely tucked in your little bed tonight, young lady. Leave the dangerous exploits to me."

"Wait a second, you weren't getting too far in cracking the code in that note until I helped. I should get to come along."

Sean grabbed me and pulled me against his ripped and powerful frame. I couldn't break free of his grip this time. "As enjoyable as your company is for me, I'd be distracted by you the entire time. It will be best for us both if you go back to your room and stay there."

"Hmph." I stared at him, feeling trapped. What could I say to get him to loosen his grip? "By the way, Sean, how exactly are you getting onto my balcony?"

"Wouldn't you like to know?" He was looking at my lips.

I acted like a helpless damsel in distress. "Well, if you can get onto my balcony, then so could the murderer. And that makes me worry. Is it easy to climb up?"

"To reach a rose, he'd have to suffer the thorns."

"Thorns?"

"Aye," he said, his Highlandish brogue stronger than usual. "Bloody thorns are everywhere, trailing up the wall. He'd have to have exceptional grip and footing to climb up the stone walls. It's a long drop, four stories below. Pray that he's deathly allergic to mint. There's a field of it at the bottom of the balcony. He would really have to want to murder you to go through all of that."

He pressed me up against the wall and kissed me hard on the lips.

I slapped him.

Shocked, he released me and raised his hands in the air. "Okay, I can take a hint."

"I just … haven't been with anyone since my husband and–" I gulped. *Why did I follow him in here? He could do anything he wants to me. Have his way with me, then chop me into a million pieces! And nobody would ever find me.* "I-I'm not really ready for a relationship."

He studied my face, as if he was deciding whether I was serious.

The man had an abundance of confidence in his ability to seduce women. *He's acting like this is the first time a woman ever refused him.*

Following an uncomfortable moment, he said, "Okay, sure. Whatever you want. I'm not the type to force myself on a woman." He walked over to his fridge and pulled out a beer. His movements were stiff. "I only have one left. Want it? Or I've got some of my green drink left."

"No, I'm not crazy about beer, thanks," I said. "And that green drink looks disgusting. I don't even want to know what's in it." I laughed out of nervousness.

You could've broken the tension with a sledgehammer.

"Are we still good?" I asked him with a tentative smile. I didn't want to make him mad, so I tried to sound light in my tone. "It kind of feels like a cement wall just dropped between us."

He took a sip of beer, then stared at me. "We're good. I'm just used to faster women."

"Oh, okay," I replied. An awkward silence passed. I was trying to think of how I could get out of there when a thought occurred. "I've been wondering something. Before you took the Royal Rodney and came to see me that day you were chased, you told me you thought Lord Robert might suspect you were spying on him. Why did you think that?"

"Because he went through my room," Sean was on the defense.

"You know for sure it was him?"

He glared at me. "My gut says it was him. But no, I didn't see him. No fingerprints were left behind. Security cameras are inoperable." He glanced my way. "Not that I'm complaining. With security cameras down, I get to climb up your trellis at night. … So, no, I can't prove he was the one in my room."

"Yet still … you assume it was him?"

"Aye," his Highlandish came out. "You should go. Time for me to prepare to go to the *South Hole*."

"Okay. But one more thing. Don't you have to be chipped to work for PAX Agencies? So, how did you get the job here when you have a chip?"

"I never told you I worked for PAX."

I crossed my arms and looked at him narrowly. "No, you never told me. But I'm right, aren't I? You're an agent. So how did you get the job here?"

"Wow," he said, glancing at the wall clock. "Already nine o'clock. You *really* need to get going." Sean grabbed my hand, a little too forcefully. "I'll take you as far as the barn. It isn't safe for you to be out there alone."

I sighed. *Good luck getting Sean to fess up*, I thought. Once we got to the barn, he said, "Be careful." I watched him disappear into the night.

An anxiousness swarmed inside me. I had mixed feelings about Sean.

Once I was finally back to the manor, I checked the time on a grandfather clock that sat on the staircase landing. It was already half past nine. The *South Hole* meeting was approaching fast.

SOUTH HOLE

Quarter to Midnight

Robert assumed the *South Hole* was the pond in The South Wing. As Robert passed the barn on his way there, Courtney's dogs *barked. Having watchdogs around isn't a bad idea. They'll sound the alarm when* Ten *and* Thirteen *are on their way.*

He walked past the staff apartments and the swimming pool, around a winding path that led to the south side of the property. A large pond with a fountain in the center sat in front of a stone building half swallowed in ivy. It was built by Ranfurly the First to be a guesthouse and hadn't been maintained.

Robert crouched and waited behind bushes next to the guesthouse.

Five minutes later, somebody was approaching. Robert wondered why the dogs hadn't barked. *Some watchdogs they turned out to be.*

The person stopped at the pond and dodged behind a tree nearby. Robert could see the person behind the tree from where he was. He could tell it was a man. *He must be waiting for the other to show.* A few minutes later the man came out from behind the tree, headed straight for Robert.

Surely, he doesn't see me. Does he?

The man changed direction and dodged into the front door of the guesthouse, then disappeared inside. Robert waited another five minutes for the second person to show.

Five minutes passed. Then ten more went by. *It's after midnight now and nobody else has turned up. Could the other person have already been inside the house when I arrived?* Robert quietly crept to the back entrance of the guesthouse.

He took out his knife to cut through the ivy and feel for the door. Thick spider webs blocked him. Such a fun way to spend the evening, Robert thought as the memory of kissing Courtney's creamy neck filled him with longing to be back in the house with her.

After slashing through the sticky webs and brushing off spiders, he turned the knob of the back door and entered.

He was in the small kitchen. He took a few soundless steps over to the wall that separated the kitchen from the small sitting room and stood with his back against it.

Peering around a corner into the sitting room, he scanned the area.

An umbrageous figure stood in the center of the room. Close enough to make out that he had the same build and height as Robert's.

Robert stood with his back against the kitchen wall, gun ready. Careful to keep his breath inaudible.

The floor creaked. Robert peered around the corner again.

The figure was no longer in sight.

Gun pointed, Robert slowly walked through the opening into the sitting room.

"Hunting someone, Ranfurly?" a familiar voice said. It came from directly behind him.

Sean Knight.

Robert turned around. Sean stepped out of the darkest corner in the room. He appeared to be unarmed.

Robert lowered his weapon. "Sean, so good to know you're alive and well. You had us all worried. Especially your father. And poor Gretchen. Is this where you've been, all this time?"

Sean pulled out his weapon and pointed it at Robert. "I asked you a question."

"Really, Sean. Is that necessary? I lowered my weapon. Why don't you lower yours so we can catch up. Have a chat." Robert was fast. He slammed a foot into Sean's knees.

Sean's legs buckled.

Robert grabbed Sean's wrist that held the gun and wrestled the weapon out of his hand.

Now he had two guns. His own, plus Sean's. He aimed them at his opposer.

Sean leapt into the air and twisted around, sending a backward kick into Robert.

The kick knocked Robert to the ground, and he lost hold of Sean's gun. It blasted toward a nearby wall and skittered back to its owner.

Sean snatched it up and took a few shots at Robert.

Robert had already kicked over the couch to use it as a shield.

The men exchanged shots until they needed to reload.

Sean sat down with his back against the kitchen wall to reload.

Robert sat behind the cover of the couch. His voice pierced the silence. "It would seem we have a stalemate, Sean."

"I suppose it would to a defeatist," Sean said from behind the wall.

"I propose we throw down our weapons and see who the real man is in the room. What do you say?"

Sean laughed. "Really. We both know you'll just take a shot at me if I walk out there unarmed."

"I'm a man of my word." Robert threw down his pistol and with hands raised, he walked out into the center of the room and faced the kitchen opening. "Are you?"

Sean appeared in the kitchen opening. He was aiming his gun at Robert. "I never gave my word to anyone." A devious smile crossed his lips.

"Fine. Go ahead and kill me. But first, tell me why you took my car to Courtney's house before you decided to disappear?" Robert asked him.

Sean chuckled. "Last minute getaway, you might say."

"Why did you try to convince her to work here?"

Sean had an unreadable expression on his face.

"Does she know you're alive?"

"Leave Courtney out of this. My relationship with her is none of your business." He emphasized the word "relationship."

The thought of Sean with Courtney sent a raging heat through him. *I want to feel his body break.*

With unbelievable speed, Robert grabbed Sean's wrist and disarmed him. He pocketed Sean's gun in his own jacket.

Sean grabbed a nearby lamp and thrusted it into Robert, sending him backward.

Robert scrambled to his feet and rammed headfirst into Sean, who fell backward to the floor. He pinned him while he was down.

The men grappled and punched at each other, until Robert sent his enemy a powerful blow in the face.

Sean was out cold.

Robert relaxed. Until Sean suddenly sprung to his feet and gave him a right hook in the jaw.

Robert grabbed Sean's neck and forced him up against the wall, then pounded his opposite fist into his face until it looked like raw meat.

Sean kneed Robert in the groin.

Robert recoiled.

Sean pushed him to the ground, then pounced on top of him. He beat his fists into Robert's beautiful face until it was covered in blood.

Robert lay on the dirty floor, unresponsive.

Why hasn't Thirteen *shown yet?* Sean wondered. Out loud, he said, "This place is a real hellhole. I have to get Courtney out of here."

While he was on the floor, Robert saw his gun within his reach and snatched it up. "Over my dead body," he said as he jumped to his feet. With a mighty force, he slammed the weapon into Sean's head.

Sean fell to the floor and blacked out.

Nearby, lightning flashed, and a second later, a rumble of thunder followed. In the distance, Robert heard *barking dogs. Now they decide to bark.*

His children had described *Thirteen* to have black short hair with a white streak. *Sean must be* Ten, *and the dogs must be barking at* Thirteen, *who is on their way to meet him in the guesthouse.*

TREADING THORNS

Quarter to Midnight

I was dying to see if *Ten* and *Thirteen* would show up on the south side of the property. *Could Sean be right about Lord Robert? Is he* Ten? Prickles formed on my arms, and I shivered at the thought.

Out on my balcony, I was thankful it was covered and protected from the monsoon that flooded the grounds below. The roar of the monsoon ended, and it was quiet and still. But only for a moment. All at once, a chorus of chirping frogs began. Their song came to a crescendo and became so loud, I wondered if the manor was being invaded by the hopping amphibians. Then I heard a more familiar sound. My dogs. They were barking in the distance. *Poor boys, they should be here in my room with me.*

The sound of rustling caught my attention. Someone was down below, walking. It was a dark night, but lanterns lit the pathway through the gardens to the barn, and I could make out the person's distinct gait. He moved like a panther.

I recalled the little argument between Sophie and Simon earlier that day. When Simon huffed off, his panther-like strut had left an impression on me.

I knew Simon's room was in the East Wing, far from where he was walking. *Odd. Why would Simon be out on a night like this?*

I know, it was crazy of me, but I couldn't resist the temptation to find out.

I really do need to check on my animals, I told myself. And while I'm out, might as well have a peek to see what's going on in the South Wing.

I quickly pulled off my pajamas and put on black yoga pants, a long-sleeved black shirt, and my black high-top tennis shoes. Not the perfect getup for sleuthing, but it was the best I could do, considering I didn't own spy gear.

I glanced at my raincoat, thinking it would be nice to wear something waterproof in case another monsoon comes down. Which would not be a surprise considering Cascadia's fickle skies. *Better not. Too swishy and swashy. And too pink.*

I prepared to get drenched.

What I wasn't prepared for was the climb down the wall. Sean had warned me, but in my haste to not lose sight of Simon, I forgot that I would first have to manage getting down four stories, clambering through thorns along the way.

I'd done a lot of dumb things in my lifetime. But once I was out on that stone wall, I was sure I'd made my stupidest mistake yet. The stone was wet and nearly impossible to grip. My tennis shoes only made it worse. I fell several feet, until I caught hold of a trellis of roses. Roses with so many thorns.

"Ow. Oh!" The exclamations slipped out. Far too loudly. Prickles stabbed into my hands, arms, legs, and tush. Simon wasn't that far away. I prayed he didn't hear me.

Note to self: stealth mode, Courtney!

Three feet from the ground, my shoe's rubber sole slipped. I fell into the mint bushes at the bottom.

If Simon heard me, he didn't seem affected. He was hurrying, headed in the direction of the barn.

My dogs were barking again.

Trees and bushes as my cover, I kept Simon in my sights and shadowed him. A picture popped into my head of a ten-year-old me with my best friend Meg, pretending to be spies.

Simon made a sudden turn before the barn, then disappeared into a grove of cedars.

Staying low, I crept from tree to tree.

I heard whispering.

Concealed by a massive tree, I tried to make out what was being said.

"I'm glad you got the message. Our first meeting place was compromised." It was Simon speaking in his strong Bellais accent. "Lord Robert found the note. If he understood any of it, he would have went to the South Wing pond to look for us. Did you have any trouble getting in the front gate?"

"None at all. No guards, no cameras. Used your code. It was easy. You're sure he has no idea that you're *Ten*?" the other person, a woman, whispered.

That must be Thirteen.

Simon chuckled. "No, I'm certain he has no idea it's me."

"When are you going to make your move on him?"

"I've been patiently waiting for my moment. But J.J. said I needed to focus on Sean right now," Simon said.

"Sean isn't even here."

"J.J. knows Sean will be coming back if he hasn't already. Jasmine is here. He'll be back," Simon said.

Jasmine? Is there something going on between Sean and Jasmine?

"But I want my Bellais sausage by my side tonight. It's too cold in this miserable place. I can't wait until you take me to the south of La Belle Terre like you promised," *Thirteen* said.

It suddenly became very quiet. I peered around to make sure they weren't coming my way.

They weren't. They were giving the cedar trees a lesson in human hanky-panky.

"Didn't J.J. tell you we would get to level up and work on something big soon?" *Thirteen* asked.

Who is this J.J. they keep talking about?

"*Ma cherie*, you have always been impulsive. Sean will be back. Then PAX wants to bring him in. They plan to deal with him for being a traitor."

"So, you found proof he is with the Resistance when you searched his room?" *Thirteen* asked.

"Not exactly. The annoying old man came in and interrupted the search. I strangled him and had to get out of there quickly, before being seen. But another staff member saw me and confronted me about it later. I had to strangle her, as well."

What?

The murderer was Simon! I desperately wanted to run and tell Lord Robert. And Sean!

"Simon, you're getting sloppy. You'll blow our cover if you keep getting caught."

"It wasn't *my* fault! But PAX has other reasons to believe Sean is a traitor," Simon said.

"What reasons?" *Thirteen* asked him.

"They didn't tell me. They just said they know, and we need to bring him in alive."

"So, we just have to wait around for Sean to come back, then? I could do some beautiful work on Ranfurly right now while we're waiting."

"You'd like that, I'm sure. But Wellington said we're not allowed to touch him. Still, I can twist a knife in him a different way, when I tell him the truth about how I made love to his wife." Simon laughed. A sick, evil laugh. "He is still the same blind fool he was when Desiree was alive. Desiree and I probably slept together in every room on the second floor of his mansion in Upland. That woman taught Satan how to lie." He snickered.

I froze. Was I hearing correctly? *Did Simon just say he slept with Robert's wife?*

Thirteen snickered. "It was a pleasure to cut her into pieces, knowing how she'd been lying to you, selling your secrets all that time to the Crown."

Wait! She killed Desiree?

My heart was pounding fiercely. Then I had guessed right. Desiree had been sleeping with a criminal. Simon! Selling his secrets to the Crown, back when Zone A was ruled by monarchs. He must have found out Desiree was ratting on him, so he had *Thirteen* kill her.

Thoughts raced through my head. If only I could break away from there, find Lord Robert, and tell him. Find Sean, who was probably still hanging out in the South Wing. Both Sean and Lord Robert were in danger!

My dogs were still barking and scratching on the barn doors, sensing I was close. If they were free, they would be able to help. I needed to let them out.

Thirteen noticed the barking too. "That woman had to bring her annoying dogs here. It's a good thing they are locked in the barn. One of them took a bite out of my arm before I broke into her house today," the woman said.

I beamed inwardly with pride.

"Was there any sign of Sean at her house?" asked Simon. "I thought for sure he was working with her, staying at her house."

He thought I was involved? Working with Sean? Where did he get that idea? *I wondered.*

"No," *Thirteen* answered. "I combed through the place before Ranfurly and that woman showed up. I didn't find any evidence that she's working with Sean."

"He must have gone to her house for some reason," Simon said.

"He's a lady's man. Probably went there to shag," *Thirteen* said.

Here I was, mere feet away from two psychopaths. How could I slip away without them noticing me? If only I could use telepathy, I'd sick my dogs on them.

Darting to the next cedar, I stood still a moment behind the giant trunk of a tree. *Just one last tree, and then I'll reach the barn.*

I made it to the last tree and caught my breath. Just one last straight dash to the barn doors. My heart was racing as I listened for *Thirteen* and Simon.

It was quiet. Even my dogs had stopped barking for the moment. I imagined the pair were back to their midnight canoodling in the woods. I peered around to check.

I couldn't see them anywhere. *Where did they go?*

"Not so fast," *Thirteen* popped out from around the tree and held up a knife. Simon stepped out on the other side of me, trapping me in.

I could have kicked myself for leaving my gun back in the bedroom. In my haste to follow Simon, I'd forgotten it.

"So, it was *you* who killed Lord Robert's wife," I said to *Thirteen*. Fear was evident by my shaky voice. "And *you* killed Jake and Marie," I said to Simon.

"Oh, so you were listening in, were you?" *Thirteen* asked, calmly. "Isn't that cute, Simon?"

"Oui. Elle est adorable." *Yes. She is adorable.*

"Simon took care of Marie and Jake, as was necessary," *Thirteen* said. They were weeds that needed to get yanked out. And at last, I get to brag about what I did! My favorite work of art was Desiree Diamond. Ask Simon. He'll tell you. I'm a master with my knives. Isn't that right, love?" She flashed a grin that reminded me of a rat.

"Oui. Ma cherie Rayeena est La Reine du Couteau." *My dear Rayeena is the Queen of the Knife.* Simon pressed against my back side and pushed me against the tree.

I struggled to break free, but he had iron strength.

"Now, little nosy woman, want to find out for yourself what it is like to become one of Rayeena's masterpieces?" Simon asked me.

Rayeena/*Thirteen* touched my neck with her icy blade, while Simon's hands frisked me, violated me. "Ah, good girl. No illegal weapons hidden in your private parts."

Rayeena watched, licking her lips as Simon groped. I fought the urge to vomit and forced myself to be still and slow my breath, lest I jerk and the knife pierce through my skin and hit a crucial artery.

"Now you get to find out firsthand what we do to pretty little spies before they die," Rayeena said. The sky lit up as lightning flashed nearby. I heard a rumbling sound. Heavy rain poured down on us.

"I promise you'll enjoy it. They always do," Simon whispered in a sick, seductive tone. He licked my neck with his scaly tongue. "Mm. Crème de minte. Delicieuse." He bit hard into my neck with teeth that he must have sharpened.

I screamed.

It was a mistake. My scream only heightened their excitement. Rayeena and Simon were sadists. I forced myself to scream on the inside.

Even if I could have fought off Simon, it wouldn't have mattered. They had me in checkmate. Rayeena slowly etched her knife along my throat, until its tip was on my larynx. As she watched my fearful reaction, her expression was orgasmic. She was savoring every second.

Not wanting to give her any more satisfaction, I went somewhere else in my mind. *Meg. My best friend for life. What's heaven like, Meg? I bet it's a lot better than this.*

Simon continued biting, then licking in circular motion. Rayeena pulled out a pen with her free hand and began drawing on me. Wherever Simon licked, she followed with her pen, while holding the knife to my neck.

"He is licking a trail for me, which I'll carve into once he is finished. We make a fantastic team, don't we?" She flashed her rat teeth into a detestable grin.

I closed my eyes, and tried to shut out the sights, smells, sounds. *God, if you're real, send a bolt of lightning down to strike them. Or strike me and let me be the one to die.*

AFTER MIDNIGHT

∾*Peter Williams*∾

AFTER MIDNIGHT

Peter was exhausted. A long flight, and a longer interrogation. He'd left Capital City on the east coast of Zone B early that morning. Spent the day interviewing Ranfurly's entire staff in the common room of the staff quarters, to no avail.

He hadn't seen Robert yet. *Where could he be?* Peter wondered. Winnie told Peter the last time she'd seen Robert was at a staff meeting early in the afternoon.

Winnie wasn't too thrilled about being at Ranfurly Manor. "I'm bored, Uncle Peter. I don't know why I'm even here. I never see Uncle Robert. He doesn't give me assignments. And Ms. Stern is over me like a hawk, watching me all the time. If I don't look busy, she makes me clean something!"

Peter sighed. Robert had always been a solo flyer. Even back in university when Peter was his professor. He kept to himself, didn't let people in. Never got serious about a woman. Not until Desiree came into his life.

Peter and Nina never met Desiree, but they saw the effect the woman had on their friend Robert, and they weren't impressed. It was obvious she brought out the worst in him. After her death, Robert was still trapped by the woman's memory.

Thank God for my Nina. I have the best wife a man could ask for. Peter knew he didn't deserve her. *If only she was here with me now.* Nina's arms after a long day were his haven. Often, he prayed a woman as amazing as Nina would come into Lord Robert's life. Then again, there weren't too many women on the planet who could hold a candle to Nina.

He looked at his watch. After midnight. No wonder he was so tired. He left the staff quarters and started through the courtyard back to his room in the main house. Lightning flashed close by; a fierce clap of thunder followed. He heard dogs barking. Where were they? In the direction of the barn? Then, a woman's scream pierced the night.

Peter ran toward it.

Approaching the barn, he heard the dogs frantically scratching at the doors to get out.

Low voices were nearby. Stopping, he listened. He quietly stepped off the pathway and through the cedar grove toward the voices, until he saw who they belonged to.

A man and a woman had their backs to him. It looked like they had someone pushed up against a tree. He saw the shine of a knife's blade in the woman's hand. The person against the tree was softly whimpering, as if being harmed.

"Stop what you're doing, or I'll shoot. And trust me, I won't miss." Peter pointed his gun's scope at the back of the man's head. The man spun so fast, his victim with him, using her as a shield.

At the same time, the other woman with the blade whipped around and held it to the victim's throat.

"Drop your gun or I'll slice her pretty little neck," the woman with the knife said.

❧ *Courtney* ❧

"Stop what you're doing, or I'll shoot. And trust me, I won't miss."

It all happened so fast, it's hard to recount the exact order of events. I was spun. A man was pointing a gun at us. Then, Rayeena's knife was on my throat.

Then … I think it happened then … a deafening shot blasted. I wondered if I'd been hit. If I was dead.

Then … I saw Rayeena. She collapsed to the ground. Her terrifying knife with her.

Simon must have let me go … my arms and body were free. I felt limp.

I couldn't hear anything but ringing in my ears. My first thought: *My dogs!* That plan to let them out was still in my head. I made a beeline to the barn, opened the doors, and set them loose.

That's when I caught sight of Simon. He was headed for the forest.

The large, black man with the booming voice who had saved my life was in pursuit of him.

Pointing to Simon, I shouted, "Attack!"

Thor and Loki, who I've always sworn could read my mind, had already joined the chase before the words came out of my mouth.

❧ *Lord Robert* ❧

Robert believed Sean was *Ten.* He had a feeling that *Thirteen* might have come to the South Hole and fled upon seeing Lord Robert with Sean. He threw Sean–still unconscious–into a nearby wheelbarrow and headed back toward the house.

On his way, he wondered why it suddenly sounded like a mad frenzy at the barn. The dogs were barking without ceasing and scratching the barn doors. He made a slight detour to see what was happening there, half expecting to run into *Thirteen.*

To his surprise, he found someone else. "Courtney?"

"Lord Robert!" Courtney ran to him and crashed against his chest. He held her, wondering why she was out there. Why did she look so frazzled.

"Shh. It's alright. What's going on? Are you crying?"

She backed away from him, her eyes on Sean who was out cold in the wheelbarrow.

"What did you do to him?" She searched Robert's eyes. She reached up and gently touched his cheek. "And what happened to you?"

Robert shifted his eyes to the woman who was passed out and bleeding on the ground. Someone had sent a bullet into her abdomen.

"*Thirteen*," Courtney said.

He noticed the short black hair with a patch of white. "That's *Thirteen*? Elizabeth was right. A woman."

Courtney shook her head. "That's no woman. That's a rodent." She started to fall into his arms.

Robert's head was in a fog. *Was Courtney the one meeting* Thirteen? *Could it be that Courtney was* Ten, *all along?* "What are you doing out here with *Thirteen*?" Lord Robert slowly raised his gun until it was aimed at Courtney.

Her blue eyes were wild and wide. "What? Seriously? This is the second time I've had a gun pointed at me tonight!" She tried to laugh, but her voice faded, as Robert watched her collapse.

EXPLANATIONS

THIRTY MINUTES LATER
The Horse Stables

The smell of hay filled my nostrils. *Achoo!*

Wet slime. Foul canine breath. Thor and Loki were slathering me with kisses.

An owl was gazing down, watching me.

I realized where I was. Lying on a bed of straw inside the barn.

A wide, dark face with kind, wise eyes was standing over me. He bent over and felt my forehead. "She's come to," he said.

"Who are you?" I asked him.

"I'm Peter Williams. Lord Robert hired me to investigate the murders."

"Oh. The detective." Suddenly my memory kicked in. Simon. Rayeena. The way he groped me. Her knife on my throat. I felt like passing out again.

"Courtney?" Peter slapped my face. "You're alright now."

The slap brought me back.

"You're the one who saved me," I said. "Thank you." I tried to push up with my arms, but the queasiness hadn't worn off, and my head throbbed. I rubbed it and felt a bump. "I sure didn't foresee that I would be the benefactor when I put a fresh bale of hay down here earlier."

Peter chuckled. "I bet you didn't."

Lord Robert came into the barn. Followed by Sean. They both looked like they'd been through a meat grinder.

"What happened to the two of you?" My throat felt painfully dry.

"He happened!" they said in unison, pointing at each other. Lord Robert bent down next to me and touched my hand.

Sean rushed to my other side. "Courtney, what happened to you? I told you to stay in your room!"

Lord Robert looked at Sean, then at me.

Oh boy.

Before I could explain, Peter chimed in at my defense. "Well, son, it's a good thing she didn't listen to you and stay in her room. Thanks to her, we have a couple of psychopaths in handcuffs."

"I just woke up in a wheelbarrow," Sean growled. "What are you talking about?"

"Please," I said. "I can explain." I tried to sit up. My throat was parched. I looked into Lord Robert's eyes. Hard. Dark. Not the eyes of the Lord Robert I knew.

"I saw Simon DuPont walking below my balcony. I thought it was a little suspicious. I mean, we were getting a monsoon rain right at that moment, so why would anyone want to go for a walk? Plus, after reading the note, well, it just felt *off.*" I looked at Sean. "So, I decided to follow him."

"Note? What note?" Lord Robert asked, looking from me to Sean.

"The note Sean found in your room. He thought you were *Ten,*" I explained, feeling terrible about agreeing to let Sean use that secret passageway.

"Why wouldn't I think that? The note was on *his* bloody desk!" Sean said.

"On my desk. You were in my room?" Lord Robert narrowed his eyes at Sean.

"Sean … you have to explain about that," I said quickly.

Sean looked at me as if I was betraying him. The misunderstanding had to get cleared up, but my head was so jumbled. I didn't know how to put anything in the right order.

"Lord Robert didn't murder anyone, Sean! I know it. It was Simon and Rayeena. All along!"

"What are you talking about, Courtney?" Lord Robert looked at me, stunned. Then at Sean. "You thought I was the murderer?" Then he turned back to me. "Y-you didn't actually think that about me, did you, Courtney?"

"No! I never believed that about you. Not for a second." *Okay, well, maybe just for a millisecond.*

"If you aren't the murderer, then what were you doing with a note to *Thirteen* on your desk?" Sean demanded.

"The note you are referring to was on my desk because Spencer dropped it. It was mixed into his music sheets." He still looked stunned. "I was looking into it, wondering if it might have to do with the murders." He paused, as if realizing something. "Wait. This morning, I ran into Simon. He looked agitated, in a hurry to find Spencer." He shook his head. "He must have realized he had left behind his note in Spencer's music."

Robert walked away from us and pushed his hair back from his forehead with a hand. "Simon, of all people … the murderer? I just can't believe it. I trusted him. Desiree trusted him."

It made me sick. Lord Robert had no idea what kind of woman his dead wife had been.

Peter interjected. "I saw Simon and the woman attacking Courtney, Robert."

"Courtney, explain what you know," Robert said.

"The woman—*Thirteen*—her real name is Rayeena," I said. My head hurt, but I recounted the details of what happened, trying my best not to leave anything out.

When I got to the part about Desiree, I treaded lightly.

A shadow fell over Lord Robert as he listened to me retell Rayeena and Simon's discussion. Part of me wondered if I should have held back some of the details. I didn't.

Lord Robert's eyes went black. He stood up slowly and walked out of the barn, without a word. Peter followed him out.

Poor Lord Robert. He had just learned that his wife had been keeping secrets, working for Intelligence, and was sleeping with a man he thought was his friend.

I tried to get up to follow him.

"Whoa there! Stay put! You are suffering a concussion," Sean said, stroking my hair.

He was right, I was unable to stand without feeling like I'd be sick. All I could do was lie there and wish I could do something for Lord Robert.

❧ *Peter Williams* ❧

"Robert, wait!" Peter's deep voice echoed through the night.

Robert stopped but didn't turn around.

"I know what must be going through your head right now, brother," Peter said. "Believe me, I'd like to see them pay for their crimes as much as you."

Robert was silent.

"They deserve justice," Peter said.

"Yes, they do. And I intend to carry it out," Robert didn't turn around when he said it. "Are you going to try to stop me?"

"I won't try to stop you."

"Good."

"But I will remind you of the oath," Peter said. "We all made it. Protect the helpless, keep order, be peacemakers, and bring offenders to justice. Leave vengeance to God."

Robert never turned to face him.

He just needs time, Peter thought. His heart broke for his friend. He had been there when Robert fell apart after he lost Desiree. He would have his back through this, as well.

A strong believer in fighting for those who could not defend themselves, Peter had put together a powerful network of like-minded people who managed to stay under the radar of PAX. Money was not the force that drove these amazing individuals. Everyone who joined the fight had lost someone in The Cleansing, or on the streets. Some had been replaced by AI. Some were like Peter, in hiding, living under false identities.

When Peter started CAPE, he knew Lord Robert had the training and the physical ability, not to mention the financial means, to make an astronomical impact for their cause. He knew Robert was always the first man to step in and help when a person was in need. But Peter's concern was that Robert would want vengeance on the murderer of his wife. That's why he waited to tell him about CAPE.

After some time, when Peter believed Robert was ready, he invited him to join the team. Robert became an integral player in the Resistance.

Peter wondered what Robert would do now that he knew who Desiree's murderers were. Not to mention all that he'd just learned about Desiree. Would it change him? Would bitterness burrow and take root? He was being tested beyond what most men could endure. Peter prayed Robert would be able to get through the test, stronger and wiser.

PLAGUING THOUGHTS

Ranfurly Manor

I couldn't scream. The frightening creature was choking me. Then the creature turned into Simon. Peering out from his distorted features were two bright green eyes. Elizabeth's green eyes.

Could Sean be right? Could the children have a different father?

Was it Simon?

***

The awful dreams made me wish I could stay awake. But I kept drifting off into similar types of dreams. The Roths and Sean kept coming in to wake me up. They said I shouldn't sleep for too long. Apparently, I had a concussion.

My memory of the entire night was cloudy. Lord Robert had given his staff strict orders that I remain in bed. Enforced by the formidable Ms. Stern. Yet he never came to see me while I was confined to my room.

Sean, on the other hand, was a different story.

"I feel so stupid for passing out when Lord Robert pointed his gun at me," I told Sean the first time he woke me. "I still have no idea why I did that."

"Because you lost a lot of blood from the knife wound," he explained.

"Knife wound?"

Sean gently touched my forearm, which had been bandaged. "Rayeena's knife managed to slice you before she went down."

"Oh."

"I'm surprised you didn't see all the blood squirting out of your arm, Courtney. She hit an artery. Peter tied his scarf tightly above the wound, so you didn't bleed out, then carried you into the barn. Mr. Roth brought out his medical bag and got the wound cleaned and stitched up. You were out cold the whole time." Sean scowled. "And as for Ranfurly pointing a gun at you, the old dimwit told Peter that he thought you might be in on it with *Ten* and *Thirteen*!"

That made me mad. "You were the one who thought he murdered his wife and staff, when all along he was innocent!" Getting mad sharpened my mind. I suddenly recalled everything. "And why didn't you say anything last night?"

"What are you talking about?"

"I asked you to explain about why you were in his room, and you said nothing, Sean. Nothing! You owe him an explanation!"

"I owe him? Do you see my face? He did this to me, Courtney. I don't owe him a *** thing!"

"You were both wrong about each other. Peter said Lord Robert thought you were *Ten*. You thought Lord Robert was *Ten*. It was all just … mayhem! A misunderstanding! We know who the real murderers are now. Shake hands! Move on from it!"

Sean just let out a low growl. The Highlander was impossible.

"And also, I don't remember if I mentioned it last night. But I overheard Simon and Rayeena talking about you. She was the one who searched my house, because she thought you and I might be working together. They said PAX knows you're not loyal to them."

"What are you talking about?" Sean looked at me, his face unreadable, as always.

"Sean, there is no point in lying to me. Because I know for sure you are a PAX agent. But they believe you're a traitor."

Sean didn't have anything to say. Yet he came back to check on me the next day. And the next.

TWO DAYS LATER

"Wow. You're back again?" I said when Sean popped into my room.

"I've told you before, it's your magnetic powers that keep drawing me." Sean said, right as Mrs. Roth bustled in, pushing a cart with medical supplies. "Your nurse has come to the rescue," Sean said, smiling tenderly at the woman.

"Hello, Sean dear. So good to see you." Mrs. Roth patted him on the shoulder. She was so sweet and nurturing. I was glad it was the Roths in charge of my medical care, and not Ms. Stern.

The old bandage was removed, the knife wound cleaned. Mrs. Roth re-applied a new bandage and gave me a pack of ice for the bump on my head.

"Looks like I should have brought two ice packs," she said, looking at Sean's pathetic face. "You still look bad, Sean."

"You should see the other fella. He looks way worse." Sean flashed her a smile.

Mrs. Roth shook her head. "Boys! Never had boys. Marie was enough trouble for us."

She left the room to fetch another ice pack for Sean.

"How is she?" I asked Sean, wondering how Mrs. Roth was dealing with the loss of her daughter.

"She's hurting. Mr. Roth is too. Marie's parents are good people. You're in the best of hands." He gently brushed a strand of hair out of my eyes.

"Even your knuckles look like they could use ice!" I said, noticing how puffy and bruised they were.

"We're quite a pair, aren't we?" He laughed.

Mrs. Roth bobbed in with more ice packs. "Keep that on your head for twenty minutes, no less!" she ordered Sean. "I know how you are, Sean. Always wiggling out of things!"

"You're referring to one time when I was ten. That's the only time I ever wiggled," he said.

"Hmph." She smirked. As she started to head out of the room, she suddenly stopped. Her countenance shrouded, she asked, "Can someone just explain to me why?"

Sean and I both looked at her, confused.

"The whole staff knows by now," she said. "Word spreads fast around this place. We all know it was Simon who killed Jake." Her jaw clenched, her face reddened, it was evident she was fighting back tears. "And that he killed my Marie," she whispered. A single tear escaped her eye. "But why? Nobody can give me a good reason!"

Sean got up and went to her, wrapping his muscular arms around her frail frame.

"I'm so sorry, Mrs. Roth," he said, hugging her.

Sean walked Mrs. Roth out of the room, an arm around her, leaving me alone with my thoughts.

I wonder how Nick and Laurel are? I hate that I can't talk to them right now.

All I wanted was to go home and forget everything that had happened at Ranfurly Manor.

I sank back, hoping to fall asleep and wake to find all of it nothing but a horrible nightmare.

On the days that followed, I was well cared for by Mrs. Roth. She and her husband checked on me regularly and fed me well.

Lord Robert's clearly forgotten about me. He must not care whether I live or die. The thought made me more miserable.

But Sean ... I was starting to warm to his attention. When he waited too long to check on me, I craved to see him.

I even felt a little fluttery feeling inside when he came to see me the third day. "Why are you back in my room again, Sean?"

"I can't seem to keep myself away from you." He stroked my cheek. "Do you want me to leave?"

"No. I don't mind." I smiled at him.

Attraction is a strange thing. The way it can attack hard and fierce, then disappear in a puff of smoke. Like a crafty enemy.

Later that very same day, I was finally well enough to get out of bed. I needed some fresh air, so I went out on the balcony. That's when I saw him. ... Sean.

And the woman he was with?

Jasmine.

It was obvious there was more than a friendship between them. The way they stood together, the way she wrapped her arms around him and whispered in his ear.

Could I blame Sean if he was head over heels for *her*? She was a goddess.

Still, it stung. After all the attention he'd been giving me. He was just a player.

Poof. My attraction for him disappeared in a puff of smoke.

Once, while she checked my bandage, Mrs. Roth said, "I've known Sean since he was a boy, you know."

"Sean mentioned to me that he and your daughter dated."

She nodded. "I used to hope they would end up together. But then Sean left for the army, and Marie … well, she changed. Wanted different things. But I know she always loved Sean." She smiled through her tears. "I believe Marie and Sean were first loves. But now he certainly seems taken with you."

I crinkled my eyebrows, wondering if Mrs. Roth was aware that Sean was also taken with Gretchen. And apparently Jasmine. And it wouldn't surprise me if he'd been taken with Winnie too. But I kept my thoughts to myself.

Sean brought me coffee the next morning. I had lost track of the days.

"Your face is still bruised. Are you still icing it?" I asked him.

"Yes, Mum," he mumbled.

"Have you spoken with Lord Robert at all?" I asked.

"Haven't seen him. He probably flew off to one of his other houses to frolic with one of his other wives."

I rolled my eyes. "So, you haven't made up with him, then?" I sighed. "You never liked him, did you?"

"Not a bit," he admitted. "Now I like him even less."

"Why? You know he didn't kill his wife and he didn't murder anyone. And we know now that it was Simon who searched your room, not Robert. And Rayeena who chased you into the Wildwoods, not Robert." I folded my arms. "If anyone has the right to be mad, it's him. We lied to him, Sean. We betrayed him."

"You want to know the real reason I'm mad, Courtney?" Sean leaned in, so his face was inches from mine.

"Hmm?" I said, my breath quickening at his closeness.

"I don't like the way he looks at you. Or the way you look at him."

"I don't know what you're talking about," I whispered. "I haven't even seen him since I've been stuck in bed."

Sean searched my eyes, trying to get a read.

"How many days have I been in here, anyway?" I asked him.

"Five."

"Really? I thought for sure it was only three!" I couldn't believe that much time had passed. I needed to call my kids! "Has anyone even fed my poor animals?" I asked him.

"They're being well looked after. By yours truly. You're welcome." He was an inch from my face.

"I really need to get out of this bed. I'm feeling fine now," I said, trying to stand, unsuccessfully. I had no strength in my legs.

"Careful! Slow down a bit!" he said, putting his hands on my waist to steady me.

"Well, now you're telling *me to* slow down. I didn't see that one coming." I laughed.

He started to get up. "Behave yourself when I'm away," he said.

"Going somewhere?"

"Yes. Don't miss me too much." He leaned in and breathed me in as he kissed my cheek. "At least I don't have to climb through those brambly thorns now to see you," he said as he got up and left through my bedroom door.

WILD AND DANGEROUS

A DAY AFTER THE MURDERERS WERE CAUGHT
Ranfurly Manor

Peter handed a tiny flash drive over to Robert before boarding the private jet in Ranfurly Park.

"Here are the recordings of the statements of Simon DuPont and Rayeena Corpus. The two of them are headed to CAPE Headquarters and will soon be locked up in our prison there."

After Robert and Peter said their goodbyes, Robert headed to his secret lair to review the video recordings.

Simon's interrogation was first.

Peter: "Did you write this note?" He held up the note that Robert found mixed in with Spencer's music.

Simon: "Oui."

Peter: "Six-four-two. What does that mean?"

Simon shrugged.

Peter: "Is it code for traitor?"

Simon clapped sarcastically.

Peter: "Why did you kill Desiree Diamond?"

Simon: "I didn't kill Desiree. She was the only woman I ever loved. Even if she was a serpent and betrayed me. When I found out she was working for the Crown, lying to me, telling my secrets to Intelligence, I was destroyed. But I could never have killed her."

Peter: "Courtney heard Rayeena say she killed Desiree *for you.*"

Simon: "Oui. That's exactly what she did. She killed Desiree so she could have me. *Tu comprends?* Rayeena was jealous and wanted me for herself. I *never* told her to kill Desiree. If I wanted Desiree dead, I could have strangled her myself."

Peter: "What kind of criminal activity were you involved in that led the Crown to have Desiree spy on you?"

Simon: "I was doing business with some people who were on the Crown's most wanted list."

Peter: "What kind of business?"

Simon: "Transactions, exchanges, eliminations. Now PAX has me doing the same thing for them. With their official stamp of approval."

Peter: "If you have a job with PAX, why did you come to work for Lord Robert?"

Simon's expression changed from nonchalant to stone-faced: "I have my reasons."

Peter: "Did you have a plan to kill Lord Robert? Is that why you were there?"

Simon ignored the question. "Isn't it funny? I am no longer a wanted criminal. I'm the one working for the government now. But you! You're the rebels! Tables have turned!"

Simon's laugh made Robert want to heave.

"PAX has already won," Simon spat out the words. "You might as well get in bed with them and have some fun."

Robert had had enough. He fast-forwarded to Peter's interview with Rayeena.

Rayeena: "Yes, PAX hired me to track Sean Knight. I followed him to the home of Courtney Drake on my motorcycle. He was driving the Royal Rodney. Once he left the Drake place, he caught on to being followed and abandoned his car in the Wildwoods. I chased him on foot but lost him in the wilderness there."

Peter: "What about the night you met Simon at Ranfurly Manor, how did you get onto the premises?"

Rayeena: She snickered. "Simon gave me the gate code."

Peter: "Did Simon hire you to kill Desiree?"

Rayeena: "The woman was spying on him, lying to him. He was a blind fool for her. I saved him and gave that whore what she deserved. Now I'm the one he lives for."

Peter: "Why do you work for PAX, Rayeena?"

Rayeena: "PAX is quite enlightened, and they appreciate my artistry. They are generous employers, too."

Peter: "Your artistry? Is that what you call it? Mutilating people after you kill them?"

Rayeena: "I wouldn't expect someone like you to understand. You think in black and white. Inside a little, tiny box. The people who work for *The Ten* have reached a higher plain of consciousness."

Peter: "That's one demented plain, if you ask me. God help you."

Rayeena's sinister laugh echoed through the room.

Rayeena: "God? I am my own God. I make my own destiny. All you know is control. You want power. You make us swear on your book of rules that restricts people from becoming their full potential. People like you kill freedom of expression. PAX set me free. They set Simon free! They delivered us from your laws and tyranny! And they're going to gas you and all the other vermin out of their holes, sooner than you think."

Rayeena's laugh was even more dastardly than Simon's.

Lord Robert had seen enough of the video. He shut it off. His thoughts were swarming, picking up speed, escalating into a raging tornado. He'd been lied to. By the only woman he'd ever loved. Desiree. How could he even know what was true anymore? How could he trust again, look at the world the same way?

He got up and went into the room with the medicine cabinet. Rummaging through it, he searched. For what? He didn't know. Something for the pain.

A blow in the jaw, a stab in the side, a bat hitting his head … he'd endured all those things. More.

This kind of pain he was in … he didn't know how to heal from it. The medicine cabinet wasn't stocked with tonics for the lacerations that bled within. There was nothing to cauterize the open wound. *If only a doctor could open me up and cut out the cavity inside that holds my emotions … my torturous thoughts. Damn you, Desiree!*

He had worshipped her. Seated her on the throne above all others. Now, she was immortalized. No woman would have ever been able to compare. *Not even Courtney.*

Desiree. Was it all a lie? Did you ever even love me, or were you just playing the role of my wife because it was an assignment?

Was any of it real? Your faith – was that a lie too? Was my own conversion all based on lies? I don't know what to believe anymore.

If only she were there in the flesh. He would have been able to see her reaction. Get some answers. But he would never have answers.

Furiously, he swiped all the medicine bottles in the cabinet with his hand, and they crashed onto the floor. Glass shards went in every direction. He slammed the mirrored door of the cabinet shut and punched it.

"Ach!" he roared at his own reflection, blood starting to spill out of his knuckles. "Cut me into a million pieces! I don't care!"

He ran down the steep steps into the cavern far below the manor, jumped in his boat, and drove down river. He pulled into a remote cove and hiked into the thick forest. Water, food, shelter, blankets, comfort … he'd lost all physical feeling, so he wouldn't need those.

Where does an animal go to bleed to death?

Through prickly berry vines and thick brush, amid towering firs, maples, and cedars, he wandered deeper into the wilderness.

❧ Courtney ❧

ONE WEEK AFTER THE MURDERERS WERE CAUGHT

The children were happy to see me when I was finally well enough to join them for lunch. Up until that point, the staff had kept them out of my room while I was recovering.

Lord Robert gave everyone strict orders to not answer the children's millions of questions regarding the murders. He was very concerned about giving them nightmares.

What the kids were told was that the murderers were caught. They also knew one was the motorcyclist with the number Thirteen. We credited the kids for helping us catch that one. They liked that.

We were told to hide the fact that their gymnastics instructor was the other murderer. That wasn't as easy to do as Lord Robert thought it would be.

"My music teacher and Bellais teacher say Monsieur Dupont killed Marie," Elizabeth said.

"Oh?" I didn't want to lie to their faces. I tried to think of a response.

"I knew it all along," Elizabeth continued.

"I knew it first! I told you the first day of class he was an evil fairy!" Luke said, excited.

"Well, we really need to make sure to put you two detectives on the case if there is ever another crime committed around here," I said.

They didn't seem traumatized. But Lord Robert wouldn't be happy they found out. Speaking of Lord Robert, I still hadn't seen any sign of him. "Have you two seen your father much since I've been locked in my room?"

"Ms. Stern told us Daddy had to go on a long business trip. We haven't seen him at all," Elizabeth whispered sadly.

"Oh." So, I wasn't the only one who was missing him. That made me feel a little better. "I'm sorry. Who's been taking care of you?"

"Winnie!" Elizabeth said.

"Winnie? Oh. Do you like her?" I asked.

"She's the best!" Elizabeth said.

"Yeah. We love Winnie!" Luke said.

"Oh. Good." *The best? Do they like her more than they like me?* "Well, I'm sure your dad will be back soon," I said with positivity. "Have you been taking good care of my animals while I've been sick?"

"Yes," said Elizabeth.

"Yes! We heard that the dogs helped catch Simon and *Thirteen*!" Luke said with excitement.

"They sure did!" I beamed.

"I've been giving them extra bones. They bury them in the hay," he said.

I laughed. "I'm not surprised! Thor always likes to bury things and Loki delights in digging them up. Once I found a neighbor's cell phone buried in my rose garden."

As I thought of all that had passed since I'd arrived at Ranfurly Manor, it dawned on me how little time I'd been there. It had only been a week, and out of that time, only two days were spent with Lord Robert. Two tumultuous days.

After all the excitement, the foremost thing on my mind was how much I missed my own kids. I couldn't wait to get back home and call them. Neither of them had any idea where I was and that I was unreachable by cell phone.

The next morning, the children and I sat down to eat our delicious omelets prepared by Mr. Roth. I told the twins I was planning to go back to my house the next day to check on things, and to call my kids.

Elizabeth and Luke were excited to learn I had grown up children.

"When can we meet them?" Elizabeth asked.

"Hopefully soon! Laurel will be coming home from college next month." As I was saying this, Lord Robert came in and sat down in his chair at the head of the table.

"Daddy! You're home!" Elizabeth and Luke squealed and ran to hug their father.

Could Robert hear the fierce pounding in my chest across the table?

"Yes, I'm home," he said, smiling at each of his children.

Is he avoiding eye contact with me? He must hate me. And he has every right. I should have never agreed to help Sean. What was I thinking?

I had to find a way to win back his trust. *If only I could look into his eyes, feel that connection with him again.*

But what am I thinking? I shouldn't be fantasizing about him, as if he would consider being in a relationship with me. He's my employer and probably wants to fire me after everything that has happened.

Not to mention, he's way out of my league! He's a freaking lord, for heaven's sake. Rein in your heart. Don't dream too far, Courtney.

But my heart refused to be reined in. It was like a wild stallion that leapt over boundaries and did whatever the heck it pleased.

The children ate their breakfast, and I picked at my food.

Lord Robert cleared his throat. "Elizabeth, Luke. Did you know that when I was your age, I would go to a place called Highland every summer?"

"Really?" Luke said. "Where's that?"

"It's across the great pond, in a place called The Green Isles."

"You told us about the Green Isles, Daddy. It's where you're from," Elizabeth said.

"Yes. I suppose I've mentioned it a few times. But I've never told you about Highland. There are mountains ten times taller than Mount Ziwa in Highland," Robert said.

"I wish we could go there!" Luke cried.

"We can. I'm planning a trip for us. Just the three of us." He averted my gaze.

"What about Mrs. Drake? Won't she come too?" *Thank you, Luke. That was the same question going through my mind.*

"I'm afraid not this time, Luke. But guess who you *will* finally get to meet?"

"Who?" asked the children in unison.

"My childhood nanny."

"She must be very old." Elizabeth wrinkled her nose.

"And we have our own nanny. We want Mrs. Drake to come!" Luke whined.

Robert went on as if he didn't hear them. "We will also be taking a trip to *Le Monde d'Enchantement* in La Belle Terre."

"What's that?" Elizabeth asked.

"Haven't you learned those words by now?" Lord Robert asked her.

"*Le Monde.* That's *the world.* And *enchantement* means good to meet you, doesn't it?" Elizabeth said.

"No, *enchante* means good to meet you. *Enchantement* means magical, or enchantment. Put the two together and what have you?"

"The world of magical enchantment!" Luke said.

"What place does that remind you of? It's in The Goldens."

"*Enchanted World!*" Elizabeth said, now excited. The children squealed in elation.

"We're going to *Enchanted World!*" They both held hands and bounced up and down for a few moments. After that, they could speak of nothing else. "We get to meet *Max and Maxine Mouse!*"

I was usurped by magical mice.

After breakfast, Lord Robert left us to take care of business.

Masking my gloom, I took advantage of the lovely spring weather we were having. "Our lesson will be outside today," I announced to the children.

This made them happy.

Toward the end of the lesson, while we were having snacks out on the lawn, Lord Robert joined us. "I'm afraid Ms. Sophie is unwell and won't be able to teach your language lesson today. And Mr. Lee has a concert in Emer Aude, so he can't teach your music lesson."

"Goodie!" Luke cried.

"Since we don't have a gymnastics instructor anymore, it looks like you will have to miss out on school for the rest of the day."

Luke and Elizabeth both shouted "hurray" and broke into a routine of somersaults and leapfrogs across the grass.

After they had some time to get out some explosive energy, Robert said, "Instead, how about horse riding lessons? Davey Reed is taking over for Mr. Knight as your new riding instructor. After that, you get free time for the rest of the day and we'll enjoy a movie tonight in the theater. Mr. Roth has already agreed to reward you with his famous kettle corn."

The announcement brought on another high-pitched, exuberant response from the children.

"Woohoo!"

"Yippee!"

"Race you to the horses!"

They ran off, leaving us alone.

The strange, swirly feelings were back. But I was hurt by the way he was excluding me from their lives, and I could hardly look at him. We sat in awkward silence.

I cleared my throat and stood. As I tried to clean up the blanket and snacks, he got up and grabbed my hand.

"Leave it. Let's catch up with the children," he said. He let go of my hand.

I caught my breath and nodded.

Lord Robert walked slowly. Our hands were so close, his fingers brushed against mine at one point. I ached for him to grab my hand again.

"Wild stallions can't be tamed, can they?" he asked.

I glanced up at him. *Wild stallions?* It was what I'd been thinking earlier. *Can he read my mind?* I wanted desperately to set things right between us and tried to think of the right words. But I couldn't find them.

We arrived at the barn and were no longer alone. I had missed my chance.

Lord Robert helped Davey saddle Sir Edgar and Lady Rose, while I brushed two of the larger horses and refilled their water trough. I expected him to mount his horse and ride with the children. But instead, he saw the children and Davey off and came back into the barn.

Once again, we were alone. I knew I needed to try to say something.

His voice broke through the awkward silence. "Courtney, may we speak?"

"Yes." *Oh no. Is he going to fire me?*

"I've had some time to think about what you shared with me that night when the murderers were discovered," he said.

As terrifying as it was, I forced myself to look into his eyes. He wasn't avoiding me anymore. He was intently watching me.

"When *you* discovered the murderers, I should add."

I didn't expect him to say that.

"Oh, well…" I blushed. "Lord Robert, I…"

"I'd like to finish what I was saying, please?"

I nodded. *How is it even possible that I can't remember how to breathe normally?*

"I was angry, Courtney. I even considered firing you and blowing a hole through Sean."

I made a noise to say something.

He held up a hand. "I'm not done."

I looked down, fighting back tears that were threatening to escape.

He continued. "Help me understand, Courtney. … You and Sean. Are you in a relationship? That's why he went to your house before he went missing. Is that right?"

What? Is that what he thinks? I shook my head. "No. You've got it all wrong. No! I-I only just met Sean when he picked me up for the job interview."

"Then why was he sneaking into your room?"

"Certainly not for the reason you're insinuating! I never invited him in. I was shocked to see him pop out of my curtains."

Robert narrowed his eyes.

I continued. "He heard about the secret passageway in my room from his dad and wanted me to let him use it." Then it dawned on me. "Maybe that's why Sean wanted me here. To use me to get to you."

He shook his head. "He wouldn't have known that I would put you in that room. The nannies usually stay in the staff quarters. I'm sure he wanted you for *other* reasons."

I felt the heat of his gaze on me.

He lifted my chin and searched my eyes. "You're sure you and Sean aren't…" Gold flames were in his green eyes.

"I'm *absolutely* sure we aren't."

Robert looked down and nodded.

When he looked up again, I held his gaze so he could read the truth in my eyes. "Robert, I gave him permission to use the secret passage in my room because I was certain you were innocent. I thought I could help prove you weren't a murderer. That's the truth."

"Hmm," he breathed out softly. "I believe you, Courtney."

A tear slipped down my cheek. He brushed it away.

"I'm sorry," I whispered.

He drew me into his chest, and I burrowed my face in his neck. His arms tightened around my waist. "And you did end up helping prove I was innocent, when you spied on the real murderers. I owe you my gratitude."

He held me for a minute, and at last I was able to breathe out a long sigh of relief.

Until we were interrupted by Thor, who jumped up and broke us apart.

"Well, you are quite in demand. First Mr. Knight, now Thor," he said.

I pet Thor, giving him the attention he was craving.

"So, I was thinking…" Lord Robert began.

"Yes?"

"Perhaps we need a fresh start," he said.

"Mm. I like the sound of that. What do you suggest?"

"First, rewind the clock." He ran backwards and then stopped. He slowly walked up to me. "Hello there. I'm Robert Ranfurly, and you are?"

"Courtney Drake."

He bowed. "Pleasure to meet you, Mrs. Drake. So, tell me a little about yourself."

"What would you like to know?" I asked.

"Hmm. … What's your favorite dessert?"

"Mm. It's a tossup between espresso gelato and freshly baked gingerbread cookies. What's yours?"

"Mine is any ice cream that has caramel and chocolate mixed in."

"Really? For some reason I didn't see you as the type who liked sweets," I said. "Tell me more about yourself, Lord Ranfurly."

"I never mentioned I was a lord. And now that we know so much about each other, that qualifies us to be on a first name basis. It's just Robert."

"Alright then, Robert. Tell me more about *you*."

"What's there to tell? I'm a dad of two very clever and mischievous five-year-olds. I enjoy riding motorcycles along the coast at sunset. Seafood is my favorite. I don't care much for parties." He turned and looked at the forest behind us. "But I do love these woods. Your turn."

"My turn? Okay. Let's see. I'm a mom of two brilliant college-aged adults. Macadamia nut encrusted halibut is my favorite. And I, too, enjoy motorcycle rides along the coast at sunset! In fact, I used to have a motorcycle."

"Now that surprises me!" he said.

"It's been a long time since I've been on one, though."

"Well, we'll have to remedy that, won't we?"

I extended my hand and he held on to it.

We didn't need words. We were there. Our souls had found each other, at last. As we stood, gazing into each other's eyes, it was like we were on another plain. A place where nothing else mattered. A place I wished I could stay forever.

"By the way, you don't happen to carry a gun around, do you?" he asked, a twinkle in his eye.

"Not exactly. But I own one. Why? Do you carry a gun?" I glanced at him sideways.

"Always." He dabbed my nose with his forefinger.

Then, in an unexpected swoop, I was in his arms. He lifted me up and twirled me, as if I was as light as a dove. Then he set me down and pressed his cinnamon lips into mine.

It was a moment of euphoric bliss. For the first time in my life, I knew what it was like to experience a foot-popping kiss.

A flashback of when I was a teenager came to my mind:

I was on the phone with my best friend, Meg.

"…and then Keith kissed me," I said.

"Did your foot pop?" she asked.

I thought it was a funny question. "Why would my foot pop when I kiss someone, Meg?"

A light little laugh slipped out of me.

"What's so funny?" Robert asked, a smile crossing his lips, as he tenderly took a strand of my hair between his fingers and played with it.

"Oh … I just remembered something that my friend Meg once said. She passed before we graduated high school. But if she were alive, I know she would have liked you."

"Perhaps she is. Still alive, I mean. They say we're more alive in the afterlife than we are in this passing place. Perhaps she is watching us now, enjoying the show."

"You know, I wouldn't be surprised if you're right about that."

I wondered if kissing was something we'd get to do in the afterlife.

SNEAK PEEK

Dangling and Dangerous (The Ranfurly Mysteries Book Two)

Courtney

How I wish we could go back in time to before the moment when we kissed in the barn that day. We would never have let Elizabeth and Luke go for a ride in the woods with Davey Reed, had we known the danger that awaited them.

The magic of our kiss dissipated completely when Mr. Reed rode his horse back into the stables. Lord Robert broke away from me to greet him. I steadied my breath yearning for his closeness. But Robert's attention had shifted to the gorgeous horse that Mr. Reed was riding.

"You have a special bond with him." Lord Robert approached the horse and stroked his mane. "I've never seen him take to anyone other than me, until now."

Davey Reed looked alarmed.

"Something wrong?" Lord Robert asked him.

"Someone is out there. In your woods."

"Someone? You mean a stranger?" Davey nodded. "Where are the children?" Lord Robert asked.

"They're right behind me."

Just then, Luke rode in on his miniature horse. We waited a moment, expecting Elizabeth to come in after him. But when after a minute, Elizabeth hadn't arrived, Lord Robert asked Luke, "Where is your sister?"

"I don't know. Probably way, way back there! She was in front of me, but I ran my horse past hers and left her and her dumb pony to eat my dust." Lord Robert ran out of the barn, and I ran after him.

"Elizabeth?" we called. Davey Reed, still on his horse, came out of the stables and joined us.

"Davey, take me to where you were just riding with the children." Lord Robert ran into the barn and mounted his horse, bareback, and followed Davey out onto the trail.

Luke had dismounted and was pulling his horse by the reins. "What's wrong? Why is everybody so worried? Elizabeth is probably just mad she lost the race, so she isn't coming in."

"Oh, I hope you're right, Luke." I sighed. "Let's put Sir Edgar back in his stall now and play with Thor and Loki until they get back."

Robert and Davey returned thirty minutes later. Without Elizabeth.

"She's here! I know she is. She's probably hiding and watching us look for her right now!" Luke started calling his sister's name. "Elizabeth!"

All of us kept calling her name. Repeatedly.

Our calls turned to shouts, then Robert's and Davey's became frantic yells. Luke's and my calls turned to screams. Elizabeth and Lady Rose weren't coming back.

Robert and Davey rode out on their horses again, back into the woods, calling persistently for Elizabeth. At that point, I am ashamed to say I did nothing helpful for anyone. It was like I was paralyzed.

When Robert and Davey came back, it was obvious they hadn't found Elizabeth.

Another poisonous snake had slithered its way into paradise.

ACKNOWLEDGMENTS

I couldn't have finished this book without the help and the talent of many incredible people.

First and foremost, I must thank Jessica Powers, editor, proofreader, coach, cheerleader. I did not know what a developmental editor was before I wrote this book, and I am ever so relieved that I invested in getting Jessica to be mine. I'll never look at a paragraph the same way.

Kim Beckham, new edition proofreader extraordinaire and friend who makes me laugh at my own blunders daily. How she manages to find every minute speck of dust in a sentence, I do not know. She says it is her "disease." Well, I for one am glad she's afflicted.

I would like to thank Shanna and the designers at *100 Covers*, who designed the cover and interior of the newest 2026 edition of the printed books and eBook.

Special thanks to the following beta readers, who contributed more to the shaping of this book than you can possibly imagine:

Maxine Knox, also known as Mom. (She counts because she is not one of those moms who praises everything I write but is red-hot-chili-pepper-honest. I love it and hate it at the same time); Carrie Campbell, Bobbie Huntsinger, Jennifer Hitsman, Koralyn Driskill, Kim Wilson, Ali Simpson, Sally Bryan, Heather Hibbs, Linda Heard, and Allison Campbell.

I have the best beta readers.

Shout out to Tim Campbell, who contributed his voice talent to the audiobook version of *Danger Lies Within*. It was a joy to work with him and his team!

Thank you to my son, Nathaniel, who helped design the maps of the fantasy world of Lord Robert and Courtney Drake.

It really does take a village!

If you enjoyed *Danger Lies Within*, consider rating and reviewing it wherever you purchased the book or audiobook.

Goodreads Bookbub Amazon

Sign up for my newsletter to get updates, bonus behind the scenes material, and more:

kmkrenikbooks.com

The Ranfurly Mysteries

Inevitable Danger *(Prequel to* The Ranfurly Mysteries)

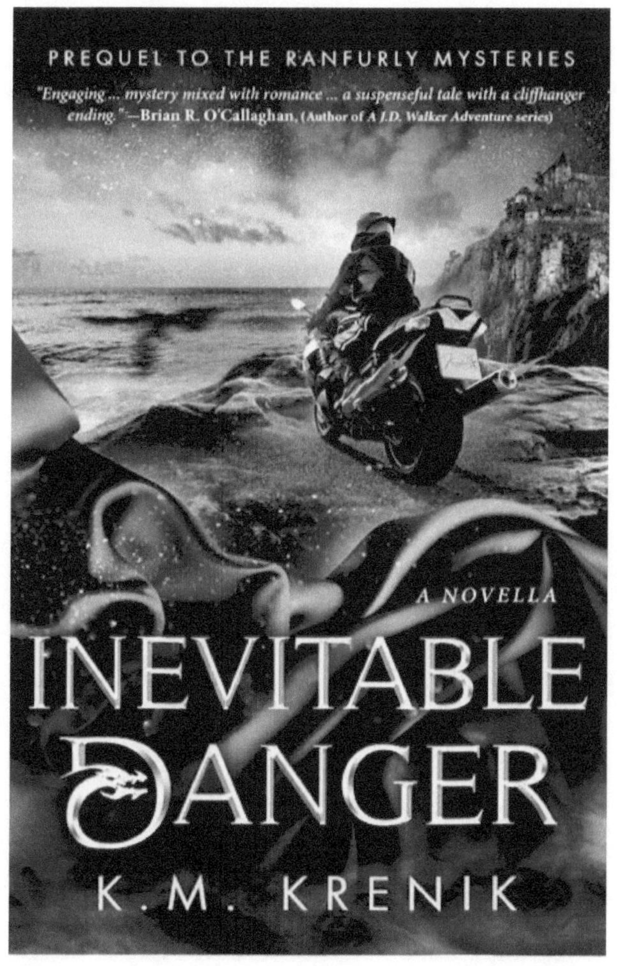

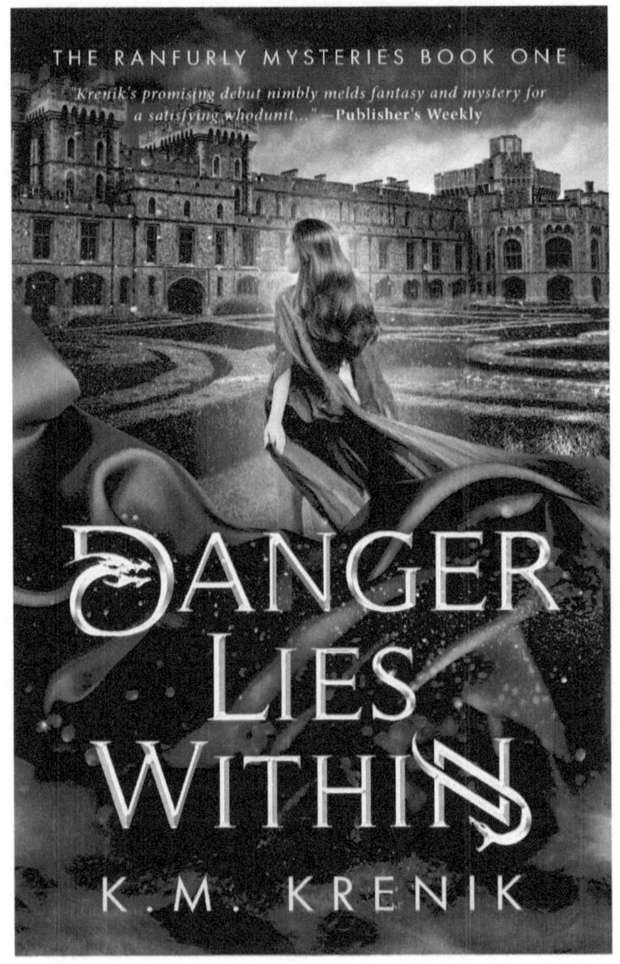
THE RANFURLY MYSTERIES BOOK ONE
"Krenik's promising debut nimbly melds fantasy and mystery for
a satisfying whodunit..." —Publisher's Weekly
DANGER
LIES
WITHIN
K.M. KRENIK

THE RANFURLY MYSTERIES BOOK TWO
"...Dangling and Dangerous delivers exactly what a second
book should: a bigger canvas, a meaner antagonist, and the sense
that these characters will not emerge unchanged..." —Booklife
DANGLING
AND
DANGEROUS
K.M. KRENIK